Forget Your Morals
SARAH BLUE

SPOTIFY PLAYLIST

Heartless - The Weeknd
Burning Desire - Lana Del Ray
Gorgeous - Taylor Swift
Boyfriend - Arianna Grande, Social House
The Heart Wants What It Wants - Selena Gomez
Meet Me in the Hallway - Harry Styles
Minefields - Faouzia, John Legend
Bad idea right? - Olivia Rodrigo
Like Real People Do - Hozier
Bad idea! - girl in red
R U Mine? - Arctic Monkeys
Dirty Little Secret - The All-American Rejects
What I Got - Sublime
...Baby One More Time - Britney Spears
Kiss It Better - Rihanna

Watch - Billie Elish
Lose Control - Teddy Swims
Shut up My Moms Calling - Hotel Ugly
If u think I'm pretty - Artemas
Wildest Dreams (Taylors Version) - Taylor Swift

FOREWORD

This is the second book in the Carlson Brothers series, however they are linear timelines. This book can be read as a standalone or read before Swallow Your Pride. There are cameos and spoilers for Swallow Your Pride in Forget Your Morals, but the context is clear.

Please be advised that this book features an adopted FMC and being adopted is a major part of her journey in this book.

Content Warnings: Adopted cousins, secret relationship, side character death (cancer), discussions of death, dealing with adoption as an adult. Sexual content: glory holes, anonymous sex, toys, sex without a condom, slight breeding kink, CNC, role-play, light bondage, spitting.

To the amount of glory hole research done for this book. You're welcome.

Penny

Hopeless Romantic

FUCK, *my cheek stings.*

I really know how to pick them, don't I?

It's raining as I stand outside of Jameson's apartment building, clutching my phone in my hand thinking of who I should call to help me get out of this situation. My parents are absolutely out of the question, I think I proved to them one too many times that I'm a complete fuckup. The disappointment in their eyes when they realize I'm nearly thirty and still don't have my shit together is too much.

Everything always feels like too much. I thought by now my life would click together, I'd be married with kids and not making the same stupid fucking choices repeatedly.

I would call Aiden, but he's going through so much right now, he doesn't need to add my bullshit on top of that.

I scroll through my phone and land on one of my twin cousin's names.

I call Gavin first, as he's more likely to pick up. Benjamin is a little more aloof, he might answer a text, but definitely not a phone call.

"Hey, Pen," Gavin answers.

"Hey, Gav. Do you think you or Benjamin could pick me up?"

"Totally would, but we're in Atlanta looking at properties this weekend," he says.

"That's right. No worries, I'll just get an Uber or something."

"Everything alright?" Gavin asks.

I have to hold back my tears, because no, everything is not alright, and all I want to do is go home and cry in bed. The thought of getting in a car with a strange man is definitely not what I want to do right now.

"Yeah, everything is fine," I lie, which I'm too good at. Sometimes my stomach sinks when I do it and sometimes it rolls off my tongue easier than a truth ever could.

"I know Aiden is probably at the hospital, but Linc should be home. I mean, you two do live in the same building," he says.

Yes, the building our family owns and I live in as a complete freeloader. It feels like another kick to the chest while I'm already down. I know Gavin has no idea what I'm going through right now, no one does with the way I bottle up all this festering failure, but I really don't want to call Lincoln.

My options are to call my cousin who seems to hate the fucking world, or have some stranger drive me home. I sigh, realizing I have to choose the former.

"Thanks, I'll call Lincoln."

"We'll hang out when we get back, okay?" Gavin says.

I'm closest to my twin cousins, since we're closer in age we grew up doing a lot of the same activities together.

"Sounds good, night."

"Night," he says before hanging up the phone.

No way do I have the balls to call Lincoln, instead I text him.

> Hey, sorry to bother you. I know it's getting late, but would you be able to pick me up?

LINCOLN

Send me the address

Curt and to the point, that's how Lincoln operates.

If he wasn't walking around, I'd wonder if he had a beating, functioning heart. He wasn't always like this, really only in the last few years has he turned into this angry shell of a man. When we were kids he was always sweet, he never let the twins gang up on me when we played and I appreciate it. I'm not sure what flipped a switch in him, but he's turned into somewhat of a grumpy old man.

I send him the address and I wait and pray that Jameson doesn't come outside. I rub my cheek, wondering if he left a mark. He fucking slapped me when I said I didn't want to have sex with him tonight. I've been with my fair share of shitty men, like Justin, Josh, Jake, and Johnathon. Now that I think about it, I'm one-hundred percent off J names for the future.

It feels like my life is slowly crumbling apart, and I'm not sure how to catch myself. The only positive thing I have going for me is that Aiden gave me a job at his company, but it's not what I see for my future.

I'm not really sure what I want to do career wise.

I have an idea of what I wanted my life to look like by now. I wanted a husband who was obsessed with me, like truly positively in love with me, and I knew I wanted to be a mother. Maybe it made me pathetic that these were my aspirations in life, but it's what I've always wanted.

My therapist says I have major abandonment issues and I'm

trying to fill that void with romantic relationships. I know she's right, and we've been trying to work through some of the things holding me back, one of the things is easier said than done. I've tried to gather the courage to look for my birth parents. All I know is that I was left at a church and spent a year in foster care until my parents formally adopted me.

I've been loved deeply by my parents and my extended family, and I know it's a choice to love me. But is it so bad to want that special someone who chooses me completely, not because I was adopted into their family? I don't know why my parents unconditional love never seems to be enough and why I keep jumping head first into these romantic relationships, every time I do I get hurt.

This time I got physically hurt, and I think maybe it's the wake-up call I needed. I've got to make some changes, because what I'm doing clearly isn't working.

I'm on the wrong side of my twenties and I have no clue who I truly am or what I want in life.

The voice behind me startles me and I nearly drop my phone as he speaks.

"Come back inside, Penny. It's raining," Jameson says calmly, like he didn't just slap me a few minutes ago.

"My cousin is coming to pick me up," I reply.

I hope that he turns around and leaves, but of course I'm not that lucky.

"I'm sorry, I lost my temper, I had too much to drink. Just come back inside," he pleads.

You've got to be fucking kidding me. He thinks he can hit me and just apologize and I'll go right back to his apartment and fuck him? He's out of his mind.

He grabs my arm and I flinch, but he's faster and stronger than me.

Thankfully, Lincoln's white Porsche pulls up at that exact

moment. I let out a sigh of relief, but Jameson doesn't let go of my arm.

A car door shuts and I can feel Lincoln's looming presence behind me.

Lincoln is imposing, and would scare the shit out of any normal person, it seems like Jameson is no exception as he drops his hand and looks up at my tall, broad cousin.

"You good, Pen?" Lincoln asks.

"Yeah, I just want to go home."

Jameson says nothing and we head towards Lincoln's car. He opens the car door for me and his face finally meets mine.

"Did he do that to your cheek?" he asks, his tone is dark.

"It's fine. I just want to go home," I tell him.

"Okay," he replies.

He shuts my car door and the locks activate, Lincoln doesn't get into the driver's side. Instead he walks up to Jameson, who is still standing there like an idiot.

I can't hear what words are said between the two, but I do watch in horror as Lincoln slaps Jameson across the face, sending the asshole down to the wet pavement. I slink down into my seat, wrapping my arms around myself.

God, I'm glad he didn't punch him. I don't want him getting in trouble because I was the dumbass who put myself in the crosshairs of another man who didn't give a shit about me.

Lincoln points down at Jameson shouting some words at him, before he calmly walks back to the car, unlocking the vehicle and getting into the driver's side.

It feels like the air leaves the cabin when his door is shut and he starts the engine. Neither of us are willing to break the silence or talk about what just happened.

He taps his finger in a rhythmic tone against the steering wheel as he drives. He doesn't even put on music to cut some of the tension. I would listen to just about anything besides the deafening silence I'm suffering through in this car.

Alright, he's my cousin. He stood up for me, I've known him all my life. I can very easily speak to this man, right?

"Thank you for picking me up," I say softly and he grunts in acknowledgement. "If it helps, I'm strictly off dating after that. I mean what a fucking asshole. I'm just going to focus on my job at Kemper's and figure out what I want to do next. No more men getting in the way of that."

He makes another noise, but doesn't speak.

Maybe I should have gotten an Uber, it surely wouldn't be as miserable as this.

"How is the new complex coming along?" I ask, trying to change tactics.

"Fine," he replies.

"Sorry I asked," I whisper.

He hears it, of course he hears it.

"Penny, please just shut the fuck up until we get home," he says, his tone even.

I swallow and look out the window and my eyes start to well with emotion.

"Sorry for just trying to have some conversation with you."

He sighs, and pushes his head against the headrest.

"I don't want to talk, because if you keep talking I'll want to turn around and run that fucker over with my car. Do you know how much restraint it took for me to just slap him? God, I wanted to hit him so hard that he would have to be fed through a fucking straw. So please shut up so I can get my shit together, take you home, and go back to my normal everyday life. My life that isn't interrupted with dramatic late night rescues because you can't seem to have any sense of self preservation or any fucking radar when it comes to a man being an absolute piece of shit," he seethes the last words and the car fills with silence once again.

I hold back my tears, because I won't give him the satisfaction of knowing he hurt my feelings. Even though there's no doubt that he knows, he probably just doesn't care.

At least he cares about me enough to want to hurt Jameson, but not enough to worry about how he speaks to me.

He has to know that I'm insecure about what a fuckup I am. That every relationship I'm in becomes my whole personality and I currently feel like a shell of a person with no path.

He's too smart not to know. And I'm too stubborn to give him any satisfaction over it. Instead, I stare out the window while he drives and I think about how exactly I can overcome this affliction of being a hopeless romantic.

We drive past Avalon on our way home, and it feels like a light bulb goes off in my head.

"Avalon looks nice," I say, completely wanting to avoid acknowledging how much Lincoln hurt my feelings, and maybe to piss him off.

"It's pathetic is what it fucking is."

I roll my eyes, taking in the bright sign.

A sex club shouldn't be the sign I've been waiting on for what direction to take in my life, but here it is, beaming brightly in my face.

I need to know who I am outside of a relationship, outside of my family. Exploring this part of myself with no one else fills me with a sense of excitement and liberation.

Some of my sexual desires have been part of the problem in my past relationships—among other deeper issues. I've had to suppress some of the things I wanted to explore because my boyfriend at the time didn't feel comfortable with what I wanted. Along with hiding who I really am.

Maybe if I'm able to get sexual gratification anonymously, I can still get laid, but work on myself at the same time. Without sex I know I'll fall for the first guy who buys me a drink and tells me I'm pretty—my standards are in the damn gutter.

I don't think my therapist would agree with this plan, but I definitely don't plan on telling Deb what I'm up to.

No one besides me and the club owner needs to know what I do at Avalon. Maybe there's some way to get a discount based on my interests. I'm trying desperately not to mooch off of my family anymore, and my salary at Kemper's is pretty sad.

This plan has some merit to it. Maybe I won't feel this urge to latch on to a man who gives me attention when I don't know who it is. I can protect my heart and try to figure out who I am in the process.

Lincoln parks his car, and I get out of the passenger's side and head straight to the elevators. I'm on floor eight and Lincoln is on floor seven. We don't speak as I hit the buttons. The elevator ride is just as stifling as the car ride was, and I take a breath of relief when he gets off on his level.

He doesn't even look at me as he leaves the elevator and heads to his apartment. I feel like I can finally breathe once he's out of my sight and I drag my sorry ass home.

My apartment is far too nice for the salary I make, but our family owns the building, and wanted me to have somewhere safe to live.

I drop my keys off by the front door and look at my face in the mirror above the entry table. There's still some redness on my cheekbone, but it doesn't look too bad.

But then I look at myself, really look at myself, and I hate what I see.

I know I'm beautiful with long honey blonde hair and blue eyes. A simple classic structure to my face, and clear skin. But being beautiful isn't enough to make someone love you, I should know, seeing as I don't even love myself.

I wallow around to my bedroom, just stripping out of my clothes and climbing into my luxurious bed.

Now that I'm alone, I finally let my tears flow freely. I'm not sure what hurts worse, the fact that Jameson physically assaulted me or that Lincoln was able to read all my insecurities so clearly.

All I know is something has got to change before I'm broken for good.

Lincoln

Fixer Upper

MY ASSISTANT, Marie, brings me my preferred coffee. She places it on the same leather coaster every morning, just as she starts going through my scheduled day.

I'm the only one who had any interest in the family business. It doesn't help that I was urged by my father and uncle for this path. It's not that I hate my job, or have aspirations for anything different, I'm just on auto-pilot. I don't find the same joy in the company that I used to, I suppose that extends to everything else in my life. Every day feels like a gloomy day, even in the bright disturbing sunshine that haunts me outside my office window.

"Krystal will be here this evening to discuss the conference in the fall to determine who from the team is going and what arrangements need to be made."

"Fuck, already?" I complain. The trade show features the same assholes every year followed by a circle jerk awards ceremony to measure dicks and strangle our pockets.

"Things book up quickly, and we need to finalize which

employees are going to be nominated and who has a reason to go to the show."

Marie is no bullshit, efficient, and effortlessly in love with her husband. She makes my life easier, and there's literally not a flicker of sexual desire between either of us. I do my best to keep her happy so she doesn't leave me to work with someone with a better disposition.

I'd never had an interest in any of my employees before, and I don't plan to start anytime soon. There's work, Avalon, and my family. I don't need anything to fill the spaces between that.

"The forms are in your email about the categories. I've already filled out who I think would be the best nominations in sales, marketing, and we will need to submit for design of the year. Krystal will handle the hotel and corporate events while in Vegas."

"Thank you, Marie."

"Oh, and your dad called. He's picking you up to go to lunch." She drops that bomb before turning away and leaving my office.

Typical.

He stepped down and had me take over Carlson Commercial Enterprises, yet the old man can't seem to let go.

I open Marie's email and scrub my face; I was half asleep when Penny texted me last night and I couldn't fall asleep after. I knew I was being too hard on her, but I was so fucking angry.

It's frustrating watching her never reach her potential. She's smart and capable but dates the biggest losers you could imagine, but more than anything, that man putting hands on her nearly sent me over the edge. I've always had a slight protectiveness over my cousin. Maybe it's because we always felt like the odd ones out.

My oldest brother, Aiden, had his sights on professional baseball early on and it was his life. My younger twin brothers,

Gavin and Benjamin, have been connected at the hip since birth. So it left me the ornery middle child, and the cousin who took a significant amount of time to piece together with the family. I'm seven years older than my twin brothers and Penny, so I remember watching her slow evolution into getting comfortable around all of us. Well, mostly.

I should text her, make sure that she's alright, and that she doesn't go back to that dick bag lawyer's house. But she's a grown ass woman, and it's none of my business what she does with her life.

Marie's email is thorough and I add a few employees in for awards, in total, twenty of us will be attending the event in October. I forward the email to both Marie and Krystal while I look over the plans for the land we want to purchase towards the border.

The day flies by as lunch time hits and my dad comes strolling into the office like he owns the place—technically he does.

"Pizza sound good?" he asks, looking over the space that used to be his corner office, which is now mine.

"That works," I tell him as I shut down my computer, grab my phone and wallet, and head outside into the sweltering fucking sun that seems to spite me.

My dad drives because he's a control freak who can't let go —maybe it's genetic.

"Collin Kemper is fading. Have you spoken to Aiden?" he asks.

I clear my throat and nod. I'm closest to Aiden out of all of my brothers. He's three years older, but we have the most in common. He co-owns a sports supply company with Collin Kemper, who is slowly losing his battle with cancer.

"He's been busy trying to keep Kemper's up and running while Collin's been sick."

"He hasn't been answering my calls or wanting to schedule anything. I thought maybe you could talk to him, get him out of the office, and take a little break."

"I can do that," I tell my dad.

"And what about you? How are things at the office?"

"Don't act like you don't have Marjorie in HR spy on me."

"It's not spying, she plays mahjong with your mother, if I happen to overhear things."

"Yeah, sure, dad."

"She says you work too much," he says as we pull up to the pizza place.

"Is that a bad thing?"

"I know times are different now, but when I was your age I had four sons, one of them entering middle school and a wife to come home to. I don't want you to lock yourself away, Linc."

"I'm dedicated to the company," I say, resisting the urge to walk back to the office so I can be spared this talk.

If there's one issue with the Carlson family, it's that they're all up in each other's shit. It's why I've kept so much to myself. It's easier that way.

"It's just I thought you and Vanessa were happy, and then we never saw her again."

"Drop it, Dad," I say as I hold open the door and we sit at a table and order food.

"It's been four years, Lincoln."

I sigh and look at my dad, trying to plead with him to change the conversation.

"It didn't work out. She's married now."

I don't mention all the other details of that horrific breakup or how long she's actually been married. Anytime I think of Vanessa I get a fucking ulcer and find myself wanting to drink myself into a coma. It's best not to remember what happened four years ago and how it's all been fucking down hill from there.

"I just worry about you is all."

"I know, Dad."

Me too.

"I SHOULD GET HOME," Aiden says, sipping his whiskey.

It's uncanny how much we look alike. He's a little taller, his eyes a little greener than blue, and right now his dark hair that matches mine is slightly shorter. But the Carlson brothers are undoubtedly carbon copies of our father in looks and size.

"We just got here," I say as Tex pours me another beer.

"It's just not going to work for me tonight," Aiden says, and I smack his shoulder.

"We can stay at the bar," I suggest.

The front of Avalon is set up like any high end bar would be. You wouldn't suspect that once you go into the backrooms, everyone is giving into their most intimate fantasies. Aiden and I are both members, but we do our best to keep some secrets between us.

Front of the house is a safe zone. Once you go into the back, all bets are off and where we head our separate ways.

"How's Collin?" I ask, and Aiden rubs his face.

"Not good. He dropped a serious fucking bomb on me today. I think he knows it's the end."

"What did he say?"

Aiden downs the rest of his drink before looking at me. "That he has a twenty-five-year-old daughter from an affair and to make sure that she's a part of the last will and testament."

"Collin?" I ask, shocked.

The man is about as wholesome as you can imagine. The

idea of him having a twenty-five-year-old kid somewhere out there that he didn't take care of is completely out of character.

"Fucking tell me about it. So on top of managing everyone at work, preparing for the inevitable when it comes to Collin, now I have this shit to deal with."

"Fuck."

"Yeah, you're telling me. Pretty sure he's telling Abigail and Zach about it tonight."

I wince over the thought of him telling his wife of over thirty years and his son this big of a secret while he's on his deathbed.

Aiden rubs his hand across his face and looks back at me.

"Everything good with you?"

"Yeah, just working."

"I'm going to head out. Thanks for getting me out for at least a little while though, I needed it."

"If you need anything else, just let me know, man."

He smacks my back as he leaves, walking out of Avalon. I pick up my drink and head to the back rooms.

Avalon is huge, but the main space when you leave the bar is mainly for exhibitionism and meeting new people. It's a luxury club, everything decorated in rich golds and luxe matte black. It's a weekday, so it isn't as crowded as I take a seat by myself.

Couples have been more popular at the club than singles lately, and shit has been getting messy.

Too messy for my liking.

I like my life in a predictable, neat box.

When I come to Avalon, I want things cut and dry. I'm only here to fuck. Nothing more, nothing less.

It's how I like my life, the more I can control, the more information I know the less I have to worry about things going to shit. Routines, organization, and structure make me feel in control.

Yet...

"Fuck," I hiss under my breath as Colleen approaches me.

It's not that anything is wrong with the woman. She's pretty, smart, no major personality disorders that I can discern, but she is clingy.

I don't do clingy.

Nothing makes my dick limper than over eagerness, I'm well aware it's a character flaw. Or maybe I'm just a prick.

But Colleen is one of the few single women here, so we've played on more than one occasion. I can tell she wants more. She tried to kiss me last time, even though that's one of my hard limits.

"Lincoln, there you are. It's been awhile," she says, her voice pleasant and soft.

I'm not sure what's wrong with me, she's open, attractive, but I find myself completely disinterested at this moment.

"I've been busy."

"You didn't answer my texts about when you would be here next," she says.

Lesson fucking learned. I'm never giving my number to anyone here ever again. Honestly, I should probably look for a different club, this one has shifted since it first opened a few years ago. I'm not sure that it fits in with my tastes the same way it used to.

"Did I do something wrong?" she asks and I wish someone would fucking smite me so I didn't have to live through the rest of this impending conversation.

It's not Colleen's fault that she likes me. We fuck. It's hot, and sometimes that can lead to feelings. But she doesn't really like me, she doesn't even know me. If she did, she'd run far away looking for a nice guy who can at least learn how to work a vibrator.

"The only thing I'm good for is my cock, Colleen. If you want anything else, you're looking in the wrong place," I tell her honestly. I'm not the boyfriend type, I'm the guy you fuck and then realize you want a husband who is actually emotionally available.

She swallows, her back going straighter as she glares at me.

How I'm the bad guy for not wanting more while fucking at a no strings attached sex club when my intentions have always been clear, I'm not sure. But I have no problems with being labeled an asshole, I could be called much worse things.

I click my teeth and shake my head. "You can't change me, Colleen. I'm not some fixer-upper boyfriend that you met at a sex club and it turned into a fairy tale romance."

Her mouth opens and closes sharply.

"A text saying you aren't interested would have been enough, asshole."

She stomps away, headed toward the locker rooms as she leaves my space. With the mood thoroughly killed, I head back to the entrance. I stop by the calendar to see upcoming events, hoping they are recruiting for more single people when I see that they will be opening more specific rooms, one of which might solve all my problems.

Maybe I won't cancel my membership after all.

BEING a glorified office bitch was not my aspiration in life, and yet, here I am sitting at the front desk and compiling a list of all of Tabitha's clients to send them an email. I swear she gets worse with every passing day.

Ever since she started fucking Zach Kemper—the co-owner's son—she's been insufferable.

I'm finally finished with the list and I send it over to Tabitha. Aiden hasn't asked me for anything today, which is odd. He's been working so hard and I know how hard everything with Collin is hitting him. It's something you can feel throughout the entire office.

Collin Kemper is loved, and he won't be here much longer. Besides his son, Zach, he's closest to Aiden.

I pull my chair back from my desk and go to his office to see if he wants me to pick him up some lunch or if maybe he needs to talk.

I find him with his forehead down on the desk, taking deep breaths.

"Aiden?" I ask, knocking on his door frame.

My cousin looks up at me, blinking away tears. I walk into his office and shut the door behind me. Out of all of my cousins, Aiden is the most kind, beneath his imposing exterior is a sweetheart.

"What's wrong?"

"Nothing, it's just Collin. It's everything. I swear to fucking God, if Tabitha comes in here with one more expense report, I might actually lose it."

"Would some lunch help?" I ask him and he nods his head. "Why don't we get out of the office?"

He sighs, but begrudgingly agrees.

I take him to the taco truck down the street. He graciously pays, like always, as we sit down at the picnic table.

"How are your parents?" he asks. He's been skipping Sunday dinners like it's his job.

"Good, retired life suits them."

"I feel like I'll never fucking retire at this point," he grumbles.

"Oh shut up, I don't even have a 401k."

He stops eating his taco to blink at me and I know I'm about to get a lecture that I absolutely do not need right now.

I hold up my hand to stop him. "I'm working on it. I promise."

He sighs and looks at me patiently. "I know this isn't what you want to do forever."

"I'll figure my shit out, Aiden. This lunch was to help you stop worrying about your shit, not to harp on mine."

"It's easier to talk about you. How's planning going for the fourth of July?"

"Amazing," I beam.

My favorite thing about this job is planning events. Did I think I'd be working here for as many years as I have? No, but this part I actually enjoy.

"Davers and Davers Law Firm and Larry's Pools have both signed the contract, so the yacht is all set up and isn't going to cost us as much as we thought."

"Thanks for handling all that. I know it's a ways off, but I think everyone in the company needs something to look forward to."

I smile. I like doing a good job. But this isn't where I want to be forever. I wish I were one of those people who grew up knowing who they were. Instead, I'm stuck changing who I am every single fucking year and not finding anything that sticks.

Maybe I'm potentially going through a quarter life crisis, but then again, my whole life till this point has felt like one crisis after the next.

"Do you ever feel like you don't know who you are?" I ask, catching Aiden off guard.

"All the fucking time," he replies.

It's not reassuring in the slightest.

WHAT'S the best way to figure out who you are? Anonymous sex, obviously. My consultation for membership is private. I didn't want to strut through the club, not knowing if Aiden is here.

I might have accidentally stumbled onto one of his personal emails from the club listing what his preferences are. Even though I know I should have exited out of the email immediately, my nosey ass did not.

I should probably go somewhere else, but maybe it's because I'm hard-headed or the fact that it's right down the street from my apartment building, I can't pass it up.

Plus, with what I'm interested in, we would never cross paths.

What I want is beyond just sex with strangers. I want to push the limit.

I'm in the back office with Clara, who handles membership management, as she tells me about the bells and whistles of the club. I don't want to waste her time, so I interrupt her.

"This is all lovely, Clara. I appreciate you wanting to tell me about all the aspects of the club, but I'm looking for complete anonymity."

"Ah, then this is what you're looking for."

She slides me over a brochure with a key hole on the front and it all clicks for me at that moment. It's everything I've been wanting to explore. The desires no one has wanted to delve into with me, that I've been judged for. Maybe Avalon can be the place where I can express myself and figure out who I am, at the very least explore my sexuality without the fear of my heart being involved.

"You'll go by an alias as a member, of course, only the back end staff will know your true identity. If there is anyone you do not want in your room, you'll just have to let us know. Or if you have a scene with someone and would no longer like to partake in activities with them, we can add them to your hardline list. While we understand the point is anonymity, we also want you to be comfortable. Of course, this is a new aspect of the business, so we would have pre-scheduled times through our portal and you select other members' profiles who are interested in the same things as you. This is also where you will list your limits, there will be safeguards in place in the room, but we can go over that next week. The profiles are how we use the online scheduling portal to ensure everyone gets what they want out of the experience. I'll be sending you home today with the paperwork on how to sign into the portal and how to create your profile for the Key Club."

"So if there's someone I know who is a member, I can list

them as someone I would not entertain, ever? Even if they don't have a profile under the Key Club?"

"Yes, as well as if you didn't have a good experience, you could put them on your banned list."

"That will be perfect."

"We're still a week from opening up this section. There will be a private entrance for this space, and security measures in place to keep everyone anonymous, since that's the allure of the Key Club. I can schedule you in for Wednesday for a tour."

I flip the brochure over looking at the price and give Clara a tight smile.

"I don't know—"

She waves her hand. "We can work a discount for the first two months," she says with a smile and I wonder if they don't have many single women interested in Key Club. Either way, I will eagerly take the discount.

Clara waits, and I almost wish the idea of bartering didn't make me want to throw up to lower the price even further, instead I just out reach my hand and shake hers.

She smiles and puts me on the calendar and gives me all the information needed to sign up for Key Club and what I specifically need to do for my portal.

For the first time in a long time, it feels like I'm doing something for myself. I'm not signing up because of a boyfriend or doing what they like. It's something I've fantasized about.

This is for me and for no one else.

I'm so sick and tired of being the girl who changes who she is to adapt to a man. I'm ready to do something just for me. It might not be in the form of me figuring out what I want to do with my life or truly getting my shit together, but despite that, it feels like a start.

It feels like I'm on the right path of figuring out who I am.

THE AVALON PAPERWORK is in my bag as I walk home. I'm slightly sweaty by the time I get my mail and head to the elevator. Even though it's not far, I'll definitely order a ride when I come back, especially at night time.

As soon as I hit the button, Lincoln comes strolling in through the apartment doors and stands next to me.

We're both quiet for a long time.

"You haven't spoken to that douchebag, have you?" he asks.

I knew not to expect an apology for the way he spoke to me. I'm not even sure that Lincoln knows how to say the word sorry. He did me a solid by picking me up, expecting anything beyond that from him would just be a let down, at least that's how it's been for the last four years.

"No, and with no plans to. But I told you that already."

"So you did."

"Are you coming to dinner on Sunday?"

"Unfortunately," he says, and I push the elevator button again, even harder this time.

"God-fucking-forbid your family wants to spend time with your grumpy ass."

"It truly is remarkable how they keep inviting me week after week, isn't it?"

I roll my eyes, and Lincoln jams his finger against the button.

"Wow, whoever built this place should have to do time for how shitty this elevator is."

"Shut up," he says, pushing the button again. Carlson Commercial Enterprises built the building. My asshole cousin more than likely pre-approved this elevator company.

The bell chimes and Lincoln holds out his arms as we both walk into the space that feels smaller all the sudden.

I'm not sure when things with Lincoln got so bad. No, I remember when it all went to shit. He had a long-term girlfriend, Vanessa. He brought her to a bunch of family functions and then suddenly he no longer brought her places and that was that. He didn't say why they broke up or what happened, he just turned into this person we all see today.

I don't think I've ever had that effect on a man, and it's probably fucked up to feel this way, but I can't help it. I want someone to care about me so deeply I have the power to destroy them.

Wow, maybe I need to increase my sessions with Deb this week.

The door slides shut and Lincoln leans against the back of the elevator. "How was my brother today?"

"He's losing his mentor, his close friend. He's not doing great."

"You'll let me know if he ever seems too bad?" Lincoln says, and I look over at him.

There are these small moments—little glimpses—of who he used to be. Under whatever baggage he's been carrying, he still cares about his family. He didn't second guess me the other night; he came and picked me up right away. He's taking the time to check in on Aiden when so many others think he's strong enough to handle the pressure he's under.

Lincoln might not be nice, but he is kind.

"I think if Tabitha quit, his life would improve drastically."

"I don't know why he doesn't fire her," he says, like he truly doesn't get his brother's thought process. Maybe Lincoln just has no problem firing people.

"Collin never made his employees sign non-competes. Tabitha has the biggest Rolodex out of all the salespeople."

"I wonder why," he says while making a ridiculous dick sucking motion.

I can't help it, I laugh.

I really try to be all for women's rights and wrongs, but God, that woman is fucking insufferable. She makes my life a living hell some days, and it's nice to know I'm not the problem. She is.

The elevator opens to his floor, and he leaves without saying goodbye or anything else. It's not a surprise, but I start to wonder why Lincoln is the way he is, and maybe he's more misunderstood than I realized.

Maybe me and my aloof cousin have more in common than either of us could have ever imagined.

Penny

Sunday Dinner

I HAVE a few hours before I head over to my parents' house for family dinner and the Avalon paperwork is taunting me from my desk. I yank it off the counter and grab my laptop, I know if I don't do it now, I never will.

This is what I wanted. To try something new and exciting and learn about myself while also shielding my heart.

Since my heart might be located in my vagina most of the time, it makes the Key Club perfect for me. Anonymity is going to open a new world of exploration for me. Add in copious amounts of therapy and avoiding men like the fucking plague—I think I can do this.

Maybe one day I'll graduate to actually going into the club itself. But something about the mystery and this being a secret only I know about is empowering to me. While others might find it degrading or seedy, the primal nature of it all calls to me.

A lot of my previous sexual partners were very against the things I wanted to explore. This gives me the freedom with no strings, no feelings, and no fear. It can be my own little secret.

The site loads and I put in the username and password assigned to me as well as my main profile that is only accessed by Avalon employees, which includes my billing information, address, club status, and medical information.

I scroll through the different sections of the main club, and there's a lot that intrigues me, but nothing like the Key Club does.

My next step is to create an alias and my specific profile for Key Club that other members will see to potentially match with me. It looks like there are options to be set up with anyone, completely anonymous, or you can click through aliases and see who might work for you and request a meeting time.

I like the idea of clicking through to make sure they have the same interests as me, going all in with no idea whose on the other side is too nerve wracking.

I've been thinking about my alias name for days now and I'm torn as I sit here, the screen staring back at me. I don't want to use a common name; it feels like it should be more code than anything. Or perhaps, just something sweet.

I put my alias as Honey, and move on, not wanting to over-think it and wind up with something ridiculous.

As I scroll through the form, the common questions you would put on a dating profile are nowhere to be seen. You don't put your age, your photo, or anything that is personal enough to make you identifiable. But you put your limits, what kind of play you're interested in, and what you want out of the experience.

The first row is formatted as yes, no, or maybe.

It's thorough and goes over things I never even thought about, like do I want to be able to hear the other person, which is a hard no.

God, how pathetic is that? I feel like I could fall in love with a complete stranger by just hearing them talk to me during sex.

But knowing myself is part of my growth, so I stop my spiral and move on with the rest of the questionnaire.

There are a slew of questions about personal preferences, do's and don'ts.

The last section is where you can write what you're looking for from this experience and to me it feels like it's beyond the physical. It's about what I want not only for my body, but how I want to leave this place feeling.

I fill out the form and take a huge breath as I hit submit. I'll see the room on Wednesday and then I'll be able to schedule my first encounter. I'm as nervous as I am giddy, but it's been a while since I've felt so excited about something. As silly as it is, I feel like this is the right first step on my growth journey.

LINCOLN GIVES ME A SILENT, tense ride to my parent's house, which is only twenty minutes away. They haven't moved since I left the house years ago. Thankfully, when I fell on my ass, the first time I got dumped and with nowhere to live, they decided to gift me the apartment I'm currently living in.

I'm smart enough to know that if I didn't have the family I do, I'd be in much worse shape than I currently am. My parents have given me the world, and yet, I still don't feel good enough to be their daughter.

I might not be living up to the Carlson standard with where my cousins are in their life, but the Myers' standard is just as high.

"Penelope, sweetie, is everything okay?" my mother, Holly, asks as she gives me a big hug.

I scrunch my nose at the use of my full name and just hug her back.

"Everything's good."

"Aiden was telling us how much work you've put into the company outing you're planning," she tells me with a huge smile.

It's embarrassing, I'm hitting thirty sooner than later and my mother has to act like my planning a company function is a big deal.

All of my cousins are ridiculously successful. Aiden played in the MLB and is CEO of a company. Lincoln took over for my uncle and father when they stepped down from Carlson Commercial Enterprises. Even the twins are successful in the clubbing sphere.

Then there's me. Penelope Abigail Myers, front desk at Kemper's Sport Supply with my twenty-two college credits, embarrassing dating history, and no fucking clue where I want to go from here.

My mother pets down my hair and kisses the side of my head.

Holly Myers is as beautiful as women get. She's sixty-five, but you would never guess. She has perfectly dark hair, not a single gray in sight, her skin is tight and clear and her brown eyes still have a youthful sparkle.

I grew up constantly wishing I looked like her. That I looked like anyone in my family. It's not that I don't realize I'm attractive, I just never fit in. Anywhere she took me, strangers would ask about my blonde hair and what relative I got it from, and I didn't have an answer.

"I reached out to the PI," she says, interrupting my thoughts.

"You didn't have to do that, Mom."

My mom cups my cheeks and looks at me. I feel like I might cry. Why do moms have the ability to just make you want to shed your whole damn soul in front of them?

"Knowing this information doesn't change anything for me or your father, sweetheart. Nothing could change how much we love you. We should have started this process sooner. I'm sorry for that."

My eyes are welling up with tears as she touches my face.

"Unless something has changed for you. Oh, God. I'm not pressuring you, am I?" she asks.

"No, Mom. I still want to know."

I want to know because it's hard to not only not know where you come from biologically, but it's the fear of the unknown. Why didn't they keep me? How could they keep me until I was two and then disappear? And most of all, why has it been so hard to find them after all this time? I've signed up for every ancestry site and I still don't have any hits.

My mom pets down my hair. I know I have it good, beyond good.

Yet there's always this lingering missing piece that no matter what I do, I can't seem to stifle.

My parents were everything you could want parents to be; loving, kind, generous. But most of all, understanding. I never had to hide my feelings about being adopted, or try to shield them from my feelings of not fitting in.

They know by getting this information, they won't be replaced. No one could ever take away the bond I have with my parents. But there is this incessant need to know the whole story of where I come from.

"I'll give Loyd your information and he can update you on anything he finds."

"Thanks, Mom."

She squeezes me tight as she leads me through the house and to the kitchen, where the rest of the family is waiting for us.

SUNDAY DINNERS always wind up the same. Our parents hang inside and even though we're all grown adults now, we always wind up outside.

Gavin laughs as he passes me the joint and I take a deep inhale before handing it to Ben.

"How was Atlanta?" I ask, and Ben whistles before blowing smoke out of his nose.

"It's called Hotlanta for a reason. God damn."

"Do I even want to know what you two got into up there?"

"You definitely don't, little cousin," Gavin answers.

"You two are gross," I reply as they laugh at whatever inside secret they aren't sharing with the group.

"Disgusting," Gavin says jokingly.

"Degenerates," Ben adds on.

Lincoln rolls his eyes and puts his hand out, where Ben hands him the joint.

"I don't understand why you two are looking for an existing property when we could build you your dream club."

"You're not invited to the next rotation, such a buzzkill," Ben jokes and Lincoln passes it back to him.

"I'm just saying. Why fuck around with all of these older, dated buildings that need so much work to make them what you want them to be? Let's build the club the way you want from the start."

"He's got a point," I say and the twins roll their eyes.

"You two are still teaming up against us? Listen, we'll think about it. The Tampa club is doing well and so is the one in Ft. Lauderdale. But it's a lot of money to build a property from the ground up, not to mention the time and legislation." Gavin groans and glares at Lincoln. "You're really ruining my evening with all this work talk, to be honest."

"What should we talk about, then? How Aiden isn't here for the fifth week in a row? How Penny had me pick her up from some creep's house who hit her, or how you two are so codependent you can hardly be apart for more than a few days at a time?" Lincoln says, and I look to the sky for strength.

"I'm out," I say, hopping up out of the lawn chair and walking toward the lake.

I'm not far when Gavin reaches me and bumps me with his shoulder.

"What a dick," he says, handing me a beer.

"Who, the creep or your brother?"

"Both."

"I'm swearing off men for a while. Going to work on myself, figure out what I want to do, figure out who I am before I start dating again."

"That's very mature of you," he says.

I turn and glare at him.

"You think I can't do it?"

He sighs and throws an arm over my shoulder.

"You're the biggest hopeless romantic I know, Pen."

"I'm working on it."

He squeezes my shoulder as we sit at the bench overlooking the lake. The sun is nearly set and I take a deep breath while taking in the view.

"You deserve someone who doesn't change you, who lets you be yourself."

"What if I don't know who I am?" I ask, turning to face my cousin.

"You're Penny. You're caring, loving, always have a smile on your face no matter what you're going through. You're sunshine, and I don't want to see you with anyone who tries to dull your shine ever again."

I sniffle and bump him with my arm.

"You're actually quite sweet when you want to be."

"You better not fucking tell anybody."

"My lips are sealed."

"Good, now let's go back inside. I think your mom made cheesecake."

I laugh and nod my head, because honestly, cheesecake sounds amazing and any more introspection I might just combust.

Lincoln

Honey

THE LOCATION for the Key Club is wholly separate from Avalon. One guest will enter through the current pathway that I'm entering from and the other entrance is on the other side.

Clara gives me a warm smile as she leads me down the hall and directs me to two doors. Both of them are black, one with a gold circle and the other with a heart.

"The heart is for the larger glory hole that a potential partner's bottom half can go through. The circle is just the signature glory hole experience. I know your preference is for women, but if you are interested in pegging, you can also partake in that section."

I blink at her, and she just nods, opening the door and leading me inside.

"This would be your side of the entrance."

The room is simple. Dimly lit, a table on the left and a panel with buttons on the right. The walls are black with gold light fixtures and nothing remarkable in the space. It's simple, direct, and most of all, discreet.

"The most ideal position for this type of glory hole would be her legs pushed back against her own body. A bit of an air-tight seal," Clara jokes as I inspect the half-heart shaped entry.

"Your partner for the evening will be first to arrive. Your door will not unlock until they hit the green button. Announcing that they are ready. You will also be the first to leave after your scene is finished. We understand that anonymity is our clients' highest concern with being a member of the Key Club and we want to make sure we help keep the mystery alive."

"Limits?" I ask and Clara leans against the dark wall, her tablet in hand.

"Current membership includes use of the Key Club twice a week. When you log in to the portal, you will be able to see your selected scene partner's limits before requesting to book with them. We will provide a list upon arrival as a reminder as well. Guests are allowed to bring in any additional toys or items as long as they are approved by your pre-scheduled partner."

Clara is efficient and direct with her answer. She's part of the reason I finally caved and got a membership. She's no bull-shit and a hell of a saleswoman.

"You mentioned a green button?"

"Each side has safeguards," she points to the three buttons. "Simple red, yellow, green to signify limits if needed. There is also an alert button on both sides if you need someone from the club to step in. Music is optional, but the wall is thick enough it's hard to hear the person on the other side. The preference is up to you."

I nod my head and inspect the room. Everything Avalon does is luxe, and well thought out—this space is no exception.

It's clean, simple, and straightforward.

Exactly how I want it.

No feelings, no niceties, just raw fucking.

"Have you uploaded your profile?" she asks.

"Not yet. I'll do it tonight."

"We've gotten multiple new members because of this new room. We already have sixty people in the database."

"How many of them are men?"

"I'll have to look when I get back to my desk," she replies with a cringe.

Meaning that there aren't many women to choose from. I'm not surprised more men are signing up for this specific room. Maybe it won't be as easy to find someone to scene with as I imagined. I'll have to take additional care in my profile to ensure that I'm someone of interest.

"We also allow couples to book the room if they don't want the anonymity feature."

The couples.

They get fucking everything.

I don't want a relationship, far from it. But it feels like they own everything at this goddamn club. What happened to casual sex?

"We have other nights planned utilizing this room as well, but everything will always be updated on the portal. As you know, cleanliness is of the utmost importance to us here at Avalon, so there will only be 4 sessions available each night. You will receive an access code to the Key Club five minutes prior to your scheduled time."

"Thank you, Clara."

"Of course, as always, if you have any questions I'm here to assist. After you schedule and hold a session, we will be sending out questionnaires to see how we can make the Key Club the best that it can be."

"Maybe a new name," I say and Clara tries to hold her smile.

"Yes, well. Is there anything else?"

"That will be all. Thank you for taking the time to show me the space. I'll make my profile tonight."

She gives me a curt nod, a clear dismissal. I wonder how many of these fucking tours she has to do today. I take one last glance at the room behind me and wonder if maybe it will be the thing to help me get through this lull I've been in.

COMING up with an alias and answering eight-hundred fucking questions has me second guessing if I want to be a part of the Key Club, but with nothing to do, I somehow prevail.

I choose Wayne as my stupid alias, because fucking Batman was the first thing that came to mind, and I drone through all the mandatory questions.

No, I, in fact, do not want to get pegged.

Yes, I would prefer music on instead of odd silence on my end of the wall.

Yes, I would prefer to wear a condom.

No, I'm not okay with sounding. *Jesus Christ*. I scrub my face as I continue clicking check box after check box, somehow feeling vanilla each time I hit no.

Once I finally think I'm done and can hit submit, I'm plagued by the final section where you have to write a little about yourself.

I tap away at the keys, remembering that I somehow need to stand out in a plethora of guys who want to partake in the new club experience. Granted, a huge portion may not even be into women, but I didn't sit here for nearly an hour clicking through all this shit to not get chosen.

There's not supposed to be any identifiable information, just a little something about what you want from the experience. How do I write that I want to fuck someone without them looking at me, begging me to kiss them? That I just want the sexual gratification with no other strings attached, just dirty, primal fucking.

So, I write about what I want my experience to be like.

I want you wet and waiting, eager to please, and willing to take what you get. I'll make it good for you if you deserve it. You'll be writhing on the other side of the wall, begging for a stranger to fuck you. We might not know each other, but I'm ready to make your fantasies come true.

Fuck it.

I hit submit and wait while the circle in the middle spins and it creates my profile. It automatically compiles a list of women who would be of interest to me.

If I have to read through all these damn profiles, I might just toss the whole idea out the window. This is why I don't date, why I don't approach many women at the club. I have no interest in the personal details of these potential women beyond what's going to happen behind closed doors.

I look at the aliases and they're all stupid basic food names. I roll my eyes and click on the first one.

Scrolling past all her check marks, I look at her personal note about what she's looking for.

Looking for a safe space to explore my sexual desires. I want to be used on my terms.

That's it. Two simple sentences. I immediately submit an inquiry to the stranger who is calling herself Honey.

She could be 60, unattractive, or completely not my type beyond a glory hole, but it doesn't matter.

It doesn't matter who she is, what she does, or what she thinks about me beyond my cock inside of her.

I PUSH THE ELEVATOR BUTTON, it's been at least four minutes and the piece of shit still hasn't hit my floor. No longer having patience, I decide to hit the stairwell.

"Mother-fucking, cock-sucking, cunt."

I smile at the voice as I see Penny on the next level, collecting papers and haphazardly cleaning up spilled coffee.

"Rough morning?" I ask, bending down and collecting the dry papers I can.

"If the fucking elevator was running properly, I wouldn't have had this issue."

"I'll call maintenance when I get to the office."

She looks up at me with watery eyes and nods. I finally look at the papers I'm collecting.

Shanahan's Private Investigations is plastered on the front with their crest. The rest are details about Penny's adoption history and general information about where and when my aunt and uncle adopted her.

"You're looking for your parents?"

"My birth parents, yes."

"I didn't realize that was something you wanted."

She shrugs her shoulders, giving up on the coffee as she stands up and takes the paper from my hand.

"I just need to know," she says, and I nod.

"What if you don't like what you find out?"

"Hating the result is better than not knowing at all."

Don't I fucking know it?

We head down the stairs together; I text the cleaning crew to clean up the stairwell and send another text to Marie to have the elevator guy come out and figure out what the fuck is going on.

The sun is blistering fucking hot as we step outside.

"Do you want a ride to work?" I ask her.

Kemper's isn't far from our building, but it's still on my way to the office.

"Please," she says and we get in my car and I blast the AC as high as it will go.

"Do Aunt Holly and Uncle Tim know that you're looking?"

"Yeah, it was my mom's idea. I've held off on actually doing anything, but now it feels like the right time."

"Why?" I ask.

She pulls her dress down over her thighs and fidgets with the hem before speaking.

"I'm turning thirty and I'm not anywhere near where I thought I would be by now. I hate my job. My relationships have been one shitty boyfriend after the next. I think having some closure on my birth parents will help me move on, among other things."

"Other things?"

She looks over at me and squints. "You're being a chatty Cathy today. But like I told you before, no more boyfriends. Maybe I should go back to school or something, but the idea of going back at twenty-nine makes me want to jump off a tall building."

"Don't go back unless you want to. You'll figure something out."

She looks at me like she's never seen me before as we pull up to Kemper's.

"Thanks for the ride," she says, opening the door. I give her a sharp nod and drive off to the office.

Penny and I were closer when we were children. Once I hit my late teens, I wanted nothing to do with my younger cousin and twin brothers. Our lives went separate ways, besides family gatherings. But it's been recently that I've started to actually pay attention to her. I've been so caught up in my own shit I never really cared to dive deeper into what her life must be like.

Maybe I'm not the only fucked-up one in the family after all, and it's wrong, but it's nice to find solace in someone else's pain.

Penny
Praise Isn't Given, It's Earned

I'M at my desk fantasizing about all the epic ways I could quit my job. Throwing a drink in Tabitha's face, screaming, *I quit this bitch* is at the top of my list right now.

Sharon, from accounting, heads over to my desk and looks around. "You want to cut out early, head to Mutiny for some drinks?"

"You had me at cut out early."

I pull the drawer open, grabbing my purse and leaving all the private investigator's information behind as I hightail it out of the office.

Mutiny is a little hole in the wall place right around the corner from the office. The amount of my paycheck they get is honestly obscene.

Sharon lights up a cigarette next to me as we walk, but she's courteous enough to keep the smoke from blowing anywhere near me.

"Who's on your shit list today?" I ask her.

"Zach," she groans. "Listen, I know his father is dying, and he's more than likely going to inherit at least half of the company, but does he have to be such a stuck-up asshole?"

"At least he hasn't been in the office as much."

"Yeah, only to swing by and pick Tabitha up at the end of the day."

"They are truly a match made in Hell," I say, and Sharon barks out a laugh.

"Collin let them run wild. I think Aiden is feeling the weight of that now," Sharon says.

I nod my head, feeling sorry that my cousin has to constantly deal with them.

The air conditioning inside of the bar is welcoming as we take our seats. Sharon is a friend, I guess. But she's the kind of friend that's situational. We both work at the same place, and have the same gripes. But she's in her mid-fifties with two divorces and two teenage sons under her belt, besides working at the same place we don't have much in common.

"So what's new with you?" she asks.

I know Sharon would be absolutely riveted if I told her about Avalon and the Key Club, but it's my secret. Even if asked point blank about what I'm doing, I'm going to lie. It's my dirty little secret and I plan on taking it with me to my grave.

So, instead, I tell her about my search for my parents. "I hired a private investigator to look into my birth parents."

"No shit?"

"I just want some closure there, ya know? I don't have any grand ideas of wanting a close relationship with them. I just need to know why."

Sharon takes a sip of her drink and looks at me with a motherly softness.

"No matter what you find out, just know that you have so many people who care about you."

I swallow thickly.

"Thank you, Sharon."

"Now let's get wasted and talk shit about everyone in the office. Did you see that girl Ed is dating? Did he get her off a website?"

I laugh alongside Sharon, feeling the lightest I have in days.

＊ ＊ ＊

I DIDN'T DRINK TOO much at Mutiny, despite Sharon's peer pressure. Her son picked her up, and I walked home and immediately jumped in the shower to wash away the day.

I hate living in Florida this time of year, but as the cool water washes over my body, I forget about it. I wrap my hair in a towel, as well as my body and lie down on my bed. My apartment is frustratingly quiet. Maybe I should get a pet.

No... we are not getting a pet during whatever crisis I'm currently going through. Maybe in the future though.

I'd much rather be in a house with a husband and the sound of children playing, but this is my life.

What little buzz and happiness I had when I was out with Sharon slowly fades away as I grab my laptop and open up the Avalon site.

I have ten requests for the Key Club.

I don't let it affect my ego too much, because the truth is they're just going off my profile, it's not because they actually want me. Which is fine, because that's what I want too.

Either way, the reality is that this fantasy is going to come to life and I need to decide who I want to give that honor to.

The first three profiles are super bland, and seem like they just want to put their dick in a hole to have it serviced. Which I get, it's part of the point, but for me? It's more than that.

The next profile goes by the alias Big Daddy. I don't even bother opening that one.

The next ones aren't so bad, but they don't stand out to me either. I'm left with two remaining files, Sparrow and Wayne.

I open Sparrow's first. He seems to be really open to toy usage, both types of glory holes, and it says he enjoys praise. I squint at the screen and scroll down to the sentences he had to write about what he wants from this experience.

I want you to be a good girl for me and take my cock.

My answer was also brief, but it doesn't give me what I'm looking for. I'm not looking to be someone's good girl, I mean maybe sometimes, but that's not what this is for me. If I wanted praise and to be a good little pet, I'd just go straight to Avalon and find a partner to do that with. I only want praise when it's completely earned.

My needs are darker, and I'm not sure that Sparrow is the one to fulfill them, but he is currently my top choice.

I click on Wayne's profile, and hope that maybe he has something more interesting. Just like Sparrow, he's open to toys, impact play, but he has some additions I haven't seen in the other profiles. The ones that catch my eye are delayed gratification, edging, and spitting.

I tap the side of my laptop and lick my lips. That's definitely something I could be into.

I scroll down and see he would specifically like to wear condoms during intercourse, which isn't an issue for me, until I finally get to his bio.

I want you wet and waiting, eager to please, and willing to take what you get. I'll make it good for you if you deserve it. You'll be writhing on the other side of the wall, begging for a stranger to fuck you. We might not know each other, but I'm ready to make your fantasies come true.

I read it at least five times.

This is—he is—exactly what I've been looking for. I reply, clicking three times I would be available and take a deep breath while I stare at the screen.

It doesn't even take a whole minute for me to get a notification that he has accepted my invitation for 9pm tomorrow night. My heart thunders in my chest as I look at the scheduled time.

Am I really going to do this?

I absolutely fucking am.

I'M NOT sure why I shaved my entire body, did a face mask, and I'm wearing a dress that is both slutty and sensual for tonight. He won't even be able to see me or feel me. I thought that just doing a simple old school glory hole would be the best first start.

Maybe even between a wall there will be some level of chemistry and then the next time we can work up to me being completely exposed and for the taking.

Part of the intrigue is being on the opposite side of the wall on my knees for some stranger.

I consider getting a drink beforehand, but decide against it. I just kill time outside the building, waiting for my code to be texted to me so I can go inside.

Whoever is putting their body inside always goes into the room first. I wonder how weird it's going to be to not be able to talk to him or hear his pleasure. This is what I wanted to experience, though. To others, it might seem informal with no sensual aspect, but for me, it's quite the opposite.

I like the idea of being used. I like that when I walk into that room, my only purpose is my mouth.

I haven't been able to really explain to my previous partners this feeling I've been chasing. I'm usually met with confusion or disgust. How could I want to be used or degraded? It's not that I truly even want to be degraded with words. Maybe I just haven't done a great job explaining myself.

Putting it into words is difficult.

But the Key Club feels like a safe place to finally express this feeling. If I don't like it, I can easily walk away and never talk about it again. There are safeguards in place, and I don't have to explain myself to anyone. In fact, no words will even be spoken.

My phone vibrates, and my heart stops as I look at the code. I take a deep breath and ready myself.

This is what I wanted.

I clutch my purse as I head toward the side entrance. The hallway is short and I reach the door with the golden circle plastered in front of it and enter the code. It's like I'm barely breathing as the lock whirls and I wrap my hand around the handle and enter the space.

Sensual instrumental music is playing as I put my belongings on the side table. The room is dimly lit and small, but there's no missing the massive cock protruding through the other side of the wall, waiting for me.

The man on the other side of the wall, Wayne, doesn't

move. He just waits patiently.

Tonight is about his pleasure, and though it might not seem like it, there is power in being able to make someone fall apart.

There's innate power in getting down on my knees for a stranger, the soft material of my skirt rises on my thighs as my calves rest against the padded material.

I rub my hands on my thighs before I cautiously wrap my hand around the base of his cock. His dick twitches and shifts in the hole from the sudden touch. I smile to myself as I stroke him a few times.

The space is large enough for his entire cock and balls to be on my side of the wall as I move my fist up and down. As far as penises go, he has a nice one. The right amount of girth. The tips of my fingers barely touch one another as I slide my fist along his cock. The tip is leaking pre-cum, and I boldly stick out my tongue, licking up the release.

The music is too loud for me to hear his reaction, but I can see his balls tightening against his body.

It's an interesting feeling not being able to hear or see his reaction in a big way, but it's enough to spur me on.

I slide my one hand into my panties, playing with myself, mostly to get my fingers wet, while I suck on the head of his shaft.

It breaks his patience as he slides back and forth through the hole, the tip of his dick slipping in and out of my parted lips. It doesn't matter who I am to this man, all that matters is my mouth is making him feel good.

It's dirty and makes me wetter. When my fingers are sticky and wet, I grab his length again, covering him in my essence.

There's a thump against the wall and I swear it must be his hand hitting the wall for support as I cover him in me and then sink him back down my throat.

I taste myself. The salty musk of my juices is warm against

my tongue as I take him deeper down my throat. He can't grab the back of my head and shove me down, not that I would mind, but I also like this feeling of controlling the situation while also being used.

My hand grabs his cock by the base, my tongue sliding over his slit and the ridges of the head before I take him down deeper. He feels so much larger as I swallow him down; he hits the back of my throat. I find myself wanting to please my stranger, knowing he isn't easy to please.

Praise isn't given, it's earned.

I take him down, dropping my hand from his length and the tip of my nose touches the wall as he takes control, fucking my mouth, taking what he wants, using me.

I do my best to ease the gagging, but it's inevitable and he just shoves his cock down my throat, anyway.

Tears are forming in my eyes, but I feel like I have something to prove. I need to show him that I'm good, that I not only want this, but so much more.

My hands rest against my thighs and I dig my nails into my flesh, the bite of pain taking away some of the discomfort of him hitting the back of my throat—I welcome both.

There's another soft bang against the wall before I feel his cock jerk and warm cum trickles down my throat. I do my best to swallow as much as I can, but some slips between my lips. I suck hard as I slide back, popping off the tip of his length.

I stare at his cock that's still slightly hard. I expect him to stay there, and let me leave first, like I'm supposed to.

But he doesn't.

He slides his dick back to his side of the wall, and my heart sinks, thinking our little anonymous game is over.

Instead, he slips his hand through the hole. I'm stunned for a moment, and don't move. He takes a moment, but his hand searches around for my face, until he finally cups my chin, his thumb swiping around my lips and shoving any remaining cum into my mouth.

His hand is soft, there aren't any major calluses on his fingers. He must have been wearing a suit, but took off the jacket. All that remains is his white dress shirt. I suck his thumb, tasting his release.

He brushes my lips one last time with the pad of his thumb, the motion almost tender, before his hand slips through the hole back to the other side. The lighting is dim and I can barely see anything except his expensive suit as he turns and leaves the Key Club.

I didn't come, but that wasn't the point of this meeting. It will still be the material I'll use to masturbate until my next encounter with Mr. Wayne.

Lincoln

Did You Have a Lobotomy?

I DON'T KNOW what I was thinking, breaking protocol and sticking my hand through the hole to touch her face.

Maybe it was because I wanted every last drop of me pushed between those soft, pouty lips that sucked my cock so perfectly.

Or maybe... maybe I'm more into touch than I thought.

No, it's just new.

It was odd not being able to wrap my fist in her hair, or to speak with her. Not that she needed direction, but it was still a completely new sensation.

She was so eager to make me come.

She paid to suck my cock through a hole, and that just made me want to fuck her throat all over again. I'm not a selfish lover, but taking what I wanted? It turned me on in a way I haven't experienced in a long time.

I'm too old and pay too much money at Avalon to play games. She did good and should be rewarded. I thought that I'd get off on her being faceless and there to please, which I am. But there's also the curious side of me that already wants to know who she is and what she looks like.

Her skin was tight and soft, and her lips were plush and needy, but beyond that all I know about Honey is that she sucks cock beautifully—I wonder if her pussy will take me just as well.

As soon as I'm in my parked car, I login to the website and send a formal request to Honey, scheduling a time in the heart room.

I drive home, feeling more relaxed than I have in weeks. There's no pressure beyond the Key Club. I don't have to worry about her wanting more or dodging her at the club. What's between us stays in that dimly lit small room, and nothing more.

I grab a sandwich on my way home and park my car, and head toward the lobby. A black SUV drops Penny off and I squint at her as she shuts the passenger door.

The car is blasting music as she approaches the lobby door.

"I thought you said no more dates?" I say, wondering if she really couldn't hold off on men for more than a few days.

"He was my driver, you fucking idiot," she says, storming past me and grabbing the door handle.

"And where were you dressed like that?"

She's wearing a sleek black dress that hits all the right spots. I shake my head, feeling like an absolute creep for noticing how attractive my cousin is. It's not that I haven't noticed before, I just actively will myself to forget that she's an attractive woman.

"Obviously sucking strangers' dicks for money," she says with an eye roll.

"Did you get some friends I don't know about?"

"I have friends."

"Sharon in accounting doesn't count," I snap back.

"You're one to talk. Your brothers are your only friends."

"That's not true. Marie is my friend."

"No, Marie is your assistant that you pay to deal with you."

We both glare at each other as she shoves her finger aggressively at the elevator button. Thankfully, it comes swiftly and the metal doors open wide, letting us both enter.

"And where were you?" she asks, looking me up and down.

"Client dinner."

"Did you all jerk each other off while talking about laminate floors and overhead lighting?" she asks.

"We did. Greg really needs to work on his form. His wrist is a little limp."

That makes her laugh, even if it adds an eye roll.

"Was the food so bad you had to pick up a sandwich after?" she asks.

"Yeah, the poor hand job really put me off my meal. Good night, Pen," I tell her as the elevator opens on my floor and I head back to my empty, blessedly quiet apartment.

HOW THE HELL does an adult man get new friends?

Penny's words lingered with me well into the night, ruining my high from the evening I had with Honey.

Honey is easy, she doesn't talk, gives great head, and expects nothing after.

Friends, girlfriends, family, all they do is want me to be someone I'm not.

I'm never going to be the guy mowing the lawn on weekends in my busted scratched up Reeboks, inviting my nosey, self-absorbed neighbors to block parties.

I'm curt, sarcastic, and impatient.

The only people who want to be around me are people who's paychecks I sign and the people who are biologically required to love me.

It's fine... that's fine.

But it's not.

"Fuck," I groan as I sit at my desk, staring out the large windows into sunny Florida.

I hate this state. It's too bright, hotter than fuck, and everyone seems happy. Why? What in the world do they have to be happy about?

You live life and you fucking die.

God, I sound like a miserable eighty-something year old man who hates the world. Is this all I have left in life?

There's a notification on my phone. Honey accepted my invitation and we're scheduled to meet three days from now.

It makes my lips twitch.

Marie walks through my office and gapes at me. "Oh my God, are you smiling? Do you need to go to the hospital?" she jokes.

I just hold out my hand and she hands me the paperwork I need to sign for the Mansfield property.

"Krystal will be here this afternoon to discuss Vegas. Do you need anything else?"

"No. Thank you, Marie."

She blinks at me and I almost want to swallow the thank you back down my throat.

"Whatever this is, keep doing it," she says, waving her hand at me.

I'm such a rotten bastard that my assistant thinks I'm an alien for being a decent person. I rub the palms of my hands against my eyes.

Why do I feel this way? Why now?

I was fine. For years I was fine, just floating through life after everything that happened with Vanessa. But now? Is the way I'm living life good enough? Will I look back years from now and regret not being surrounded by more people who care about me, that I didn't start a family?

Is that what I want?

I'll never be a team dad, or the husband who's thoughtful and considerate all the time. But I could be, couldn't I? If I really wanted to do those things, I could try to do better. It's not like I have a steady partner to even consider this with. I'm thinking about someone I'm going to fuck anonymously for fuck's sake.

I pick up my phone and text Aiden.

What does a midlife crisis feel like?

AIDEN

I'm not even fucking forty. How would I know?

I thought your retirement from the MLB was your midlife crisis?

AIDEN

Maybe you should see a therapist.

I roll my eyes and place my phone screen side down on the desk. What is it I truly want?

I shake away my existential crisis and focus on work, and my upcoming night with Honey.

That has to be enough, because I'm not sure I'm capable of anything beyond that. I don't touch my phone, just plug away at work until there's a knock at my door.

"Come in," I say, without even looking up.

The person in question comes and sits in front of me, making me abandon the current report that I was looking at.

"Krystal," I say, noting the event planner's presence.

She handles everything from our building grand openings, client get togethers, to employee functions. She also helps with staging when needed.

Krystal doesn't take any bullshit, and for the most part I let her do her own thing.

"Right, the tradeshow and awards in Vegas."

"I'll have everything planned, but I won't be able to attend this year," she says, leafing through her files.

Her nails are unpainted, and her outfit is simple business casual, as well as her hair in a tight bun at the back of her head. She hands me a file, peering at me with her deep brown eyes.

"Why not?"

"My wife is having a baby," she says, sitting back and placing her arms on the arm rests.

I'm not stupid enough to ask how exactly they made it happen and it's none of my business.

"Congratulations," I say.

Krystal rolls her eyes and crosses her arms over her chest.

"She's due in October so I'm not risking missing anything by not being there."

"Okay."

"Seriously, I can't—wait. What?"

"Being here is more important. As long as you handle the major planning, I don't see why you would have any issues."

"Did you have a lobotomy?"

"Just tell me what I need to know," I grate out and she smiles, a deep set dimple forming against her light brown complexion.

"Let's start with accommodations."

I SPENT about an hour with Krystal finalizing the details and budget for Vegas. I considered going to Aiden's place and forcing him to hang out with me, but I decided to go home.

It's quiet in my apartment, something I treasured just the other day.

But as I sit on my couch in complete silence I wonder if there's more to life than just surviving, and if there's anything that might save me.

Penny
Silent Degradation

I'M DAYDREAMING at my desk again. It's been a problem all week. I'm fantasizing about a faceless man who wears suits and what he's going to do to me tonight.

I'll be exposed, completely at his will, and the thrill of it all makes it hard to concentrate.

The point of this all was exploration, giving myself something that I've wanted for a long time. Yet, I find myself falling into old habits.

Wayne, my stranger, consumes too much of my thoughts, just like every man I've fallen for way too quickly.

Part of me thinks I should stop. Actually, no, the rational side of me absolutely knows I should stop. The more I meet up with him, the more I'm going to wonder, daydream, and contemplate the kind of man he is.

I should have just stuck to masturbation, or maybe I should switch up partners at Key Club.

But the idea of choosing someone else seems like more of a risk than anything. Wayne could be meeting other people, but part of me doesn't think so, at least not yet. God, I'm truly fucking pathetic. Am I seriously getting jealous over the idea of a man I gave anonymous head to doing the same with other women?

I rub my forehead, willing the thoughts to dissipate as a grating voice interrupts my wayward spiral.

"Penny, I need these copied and ready to go for my meeting with the county athletic board," Tabitha says, dropping a stack of papers on my desk.

I give her a smile and breathe through my nose before heading over to the scanner to do the wench's bidding.

It's not like it's rocket science to stick the stack of papers on one side of the machine and wait for the others to come out. I really should stick up for myself, tell her to fuck herself and make her own copies. But despite how much I hate Tabitha, there's part of me that doesn't want her to hate me back.

I need to find a new job and possibly a spine.

What would I be good at? I like kids, but I can't imagine being around them all day. Even though the idea of being a nanny has some appeal, at least when little kids boss you around, it's not out of malice. Maybe I'll make a pros and cons list about what I like doing at Kemper's to see if I can find something else suitable that doesn't require a higher education.

If only I could go back in time and shake myself for ditching second semester to go on tour with my boyfriend at the time.

I need to schedule an appointment with my therapist sooner than later. There's too much going on to filter through this all on my own. My need for love and affection from men has led me to have no close friends, so I really only have my mom, Sharon, and my therapist to rely on.

Christ, things are looking bleak.

"Everything okay, Pen?" Aiden says behind me and I nod my head. "You really should tell her to do that herself."

"It's alright."

"I'm going to head to the hospital. Things aren't looking so great," he says.

I squeeze his arm, and he looks down.

"If you need anything, Aiden, just let me know."

"Can you just keep an eye on my email and flag anything important?"

"You've got it."

"Thanks, Pen."

He packs up for the day and heads out to see his ailing friend. Collin might have been a good twenty-something years older than Aiden, but they still had a close friendship.

New item on the finding who I am and what I want to be— get a fucking friend.

AGAIN, I know it doesn't matter what I wear, but the idea of looking good, even though Mr. Wayne has no idea, appeals to me.

I didn't go for sexy tonight, more so cute, in a yellow sundress that hugs my breasts and flares at the waist.

I'm really doing this.

My leg shakes in the backseat of my driver's car as he pulls up to the location. I give him a tip on the app, and he barely even acknowledges me as I step out and wait for my code.

It feels like my stomach is upside down while I wait. It's a mix of eagerness and anxiety.

This is something I always wanted, or at least a taste of it. Doing something seedy or seen as wrong while knowing I'm safe, that nothing truly bad can happen.

It's a fantasy, one that this stranger is going to bring to life.

I'm probably delusional, but I know it's going to be good. I know I'm going to leave this place on wobbly legs and yearning for more. Yet, I'm still going through with it. I'm not denying myself this sexual experience, even if it's only adding to my list of emotional issues.

No matter what happens in this building tonight, I'll learn something about myself, and that was why I signed up for Avalon and the Key Club. I just can't let it get to my head. It's just a sexual encounter, nothing more, I remind myself as my phone vibrates in my purse.

"Fuck," I groan as I pull out my phone and look at the code.

I open the first row of doors and the gold glittering heart on the door taunts me as I put in the code and enter the room.

Just like before, it's dimly lit with music playing. I peek through the half-heart-shaped hole to view the other side. They're nearly identical.

There's a table off to the side with condoms, and I grab the small vibrator out of my purse and place it on the table next to the basket.

A few deep breaths later, I'm placing my purse and panties on the table before climbing up on the leather bed. I don't bother with my dress or bra, because he won't be able to see them, anyway.

The leather is cool against my ass and lower back as I slide down. My hair spills around me as I scoot all the way to the entrance, sliding my exposed lower half into the vacant space.

There are stirrups if you want them. Instead, I just place my feet against the wall. I swallow thickly, my heart racing in my chest as I think about what he's going to see when he walks into the room.

I guess it's no different when I was on the other side of the wall. But I'm completely exposed to him. All he'll be able to see is my exposed pussy and ass when he walks in. The rest of me is a mystery.

The idea of him using me and taking me the way he wants is what has me pushing the button, showing that I'm ready.

I can stop this at any time, though every fiber of me knows I won't. As nervous as I am, I still want this so bad.

I place my shaky hands against my thundering heart as I wait. The waiting somehow feels like the worst part. The anticipation of what he's going to do is all-consuming.

My body is completely at his mercy. This man I don't know is about to own me for the night, and I'm eager for it.

The music is too loud, not glaringly so, just too loud to hear if he's entering the room or not. He could be staring at my pussy that is already wet with the promise of what he's going to do with me.

Will he be gentle? Rough? Quick? Or menacingly slow?

The top of the entrance is pressing against the bottom of my thighs, creating a snug fit. I know I'm going to be sore tomorrow, and that thought makes me even more excited.

This dirty little secret is all mine.

There's no judgment, just impending gratification. At least I hope.

I'm waiting for what feels like minutes on end. Did he not show? Did he change his mind?

I suddenly gasp as what feels like a thumb dragging along my pussy from my clit to my entrance. How long has he been there just staring at me?

My cheeks heat and my breathing increases. The vulnerability of my situation is heady and I swallow as he just drags his fingers through my wetness. I'm already dripping down my ass.

It should be embarrassing, but I only feel more turned on by the idea of him hard and stroking himself while looking at my dripping, needy cunt.

His fingers leave my clit and I moan, attempting not to move too much, not that there's much wiggle room with the way I'm positioned.

All I feel is the cool air against my wet pussy, making me clench.

Is he watching?

Does he like watching me beg with my body?

Not being able to see or hear him adds a level of wrongness to the situation that I can't deny. Letting this stranger touch me and use me however he pleases is thrilling in a way I didn't expect.

I'm so wet, it's nearly obscene. I can feel a trail of moisture dripping from my entrance.

The stranger on the other side of the wall touches me again, his fingers gathering the release and shoving it back in my pussy.

My lips part on a silent moan.

The only thing I can hear is my pulse and the instrumental music filling the room.

There's a soft press of lips against my mound, and I gasp. I wasn't expecting the touch or the tenderness. His tongue laps right above my clit, trailing down until he's leisurely sucking on my clit.

He's making this last.

Why do I find that so charming?

Something's fucking wrong with me.

He's slow, sensual, borderline teasing with his tongue. His goal isn't to make me come, no, he wants to draw this out, knowing that I'm at his mercy.

I savor it as much as I want to bang on the wall and beg. I'm not sure what I would beg for because he's doing all the right things, making me ache for it.

His fingers press inside of me, slow and methodical, while his tongue circles my clit. I'm not quiet and I'm not sure how much he can hear through the wall and over the music, but I don't care.

Suddenly, his fingers slide out of me and his tongue leaves my clit.

"Fuck," I complain under my breath.

I'm torn between wanting him to drag this out for all our allotted time in the room, and also wanting him to take away this endless need.

My thighs start to tremble against the wall and I swear to God I hear him laugh. It's muffled between the wall, but I know that he laughed.

It makes me wetter. It makes me more curious.

His laugh is dangerous, and addictive in a way that seduces my need for a deeper connection.

He's probably just staring at the way my cunt is milking air, begging to be fucked. He thinks it's funny watching me suffer. This stranger I don't know gets off on this just as much as I do, and I can't help the connection I feel towards them.

This understanding this faceless man has of me, that none of my previous sexual partners have had is overwhelming. I wait impatiently, my arms wrapping around my calves, trying to release some of the strain as I wait for his next move.

I gasp as his flesh smacks against my pussy lips.

Suddenly he's gone again and I want to scream, but before I can, I feel his breath along my pussy lips before a drop of spit slides down my slit.

He squeezes my ass, spreading me wide. I can only imagine what I look like as he slides the head of his cock through my spit covered pussy before sliding into me.

I hold on to the table beneath me as he pushes deep inside of me. My walls accommodate his significant length and I wonder if he can hear my needy moans of pleasure.

Unlike everything else, this isn't a slow introduction as he fucks me deeply, bottoming out, and filling me completely.

His thrusts aren't brutal, but they are deep and languid.

The way I know he's watching his length slide in and out of me has me arching my back and gripping the table to the point I know my knuckles are white.

It feels so right and wrong at the same time. How can a man I've never seen or spoken to work my body in a way no one else has ever been able to manage?

His thighs rub against my ass and I moan, feeling the combined wetness of my arousal and his spit collecting on the bench. For a long moment he doesn't move, just rests deep inside of me, feeling my pussy flutter around him.

The sound of buzzing is barely audible, but the sensation is immediate as he presses the vibrator against my clit as he fucks me.

My thighs tremble and moans of uninhibited, fearless pleasure rip from my throat. My nails scratch against the bench and I'm so fucking close.

I'm right there on the precipice. My impending orgasm is begging to be released and my back arches off the bench, my legs writhing in both pain and a need for both of us to come.

He pulls out and removes the toy.

The annoyed groan that leaves me is comical and I wonder if he enjoys how much he's torturing me.

He slaps the head of his cock against my clit three times before placing the small vibrator between us; the sensation radiating around my clit and the head of his cock.

Again, I'm so close, if he would just fill me up.

"Please," I whisper to myself, knowing he can't hear but needing the words involuntarily slipping from my lips.

He pulls away again, and I'm so close to shoving myself away from this wall and begging, when he suddenly thrusts roughly inside of me, cutting off any thoughts of moving from this position.

The vibrator is back on my clit and he fucks me like he owns me.

My body is his and I don't even know him.

He moves the vibrator to the right spot and I completely fall apart. My stomach tensing, my thighs shaking as I milk his cock and reach my peak. My breaths come out in shallow pants as he fucks me throughout my release. He doesn't move the vibrator or stop pounding into me even as my body shakes and pleads for reprieve.

There's a bang against the wall and his hips stutter as he comes. He doesn't turn the vibrator off right away and I'm about to shout at how oversensitive I feel, but he graciously turns it off.

He stays inside of me for a long moment.

How can something feel so intimate while being so impersonal? He cups my ass, sliding out of me.

I wait for the light to turn green so I can leave. I know I'm a drenched, exposed mess, but I take the time to breathe and get myself together.

There's a soft press of lips against my clit, and a few moments later the light turns green.

If I'm not mistaken, the stranger on the other side of the wall is trying to seduce me.

Lincoln

Bruised

I COME INSIDE of her with a groan, my forehead hitting the wall. Her thighs spasming from her release and no doubt from being bent like a pretzel on the other side of the wall.

It was difficult, but I still heard her moans of pleasure through the wall. I don't know why I haven't pulled out, why I'm not long gone from this room right now. But I just keep my softening dick in her and remove the vibrator.

Her pussy is a perfect shade of dark pink. As soon as I walked in the room, she was already wet, but now that I'm done with her, she's a fucking mess. I rub and hold her ass cheek, almost wishing I could see what it looked like in a doggy style position.

It's erotic being able to keep my softening dick inside of her, but I groan, knowing our time is over.

I pull out, admiring the wet sheen of her release on the leather bench and the globe of her ass. I dispose of the condom and consider reaching out to her to renegotiate that part of our limits. The idea of spilling inside of her and making her sit here while it slips out is enthralling.

I put the vibrator back where I found it and just stare at her for a long moment. Part of me just knows someone with a pussy that perfect has to be beautiful. Not that I should care or that makes sense. I shouldn't give a fuck beyond getting off and getting her off.

But there's this nagging in the back of my brain. There's something about her that I just can't shake and I'm not sure how I feel about it.

Somehow, despite how we're strangers who know nothing about each other and have never had a conversation, I feel connected to her in some odd way.

I don't want to leave this room; I realize.

Fuck.

Of course, out of all the women to interest me, it's the one who's faceless and enjoys the same anonymous kink I do. I put my suit jacket on and rub my face, the scent of her pussy lingers on my fingers as I look at her one last time.

I don't know why I do it, but I lean down and press a soft kiss against her clit before turning around and leaving the room.

What the fuck is wrong with me?

I head to my car and sit in the driver's seat for far longer than I need to. Contemplating everything. How did I get here? What do I want? And what the hell am I supposed to do now?

Thinking about it is all too fucking hard, I text my twin brothers.

> **Me: Are you two partying tonight?**

> GAVIN
>
> We're on the tiki boat.

> BEN
>
> We're going to dock soon if you want to hop on. There's a bachelorette party and a divorce party getting on board.

I'll be there in twenty.

With how much I work, I have a change of clothes in my car as I head off to the docks. It's probably not the most mature thing I should be doing, but alcohol has a way of making things clear.

I park at the marina where my brothers run their tiki boat business. I don't understand why they won't take my suggestion into consideration to expand by building from the ground up.

With it being dark, I don't give a shit as I take off everything but my underwear and put the short sleeve button up and shorts on, as well as a pair of flip-flops.

A horn blares and women scream as my brother holds the railing of the ship and screams.

"Welcome aboard, motherfucker!"

Ben is clearly partying while Gavin drives the boat.

He steers it just close enough so I can hop on and they continue cruising down the channel.

"Ladies, welcome the ugliest Carlson brother, Lincoln," Ben says into the microphone and there's a bunch of hoots and hollers.

"You're such a prick."

Ben smiles and grabs me a beer.

"What has your broody ass out this fine Friday evening?" he asks.

"Just wanted a drink, and to hang out with you two assholes."

"Hmm, likely story," Ben says. He looks back at the ladies on the boat. "Alright lovely ladies, who wants to do a shot ski?"

He starts setting up the shot ski, which I doubt they've washed since buying this boat, and I go hang out where Gavin is, captaining the ship.

"I thought you two barely captained these things anymore," I say, leaning against the back and sipping my beer.

"Kip got sick and Lucy is hungover, so we decided to take it out for a spin tonight."

"You two are lucky," I say, sitting down, chugging the rest of the beer and throwing the aluminum in the bin.

My brother glares at me and takes a seat while he coasts the boat.

"So are you."

"I just mean that you truly love what you do. You both seem so happy."

"You could be too," he says simply.

"I think I'm having a mid-life crisis."

He laughs, placing his wrist on the top of the wheel, and looks over at me.

"My millionaire brother, with his full head of hair, nice vehicle and apartment he keeps perfectly pristine in a crisis? You don't say?"

"What is that supposed to mean?" I furrow my brows, grabbing another beer from the center bar.

"You self-isolate, hate everything, and haven't been the same since Vanessa. I mean, you were always a dick, but after things ended with her, you changed."

I haven't told anyone in my family what happened; I was too ashamed. I dated Vanessa for two years. For two fucking years I had no idea what she was doing, and when I found out, it destroyed me. She didn't just take those two years from me, she's taken the four after it as well.

I don't say anything and Gavin sighs, leaning back, his head tossed back and his dark hair in loose curls.

"Call up some of your college friends. Hell, reach out to us more. We always want to spend time with you. Penny lives in your building, spend more time with her. People aren't meant to be solitary creatures, Linc."

"Maybe I should start dating again."

"Well, there are some divorcées and girls who are watching their friend get married first on this boat. It's like shooting fish in a barrel."

But I don't want any of them.

I want my mystery girl.

It's all so completely fucked.

"There's someone I have in mind."

He looks shocked, but doesn't ask me any more details. He squints at me and I glare back.

"What the fuck happened to your forehead?"

"What?"

"Your forehead."

I rub my head, and sure enough, there's a bruise forming where I banged my head against the wall when I came.

Wonderful.

The bachelorette and divorce party starts amping up. Ben plays music as the women sing and dance and he joins us on the back of the boat.

"Now we just gotta make sure no one falls off the boat and we're golden," Ben says. "What happened to your forehead?"

"Will you two fuck off?"

"Touchy touchy."

"Have either of you heard from Aiden?"

Gavin sighs, keeping his eyes on the women to make sure we don't lose one of them before they get married or get to live in post-marital bliss.

"Things don't look good."

"I'll call him tomorrow," I say and they nod.

It's how it's always been. I'm closer to Aiden and the twins have each other. If anything, the twins are codependent. Sometimes I worry about them, but they're also happy—happier than me, at least. Who am I to judge?

The women start drunkenly singing a song and I regret my decision automatically. Ben puts another beer in my hand as I rest my head against the railing and let the humid summer air hit my face.

I should stop paying for Avalon and find something else. I can't be pining after a woman who also chooses to be anonymous.

I guess it's time to finally grow up.

IT'S BEEN A FEW DAYS, and I stay off the Avalon site; I don't look to see if Honey has requested me and I don't request her.

Fuck, she's probably wondering if I didn't enjoy myself, but I can feel this sick obsession starting to creep on me.

The best thing I can do is to walk away completely.

I'll stop using Key Club and consider closing my account with Avalon as well. I haven't wanted something with someone in so long, of course it's the unobtainable that I want, so fucking typical.

It's weird, usually I enjoy working, and when I'm in my office I can easily put my head down and get the job done, but lately I can't focus. I groan, exiting out of the current report and my phone rings and I consider ignoring it until I see Aiden's name.

"Hello."

There's a heavy sigh on the phone and I already know before he speaks.

"Where are you?"

"Tampa General."

"I'll be there in thirty minutes."

He doesn't speak, just hangs up. I close out of my computer, lock my desk and head to reception.

"I'll be gone for the rest of the day. Can you handle my calls and put anything urgent on my desk?" I ask Marie, who nods curiously at me. "Collin Kemper," I say and understanding and sadness takes over her features.

I make the drive to Tampa General, expecting to go inside to find Aiden saying his goodbyes, but he's waiting at the parking garage entrance. I hit the unlock button and he gets into the passenger's side.

"Batting cages?" I ask, and he nods.

I drive to our usual spot. My brother is quiet and contemplative. I've never lost someone in this way before and I can't imagine what he's feeling. Collin Kemper was his mentor and closest friend.

"Do you want to talk about it?"

"No. Funeral is in three days."

I nod and do what I do best, giving him space. Traffic is a nightmare, but we finally get to the range and I rent a lane for an hour. I already know his preferred bat and grab him a helmet as I hand them to him. He steps in the cage and hits balls.

I wish I was more like Aiden. He called for help when he needed it, and this is the place he can get his emotions out.

Mine are bottled up and festering to the point of explosion. It's only a matter of time before I explode with no outlet. Suffering alone has always seemed simpler than depending on the shoulders of others.

Aiden hits the balls, the chime of the bat hitting the ball a small comfort. He doesn't talk, he doesn't smile, he just swings and hits the shit out of each ball.

Eventually he tires out, a sheen of sweat covering his skin as he hits the button to turn off the machine and steps out of the cage.

"Better?" I ask.

"Yeah, can I stay at yours tonight?" he asks.

Aiden doesn't ask much of me, ever. He doesn't hold me accountable for my shitty words, judge me for my moods. Whatever he needs at this moment, it's his.

"Yeah, man. Chinese sound good?"

He nods his head, and we stop at his house to collect some of his things. His large house where only he lives. While Aiden might smile, be kinder than me, I wonder if he feels just as lonely as I do.

Maybe we can help navigate this time of our lives together. I'll just have to work on communicating, which sounds revolting, but I need a change.

Penny
What I got

HE DOESN'T REQUEST me again.

I'm at my desk feeling desperate and unnervingly pathetic as I look at my phone repeatedly to see if I get a notification.

There's still a deep ache and tenderness in my thighs from nights ago. It was memorable for me and still lingering, but it wasn't for him.

I'm really trying and failing to not be in my feelings about it.

Work keeps me busy as I monitor things for Aiden and do menial tasks. Maybe I should look through the profiles again and see if there's someone else who interests me, or maybe this is a sign that I shouldn't be doing this.

Seeking validation from some random man who made me come super hard is truly a new low. Daydreaming and worrying about what he thinks about me shouldn't even be on my radar. Why did I think I could handle this?

My work email chimes, it's from Zach Kemper. His father has passed.

The office goes quiet. I can hear Sharon and Ed softly crying, and I have to wipe a tear from my face. Even though I haven't worked here as long as the others, he's had an impact on everyone in this office.

I text Aiden to make sure he's okay.

> I'm so sorry, Aiden. Let me know if you need anything.

AIDEN

Can you send everyone home early and just check in on my email?

> Of course.

I write up an email and send it to everyone in the office, telling them to take the day and that funeral information will be sent out as soon as we have the details. Everyone is down-trodden and sad as they leave. I stay at the office and wonder what that type of loss feels like.

I do everything I can to make Aiden's life easier before I head home.

There's still no notification and my fragile ego has a hard time dealing with the rejection as I sit on the couch of my empty apartment.

Nothing like someone's death makes you introspect on your own life. If I left this world tomorrow, what would I leave behind? Who would I leave behind? The thought just makes me sadder when I realize only a handful of people would care, and my imprint on the world is barely even a speck of dust.

THE FUNERAL IS TASTEFUL; the room packed with people who loved Collin. Lincoln drove me so we could both support Aiden. Multiple members of the office are here, along with his friends and family.

Lincoln looks around the room and leans in to whisper to me.

"I knew he had a lot of friends, but Jesus Christ."

I shrug my shoulders and look at the new and familiar faces alike.

"Does it make you think about who would be at your funeral when you die?" I ask, looking at him seriously.

He doesn't make a joke or look at me like I'm crazy when he says it.

"That was actually my exact thought. I didn't know you were just as fucked up as me, Pen."

"I think I'd be able to at least fill the first row. I don't know about you, though."

His mouth gapes open and he knocks me with his knee and I wince.

"What's wrong?" he says, looking down at me.

"Started a new workout tape," I lie. How my legs still hurt nearly five days later is beyond me, but I was squeezed in tight in that small little hole.

I point to his forehead.

"What happened to you?"

He touches the bruise on his forehead.

"Tiki boat with the twins."

"Been there," I reply.

The service is about to start and I look down our row, seeing a pretty brunette I haven't met before. She's laughing at something in the program before covering her mouth and the service starts.

Collin's family and friends share fond memories of him and I find myself getting choked up just because of their emotions over how much they loved him.

I want to be loved and missed even a fraction of what this man was.

It's my first funeral, and I didn't know what to expect, but it was actually a sweet farewell to the man I once knew as kind and loving.

People are starting to file out of the reception.

"I have to go talk to the lawyer about some of the will stuff. I'll see you tomorrow at work, Pen," Aiden says softly.

Lincoln and I nod.

"Want to get a drink?" Lincoln asks.

"Please," I sigh, feeling the weight of the funeral creeping up on me.

We pass Zach on our way out, who looks irritated, but that's not unusual before loading into Lincoln's car.

He doesn't ask my opinion on where we should go, which I shouldn't be surprised by. But what does shock me is where he chooses. It's close enough to our building that we can walk home, but it's definitely more of a dive, and tonight is karaoke night.

"Seriously?"

"Seriously," he replies, getting out of the car and I follow him.

We both look out of place, me in my black cocktail dress and him in his suit. He tosses his jacket in the back and rolls up his sleeves as we go inside.

We sit at the bar. The stools must have been here from the sixties with the way they're held together by duct tape and a prayer over the ass that's going to be sitting on them.

"Shots?" Lincoln turns to me and asks, placing his elbows on the sticky bar top.

"Tequila?"

Lincoln holds his fingers up and the bartender, who might have very well worked here in the sixties, slowly approaches us.

"What will it be, Linc?"

He's a fucking regular here?

"Four shots of Patron Silver chilled, please."

"Oh, don't act like you have any fucking manners," she says, grinning at him and going to pour our shots.

"You come here regularly?"

He shrugs his shoulders as a woman takes the stage and sings her rendition of Toes by Zac Brown Band.

"It's close to the building. The drinks are cheap."

"They have karaoke," I say in astonishment.

"Get enough drinks in me and maybe I'll sing too."

I blink at him as the elderly bartender puts our shot glasses on the counter.

"Your majesty, I hope they are chilled to your liking."

"Thanks Gladys."

I'm too stunned to speak as she turns to me, her hair is likely white, but it's colored bright pink. Her eyeliner is heavy on her waterline and her skin has clearly taken a heavy beating against the Florida sun.

She looks me up and down. "Who's the blondie?"

"This is Penny," he says, grabbing his shot glass and urging me to grab mine.

"You're too good to be hanging around the likes of this one," she says, pointing a finger at Lincoln, who laughs and tosses back his shot. I do the same.

"Do you have a whole separate life I don't know about?" I ask Lincoln. Something about the words bothers him as he takes the two additional shots he ordered back to back.

"Keep them coming Gladys."

"Remember, I don't take tips in the form of sexual favors," she says, and a laugh slips out of me.

Lincoln smiles as we both glance over at the woman on stage singing. Thankfully, she's actually pretty decent.

"Have you gone up and performed before?"

"A few times."

"Who are you and what have you done with Lincoln Carlson?"

He shakes his head. "It's my place, so just be grateful I brought you here," he says sharply.

I fake zipping my lips as Gladys puts more shots in front of us.

"I do have to work tomorrow, you know."

"So do I."

I toss the shot back. Drinking is definitely not a good way to solve your problems, but right now it certainly feels like it.

Too much tequila later....

"WOO!" I cheer as a heavily drunk Lincoln puts in his music choice and takes the stage.

The DJ introduces him. "Everybody, welcome Lincoln to the stage."

I cheer and clap my hands, nearly falling off my chair, which makes me laugh even harder.

Lincoln's hair is loose and sweaty, his shirt askew and more than a few buttons undone as he takes the mic. The beat starts and he starts swinging his hips. My mouth drops at how smooth he is.

There's a wide smile on his face and for the first time, he looks truly happy, it's handsome on him. I shake my head as I focus on what he's singing and I laugh even harder.

He passionately sings What I Got by Sublime, and the audience, including myself, chimes in.

His voice is actually pleasant, and he's animated when he sings. It's definitely an effect of the tequila. But this version of

Lincoln? It's hard not to love him, to not want him to be like this all the time.

It's endearing and I see Lincoln in a light I never have before.

He dances on stage, singing the song, carefree as I've ever seen him.

There are some whistles from the older ladies at the bar and I chime in, which just boosts his ego even further. He keeps up with every word, eating up the attention and moving his hips.

He ends the song and dramatically drops the microphone, exiting the stage. I clap like a madwoman, cupping my hands and wooing at his performance.

Lincoln comes stumbling over and nearly falling, using my body for balance. His hands are warm and I swallow and shake off the touch.

"Your turn."

"No fucking way."

"Come on, Pen."

"After that performance, ain't no way."

"I believe in you. Come on Penny. Go sing."

He starts tickling my side, and I nearly fall off the stool before he catches my arm.

"Come on."

I glare at him but get off my stool.

"Penny. Penny," he starts a chant and gets his band of AARP members to add into the chant and I finally give in.

I give him the finger and he gasps, but mimes like he is grabbing my middle finger before shoving it in his mouth and swallowing it. I shake my head but walk up to the DJ booth and flip through his book.

"Everyone welcome pretty Penny to the stage!" he announces, and I take the stage, grabbing the microphone.

I wave to Gladys, letting her know I'm going to need a drink as the music starts. As soon as the chorus starts, I can see Lincoln throwing his head back in laughter.

I close my eyes as I sing the song and I'm shocked as more audience members sing along. It boosts my confidence as I belt and dance to ...Baby One More Time at the top of my lungs. Feeling empowered, I dance and command the stage, but Lincoln's face sticks out among the crowd. His smile beaming bright with his hand over his heart as he sings along.

I'm sure I'm off pitch, but this is the most fun I've had in weeks, maybe months. I feel free; I feel happy; I feel like me.

My eyes water as I wrap up my song.

"Thank you, Tampa!" I shout into the microphone before putting it on the stand.

Lincoln is up front and grabs my hips to pick me up off the stage and put me back on my feet.

He's so close as he smiles down at me.

"You fucking killed it."

"I did, didn't I?"

"I felt like I was at her concert."

I throw back my head and laugh as Gladys brings us more drinks that we don't need.

We sit at our table, intermittent karaoke taking place as we laugh and joke and enjoy each other's company.

"You know you're actually fun when you're not hating the universe," I tell him, sipping the Margarita I swear is the last.

"I don't hate everything."

"You have for the last couple of years," I say and he tilts his head.

"You're no stranger to a bad breakup," he says and I sip and nod.

"Vanessa?"

He tosses back the rest of his drink and rests an elbow on the table, his chin resting on the palm of his hand.

"I thought she was my person. I mean, I know looking back I wasn't the best boyfriend, but still I didn't expect what I found out."

His blue-green eyes are glassy as he looks at me.

"You've probably been nothing but a good girlfriend to all those assholes you've dated."

I shrug, wanting to push more about Vanessa, but clearly picking up on the topic change.

"I don't know," I say, grabbing my straw and biting on it.

"What do you mean, you don't know?"

"I always changed who I was with every boyfriend. I just wanted them to want me, you know?"

"They'd be stupid not to. Let's go home," he says.

Gladys grins at us and holds up her own shot as Lincoln grabs a wad of cash and shoves it in her tip jar.

"We bid you farewell. Please visit us peasants the next time you need ale. So long fair maiden," she says to me and I wave and smile.

We start the walk to our building, which feels way fucking longer than it did the drive here.

I drunkenly bump into him with my shoulder.

"You're not so bad, you know?"

He smiles and says nothing. I wonder if I'll see this side of Lincoln again, or if this is just a rare glimpse of the man he keeps hidden under his rough exterior.

MY HEAD ACHES as I put a ridiculous amount of concealer under my eyes and pop two Tylenol.

As shitty as I feel right now, I don't regret last night.

It was the most fun I've had in a long time and seeing Lincoln actually carefree and happy is worth feeling run over by a truck.

Even though I wanted to call out and lie in bed all day today, I knew that wasn't an option. Collin's funeral was hard on everyone, but especially Aiden. I need to be there for him today.

Hangovers are a state of mind.

I repeat it to myself, even as my stomach churns. Maybe I'll go get something greasy and delicious for lunch to soak this all up.

I'm dressed and ready for the day, and I no longer look like a reanimated corpse as I leave my apartment and head toward the elevator.

It stops on Lincoln's floor and he enters; I give him a soft smile, and he doesn't return it.

"How are you feeling today?" I ask.

"Like shit," he grumbles, not looking at me.

I sigh, wondering if it's the hangover or if he regrets opening up to me last night. Either way, now is not the time to get into it.

"Do you need a ride to work?" His tone is sharp, businesslike.

"If you don't mind."

He gives me a curt nod, and he drops me off at Kemper's Sports Supply without a word between us.

The office is tense, not just because we're all still reeling after the funeral, but because word has gotten around that Aiden has offered a job to Collin Kemper's secret daughter.

I'm handling an influx of emails from other businesses wishing their deepest sympathies, when a familiar-looking woman enters and heads to my desk.

"Hello, can I help you?"

"I'm Jessa Peters. I'm supposed to meet with Aiden," she says. I then realize she was the woman who was trying to hold back her laughter at the funeral.

She looks a lot like Collin and Zach, with her dark hair, brown eyes, and olive-toned skin.

"Oh yes, Mr. Carlson is expecting you. Follow me." I stand up from behind my desk, and she follows as we walk throughout the cubicles and closed door offices on the left. "My name is Penny. I work the front desk, if you ever need anything."

"Thanks, Penny. I'm Jessa," she repeats.

I give her a smile, finding her awkwardness kind of charming and sweet. Part of me automatically wants to be her friend, not only cause we're close in age, but I doubt she knows anyone in the area.

"Oh yes, everyone knows who you are." I regret the words as I say them. I guess I'm also not as smooth with meeting new people. I direct her to take a seat and head back to my desk.

I can't imagine what she's going through. I also can't imagine

Collin abandoning his child. I hate that it makes me see him in a different light. Maybe it's my own issues floating to the surface. But if a good man like Collin can do something shitty, is there hope for any decent men out there?

With the funeral, seeing a different side of Lincoln, and Jessa's arrival to the office, I haven't had time to think about the other things looming in my life. Like how I'm still sensitive as hell over the fact that Wayne hasn't requested me again at Key Club, or how the PI hasn't gotten any additional information about my biological parents.

I feel like I'm attempting to improve myself and it's going nowhere.

Well, getting a true friend was on my to-do list. I can start there. I get Jessa set up with all the items she'll need and I overhear Zach being an absolute dick to her. Collin has to be rolling over in his grave with the drama he's caused.

What a douche. I head over to Jessa's cubicle and try not to fumble with my words.

"You've really caused quite the stir here at Kemper's."

"I didn't mean to," she says and I wince. Really fucking crushing this whole new friendship.

"Oh, honey. It's not your fault. Everyone here loved Collin. When he got sick, we were all devastated. When he was on his deathbed, we learned about his secret daughter. It was a shock to us all."

"Everyone knows?" she asks, looking around the cubicle hallway, and I wonder if she's worried about another confrontation with Zach.

I grimace and nod. "Everyone knows. I'm guessing that's why Zach's been a bigger dick than usual." I cover my mouth after I say it and shake my head. "Sorry, I shouldn't say things like that."

"If the shoe fits," she replies with a smirk, and I find myself liking Jessa Peters more with each passing moment.

"He was always kind of a tool before, but ever since his dad got sick, he's been on a real power trip. We all heard about the shares," I say softly. I'm not trying to gossip with her, well maybe I am. That's what girlfriends do, right? "Zach really likes to talk about himself." I shrug and realize getting out of the office will be the best place to really get to know each other. "Hey, want to get some lunch?"

"That would be great," she smiles and I feel some level of accomplishment.

"Do you like Mexican food? There's an amazing food truck right around the corner."

"That sounds great."

We make our way out of Kemper's and start the short walk to the food truck.

"So, where are you from?"

"I've lived mostly in Virginia."

"Never been. Well, we sat in traffic in Virginia on our way to Maine that one year, but I've never spent time there." If she doesn't think I'm a rambling idiot, it will be a miracle. "So you knew Collin was your dad?"

"I'd only ever met him twice." I nod and feel a pang of sadness for her. It's just so out of character for the man we all loved at the office. I guess it's true about never really knowing someone.

"He didn't seem the type to just abandon his kid."

"Men have a way of disappointing you like that."

"You're right about that. So the funeral was the first time you met Zach?"

"Yes, I didn't know my father had other children."

"Woof, this story keeps getting more messed up," I say, and

grimace. I've really got to work on not saying every stupid little thing that comes through my head.

"You don't have to tell me how messed up it is. I'm living it."

"Well, I'm here if you need me. I know it can be hard to make friends in a new town," I say, lightly touching her forearm. She gives me a smile and I hope that maybe she'll stick around at Kemper's and we can really get to know one another.

It's hot and I feel like I'm sweating tequila as I suggest we take our food back to the office. While we're eating at my desk, Zach walks past looking pissed as hell and I have to hide my laughter.

"Sounds like someone just got put in his place."

Aiden walks up to reception. He doesn't look fazed in the least as he rests his elbow on the table. "Jessa, when you're done, will you come to my office?"

Jessa frantically goes to pack up her food and Aiden holds out a hand to calm her down. "No, finish your food, take your time. I'll see you shortly."

"At least the person who matters the most in the office seems to like you," I say, the hopeless, ridiculous romantic in me already shipping my cousin with his dead best-friend's secret daughter. Something is supremely wrong with me.

"What?" Jessa asks and I shake my head and take a bite of my burrito bowl as I start to plot on how to both make Jessa my best friend and see if my initial reaction to these two being a match is spot on or not.

The day seems to drag on for fucking ever and I don't know if it's because I hate my job, or if this hangover is just kicking my ass.

I try to give Jessa space and pray that she'll be back tomorrow. It's the end of the day and everyone starts filing out, including an overwhelmed looking Jessa.

"See you tomorrow, Jessa," I say, and she smiles back with a nod.

"Yeah, see you tomorrow."

I gather the potential clients' lead list to give to Aiden so he can divvy it up between the salespeople so they can start cold calling. Almost everyone in the office is gone, except the man himself.

He's tossing a stress ball in the air and squeezing it in his bad hand when I enter his office. I drop off the files and look at him questioningly. Is he stressed because Collin's daughter is pretty as hell and absolutely his dream girl? Probably.

"What?" he asks, annoyed.

"She's nice."

'Okay?"

"I think..." I roll my eyes at him, and his shitty tone. "I think she needs a friend, and I plan on being that for her. I think she's sad."

"Of course she's sad."

"Maybe..."

"Listen, Penny. She's an employee, she's a shareholder. I'll be kind to her, not just because I'm her boss, but because she's Collin's daughter. Is there anything else?"

"Damn, don't chew my head off, or I'll call Aunt Maggie," I immediately throw out. Totally fine calling my aunt to tell her what a dick her son is being. Especially when Aiden is probably the kindest out of all of his brothers. This isn't like him.

"Seriously, you're going to call my mom when I tell you to mind your own business?"

"Yeah, maybe. I'm just saying. Everyone in the office is already gossiping about her; it's going to be hard. We have to make more of an effort. I'll make sure to ask her to lunch."

"That will be great. Is there anything else?"

I shake my head, clearing my throat to leave his office, when

I stop at the door frame. "Will you be at family dinner on Sunday?"

He nods and I smile. It's been so long since he's really been a part of any of the family stuff and it makes me sad seeing him suffer.

I probably shouldn't be plotting ways to make him fall in love with our latest employee. But my break from dating men has me antsy and wanting to at least see someone else get their happy ending.

They'll be none the wiser as I plant my seeds of forbidden office romance.

I collect my belongings and make the walk to my building. I really need to start driving again, but the fact is I hate it. Every time I try to get in the driver's seat of a car, I just freak out. It's not worth it, it's why I was more than happy to take the apartment when my parents offered. I can walk to work and the best food spots, plus Lincoln will drive me when needed.

I eat the leftover Chinese food in my fridge and put on something mindless, trying to ignore the overwhelming loneliness that's eating me up inside.

My next appointment with Deb is in a few days, and it couldn't come at a better time.

My phone vibrates, and I pick it up, seeing the notification from Avalon.

A massive smile takes over my face. I shouldn't be so excited over a man I don't know wanting to see me again. Maybe he had a busy work schedule, or had something come up and was just now able to reach out. My days of spiraling over why this man wasn't interested in me seems ridiculous. All the feelings of disappointment are quickly replaced by anticipation.

Lincoln

Selfish

I FEEL like shit the entire day. The entire meeting with the plumbing company had me wanting to end it all, but I somehow persevered.

I don't know why I took Penny to Calamity. After that funeral, I just wanted to feel alive, and not so alone. But as I head to pick up dinner, the feeling sinks in again.

Why can I only let my guard down when I've been piled with drinks or when I'm fucking a stranger?

It's all truly pathetic.

My number is called and I grab my bag of to-go food and head back to my car. And that's when I see her.

She's walking with her kids, who must be around eight and twelve, in my direction. She doesn't look any different. The same dark hair, same figure—same everything.

I feel like the universe is bending me over and fucking me in the ass as she notices me and sends her kids into the restaurant. The children who are exact clones of their mother look at me curiously before heading inside.

"Lincoln," she says softly.

"Vanessa." Her name tastes like ash on my tongue.

How was I so fucking blind? So self-absorbed that I didn't see the signs?

"I hope you're doing well."

She stands there confidently, like she didn't ruin my whole fucking life with lies. Her wedding ring is sparkling on her finger and my heart goes out to the bastard who chose to stay with her after everything.

I nod my head and go to skirt around her when she touches my forearm.

Her nails are painted a bright pink as I look down at where she's grabbing me. There's still resentment and anger when I glance back up to meet her eyes. The look she gives me is one of pity.

I wrench my arm away and she sighs.

"It's been four years, Linc. It was just a little fun."

I swallow, not knowing what to say. That isn't what she was to me. I mean, yes; we had a lot of fun. She was usually only available at certain times, and I didn't even consider that it was for nefarious purposes. I thought I liked that we had more time apart than together, but I still cared. I still wanted more.

She was the first woman who ever made me feel that way, and she destroyed me.

"It wasn't for me. You lied to me for two years, Vanessa."

The younger child opens the door to the restaurant and looks at his mom. "Mom, are you coming?"

"I'll be right there," she tells him.

"I mean it. I hope you're doing well," she says, touching my arm one more time.

She walks away like I mean nothing, which I suppose I don't. I was her boy toy vacation, a night away from her husband and kids once or twice a week. I wanted more; I wanted to be better for her, to settle down and maybe have a family of my own, but she couldn't commit.

It made me curious, and that's when I realized the last name she gave me wasn't her real last name and that I was her little toy. It was embarrassing. That I was stupid enough, blind enough, not to notice this woman had a whole fucking family already.

So I kept it in, didn't tell anyone while I tried to work on how I felt about it.

Four years later and I'm still bitter and holding a grudge, and it's not who I want to be.

She hurt me enough as it is. I can't keep living like this anymore.

I put the take out on the passenger's seat and blast the AC as I close my eyes and rest my skull against the headrest.

How fucking cliche? Becoming a workaholic, grumpy bastard after a woman breaks your heart.

I think about last night and how much I enjoyed myself. It's been a while since I went to Calamity, but I've never had that much fun. There wasn't any pressure to be a certain way. My guards were down. I hate that it took so much alcohol to get me there, but fuck, I felt good.

I rub my temples with my fingers and groan. No more over-thinking shit, just do what feels good.

I log into the Avalon app and request another meeting with Honey. It's probably not a healthy response to seeing Vanessa, but right now, I don't really give a fuck.

AIDEN, of course, asked me what I was doing tonight, and I stupidly mentioned Avalon.

So now, here I am, in the main area of Avalon, when I have

somewhere very fucking important to be in the next—I look down at my watch and sigh—forty-five minutes.

"Why are you sighing and shit? You're the one who said you were already coming here."

I shrug, and Aiden narrows his eyes at me.

"What aren't you telling me?"

"I don't know what you mean?" I easily lie.

"Yeah, alright. Let's act like I haven't seen you at the main club, yet you continue to mention how you're coming here. Or the way you keep checking your watch. Holy shit, are you seeing someone at Avalon?" he asks.

Oh, if only it was that simple.

How do you tell your brother that you're pinning over a woman you don't know, haven't spoken to, but could draw her pussy from memory?

What if she's here now?

I look around the room, looking at the different single women sitting around.

"You are waiting for someone," he says.

"Maybe I am."

"Never thought I'd see the day, to be honest. Who is she?" he asks.

It's then he glances over, his jaw slacked as a pretty woman with dark hair sits on one of the cushioned couches, sipping her drink.

"Her," I say, nodding my chin in her direction.

"You're full of shit. Stop fucking with me, Linc."

"What do you mean?"

"That's Collin's daughter, Jessa."

He says it and doesn't look away from the pretty brunette. He likes her, and it's going to really suck if she also turns out to be Honey.

"Excuse me," I say, nudging his shoulder and he grabs my arm.

"Do not fuck with me, Linc."

I give him a grin, noting that either way, this is going to be enjoyable. He lets go of my arm as I approach the woman in question.

"May I take a seat?" I ask, even though my ass is halfway to being sat already. I glance over at Aiden, who is red in the face.

"Of course." She gestures to the seat and I give her a warm smile.

"Lincoln," I say, holding out my hand. She shakes it, her hand soft.

"Jessa."

"I haven't seen you here before," I say, and she laughs. Is the laugh because she's currently using glory holes or something else?

"I'm here for the tour and to possibly join," she says, and I realize she's not Honey. Regardless, I take this moment to fuck with my brother. I haven't seen him get so irritated over a girl before.

"Is there anything I could do to sway your decision?" I ask.

"I have pretty strict rules being a visitor," she jokes and I can see Aiden already approaching us, his face nearly red with irritation.

"There are so many ways to make you come without fucking you, sweetheart," I say, and her throat bobs.

"That's true. What would you suggest?"

What a little minx. No wonder Aiden is torn up over his dead bff's daughter. She's a bit too sweet for my taste, but for Aiden? If he can get over himself, she might be just what he needs.

"I could—" Aiden grips me by my lapels.

"I'm going to kick your fucking ass later," Aiden whispers in my ear, and I smirk at Jessa. Oh, poor man has it down bad. I guess I'm not one to judge, considering I'm currently obsessed with a woman I met at a glory hole.

"I could... just head over and get a drink. Nice speaking with you, Jessa," I say to her, giving my brother a wink and I can tell he wants to probably hit me. It's too easy getting him riled up.

But with him occupied by his little crush, it gives me plenty of time to head to the Key Club and wait for my code to enter.

I do have to leave the building and head around back to wait at the entrance.

It's been running through my head how unhealthy this all is, but I don't care.

After seeing Vanessa, all I want to feel is the simple release that the Key Club and Honey brings me.

I rest my forehead against the door, realizing my fucking solace is a hole in a wall—literally.

My phone vibrates with the code and I input it. The door whirls. I leave my phone at the entrance before turning the knob to the heart room.

It would probably be cleaner, less attachment, if I took her to the other room. But I find myself craving what little intimacy we can get in this situation.

I chalk it all up to having what I can't have.

Surely I'm not wanting something more outside of the Key Club?

A groan escapes me when I see what's waiting for me. Honey's perfect ass and pussy are on display, but she's wearing tights that are stretched over her skin.

She wants me to rip them apart and take what I want.

Fuck.

This woman was made for me, yet a wall separates us.

I drag a fingertip along her stockings, the touch nearly

feather light. Just enough to let her know that I'm in the room and plan on toying with her.

There's this feral part of me that wants to drag her ass through this wall and fuck her on the floor while she looks at me and knows exactly who fucks her the way she needs. It's evident she needs this as much as I do.

Two peas in a very fucked-up pod.

I press my palm against her stocking-covered cunt, feeling how wet she is with anticipation.

How could she possibly know how much a pair of stockings would turn me on? I mean, of course, there's my extensive profile, but this wasn't on the list.

I press my palm harder against her pussy, almost like I'm physically showing her that it belongs to me.

Which it fucking does.

At least when we're inside of these walls—she belongs to me.

I should be thinking about what I want outside of this room and club. But I'm mesmerized by her body as I grab two sides of her stockings and rip them down the middle. She flinches, and the nylon stretches against her skin, nearly digging into her soft flesh.

Her pussy and tight little hole are exposed. Wetness is already dripping out of her entrance and I use my fingers to collect her arousal and slide it over her needy clit.

Is this the highlight of her week? Has she been thinking about how my hands feel on her constantly?

If she hasn't, I plan on fucking her so good she doesn't leave this room without the painful reminder of how well fucked she is.

I may have denied her last time, but this time we're going to aim for over abundance. At least as much as I can give her without being able to see her reactions or hear her voice. Fuck, how am I wanting more with this woman?

With a hand on the wall, I steady myself down to my knees and grip her rounded ass with both hands before I devour her clit.

The nylons digging into her skin are an addictive sensation and I use my fingers to slide under the black material, getting closer to her skin.

My lips wrap around her clit with my only focus being making her come all over my face.

Deep down I want her hands tangled in my hair and the sounds of her moans spurring me on.

The only thing I have to go off of is the way her cunt is dripping down my chin and her ass shaking in pleasure. But I want more.

I want to know what color her eyes are, and watch them roll back into her head when she comes on my tongue.

My fingers leave her nylons alone to finger her pussy while I lavish her with my tongue.

She tastes just as I remember, and I know there's no trying to hold back this infatuation anymore.

I curl my fingers inside of her and there's a bang against the wall before her cunt is clenching around my fingers and her taste is filling my tongue.

Typical, selfish me, I want more. And thankfully, she agreed to no condom tonight.

Her pussy is fluttering, and she's dripping from her entrance to her ass. I want to fuck her there, but I don't have the patience or the consent right now.

I use the wall for purchase as I fist myself, sliding the head of my cock up and down her slit, drenching myself with her cum—wishing there was no barrier between us.

When I slide into her warm, wet center, all I can think

about is how badly I want to fist her hair and look into her eyes while she takes me. There's this incessant need that's festering of wanting to know who she is, but more than anything, wanting her to know I'm the only man who can give her what she needs.

We don't need a wall for me to bring her fantasies to life—not anymore.

I'm deep inside of her, my pelvis pressing against her round, firm ass as I use my thumb to rub her clit.

Her cunt is fluttering around my length and I know I'm not going to last long. The music in the room is loud and I wish I could shut it the fuck up just to get a glimpse of how she sounds while she comes.

Does she whimper? Is it more of a light moan or a scream?

I've never given much thought to the noises someone makes when they fall apart, but I find myself wanting to hear just exactly how I shatter my mystery woman.

My balls are tightening as my hips slap against her soft flesh and my wet fingers strum against her clit, needing her to come again.

I need her to want me—I need to know I'm not alone in this fucked-up madness.

Her pussy milks my cock and I fall apart, slamming into her, fucking her through her orgasm.

The music shifts to another song and there's a low moan through the wall. I rest my head against the barrier between us as I spill inside of her, immediately craving more.

IT'S IRRATIONAL.

It's crazy.

It's fucking madness.

I keep telling myself over and over how stupid it is to want to find out who my mysterious Mr. Wayne is, but then, the perfect opportunity lands on my lap.

Avalon is doing a masquerade night right before the Fourth of July.

I can go, cover my face, be incognito and drop some little hints and see if maybe he's curious too. Hoping I'm not alone in feeling this connection.

I always knew my heart was in my vagina, but even for me, this is extreme.

But being with him with a wall between us just isn't cutting it for me anymore. Something tells me that Mr. Wayne might just be the man who can bring all my fantasies to life. The ones I've kept locked away, and didn't feel safe talking about with anyone else.

It's just a deep sexual connection—nothing else.

Either way, I need to go to this party dressed my absolute best. Jessa is with me flipping through dresses.

"So what look are you going for?"

"Sexy, mysterious, something bordering on slutty," I tell her, walking down the aisle and picking up multiple dresses in my size.

"And you still won't tell me what it's for?"

"I have a date," I lie.

"You have a date and you want a scandalous dress for said date?"

"Yes, I want to get laid after said date."

She shrugs her shoulders and nods her head. She's looking at cuter, more precious dresses for herself.

"You should get that light blue one," I tell her.

"Really?"

"Yeah, I bet he'll like it," I say.

Her cheeks flame red. "Who?"

"Oh, no one in particular."

She looks around and doesn't comment on it. I've totally noticed her and Aiden flirting more and more at the office. No matter how much my cousin is actively trying to avoid her, he can't keep his eyes off her.

They'd be perfect together.

Maybe I can find a way to push them together when we're on the boat later this week.

"I went to Avalon," she sighs.

"How was it?" I ask cautiously.

"Interesting, but I don't see myself joining, at least not right now."

Internally, I'm taking a sigh of relief. The last thing I need is someone seeing me at this masquerade. With how Aiden has been obsessing about Jessa, there's no way he's going either. He's just not like that. If he has feelings for her, he wouldn't be able to go through with anything at the club.

"Sorry it didn't work out."

"Just a little too rich for my blood right now," she says.

I totally read through her shit. Jessa is like me, a serial monogamist. With her eyes set on Aiden, it makes sense why she wouldn't want to go back, even if she isn't willing to admit it right now.

Hopefully, these two idiots figure it out sooner than later.

"You could always try another time."

"Yeah, maybe," she says, shrugging, grabbing her cute blue dress and we try on our clothes.

I buy a tight black number and wait for my mask to arrive in the mail.

I HAVEN'T SPENT any time in the main club before and I feel like a fish out of water. My little black dress hugs every curve and my bejeweled mask hides half of my face. My blonde hair is curled, and in loose waves as I grab a drink and walk around the space.

I'm not even sure how to approach someone. I'm not interested in meeting anyone new. The only thing I want is to know who my mystery man is.

All the men are wearing suits, which is so fucking unhelpful as I search for Mr. Wayne.

If only I had a little bat signal.

A man approaches me and I swallow thickly. His jaw is sharp, and his mask doesn't hide his deep brown eyes well as he steps in front of me.

"Hello."

"Hi," I reply kindly.

"Is this your first time here?" he asks, and I nod.

"Yes, well, this part of the club."

He tilts his head in confusion, and I already know he isn't my mystery man. My interest immediately depletes.

God, I'm pathetic—at least I'm self aware.

"I'm actually looking for someone," I tell him.

"Oh, room for a third?" he says, leaning against the table.

I look him up and down and actually contemplate it. You know, two guys fucking me at the same time doesn't seem so bad.

"Fuck off," a familiar voice says behind the blond man who didn't even give me his name before suggesting a threesome—you gotta appreciate sex club etiquette.

He holds his hands up in mock surrender, not wanting to deal with our drama as he walks away. I watch the blond man leave, and my heart races as I prepare for this confrontation.

He said this place was for desperate, pathetic people. The thought of Lincoln being a member of Avalon didn't even cross my mind—this place is supposed to be beneath him.

There's a golden mask covering his face, his dark hair loose and his suit pristine as he glares at me with his piercing blue-green eyes.

"What the fuck are you doing here?" he grates out, grabbing my arm to lead me out of the entrance.

I tug my arm away and cross my arms.

"What am I doing here? What are you doing here? I thought this place was pathetic," I say, sneering his words back at him.

"It is. It's why I'm here. Go home, Penny."

"No."

His jaw ticks, and he exhales through his nose.

"You don't belong here."

I laugh sardonically. "You have no fucking clue who I am."

He grabs his mask off his face in exacerbation and pinches the bridge of his nose.

"We can't all go here. Isn't that a little too royal family of us?"

"I'm not leaving until I get what I came here for," I tell him.

"And what the hell is that?" he asks. He's scanning the room like he would rather be anywhere else instead of dealing with me right now.

"I'm looking for someone."

"Who?" he asks.

How do I tell him I've been fucking a stranger, and this seemed like the best event to find them at?

Lie.

Because there's no fucking way I'm admitting that. I'll just use a play on words for the man I'm looking for.

"Batman, obviously," I say laughing it off. I always wondered if he chose Wayne for Bruce Wayne and having a secret identity. I take a sip of my glass and look up to see Lincoln's face covered in shock.

"What did you just say?" he says, his mouth slack as he stares at me.

"Nothing, it's stupid. Just let me have this night and I'll be out of your hair."

I can see the vein in his neck pulsing, and I squint at him. I swear to God he starts fucking sweating and... no.

There's no fucking way.

"Oh fuck," I whisper under my breath, and he just blinks at me, his eyes wide with realization.

I go to walk past him and he just stands there, lost in his own thoughts.

My heart is thumping so fast in my chest it feels like it might just rip out of my chest onto the floor as I try to breathe as I quickly walk out of Avalon.

No. No. No.

There's no fucking way, my stranger. The man I let fuck me through a wall, the one I've been fantasizing about endlessly, is my cousin. I rip the mask off of my face as my heels click against the marble.

My mind is a mess as I race my way out of the building. I forget about my keys and phone as I push through the heavy front doors and walk along the curb.

He didn't say anything verbally, but his face said everything he couldn't.

Lincoln is my Mr. Wayne.

My heel snags on one of Florida's fine fucked-up pieces of sidewalk and I sag against the side of the building as I try to slow my frantic breathing.

In a series of wrong turns and men who are bad for me, this is my ultimate success at being a failure.

I've been endlessly thinking of a faceless man who happens to be my adopted cousin—who hates me.

I fucked Linc.

My breathing gets even more panicked and I feel like I'm dying. I'm having a heart attack at the ripe age of twenty-nine.

I want to rip off the slutty dress I wore to impress a man who's known me my entire life.

Tears stream down my face, and I hold on to the wall for support.

Rock meet bottom.

A hand touches my back and I still for a moment. But it's a soothing touch as their large palm circles my back.

"Just breathe," Lincoln says, and I try, but hearing his voice just makes me panic even more.

"Fuck," he hisses. "Don't move. I'm getting your purse and shit."

His voice is calm, controlled, maybe even unaffected.

How can he be so fucking calm? How isn't he right beside me on the concrete having a similar ultimate life crisis?

My throat feels constricted and I reach at my back to pull the zipper of my dress down so I can breathe.

Footsteps have me looking to my right where Lincoln is holding my purse.

"Come on," he says, grabbing me by my upper arm.

He supports most of my weight as he leads me to his car. He has to lean me against the side of the vehicle before opening the passenger door and helping me get in.

How could I have let this happen?

Lincoln climbs over into the driver's seat and I glance at him in my peripheral vision. He was the best sex of my life. He ate me out, fucked me, and somehow made it intimate in a way I can't describe.

I was falling for a man through a wall, and it's him.

Oh my God. I rubbed my cum all over his dick and sucked it off.

I turn and look out the window. This has to all be a bad dream.

I'm going to wake up and it will all have been some seriously messed-up nightmare my demonic mind came up with and everything will be normal. I'll wake up tomorrow with no very in-depth memories of how Lincoln's mouth feels on me, or how he has the most perfect cock I've ever seen.

"Are you done panicking?" he says softly and I nod my head. "You're Honey?" he confirms and I nod my head. "Jesus fucking Christ," he mumbles.

I'm not sure what words can be said between us right now.

"This is fucked up," I say under my breath and Lincoln laughs next to me.

It's not a cruel laugh. Maybe this is his way of handling the situation. He doesn't cry, so he might as well laugh it off.

He rubs his jaw and parks by our apartment and neither of us gets out.

The silence is deafening and I feel like I'm being crushed by the overwhelming weight of what I learned tonight.

He turns, so his head is resting against the headrest while he looks at me. My position mimics his.

Mr. Wayne had to be beautiful. I knew that through a wall and I wasn't wrong. Lincoln is handsome, and broken, and beautiful all the same.

His eyes are piercing mine and neither of us looks away. There's so much to be said, to talk about, yet words don't feel like enough.

Where do we go from here?

"We'll keep this between us. We can act like it never happened," he suggests.

His tone is unnaturally soft and kind. A small glimpse of the Lincoln I got to see that night after Collin's funeral peeking through.

"Okay."

He nods his head, his eyes searching my face like there's so much to say, but no other words are spoken as we leave the car in silence and go to our respective apartments.

I DON'T SLEEP. I lie in bed, just replaying the night repeatedly.

Penny is Honey.

I fucked my adopted cousin through a wall.

Before I even decided to join Key Club, I thought I was in a mid-life crisis of sorts, but now I absolutely find myself wondering what the point of my life is.

Especially because now I'm connecting Penny's face and body with the most perfect cunt I've ever seen.

I'm picturing her face and body on the other side of that wall, and I can almost imagine the noises she made.

It's wrong. I know it's fucking wrong, but apparently my dick doesn't.

My shaft is hard, straining against my boxers while I lie on my expensive, lonely sheets.

I'm hard for Penny. My annoyingly sweet, slightly messed-up cousin. Who is undoubtedly charming and, as of late, has made me feel more human than anyone else has.

The woman in the apartment above mine haunts me.

The worst part?

It's not even about everything we did at the Key Club. I wish it was. I wish that I was just craving the physical nature we were chasing together. Now that I know it's Penny, I feel more.

Fuck.

I grab my cock and squeeze it from outside of my boxers, willing it to go down and for these errant, immoral thoughts to slip away from my mind.

When I realized it was her, there was, of course, a moment of shock, but I didn't react the same way Penny did. Her tears and panic have me moving my hand off of my erection and flinging my arm over my eyes.

She was shattered that it was me.

It's how I should feel. I should feel disgusted, revolted even that she was the woman I was doing nasty things to.

Yet...

No.

We made a deal in my car. Honestly, I would have probably told her anything to make her stop crying and calm her panic, but it's what she wanted to hear and what I need to live by.

We have to forget it ever happened.

Though there's no way I can truly forget. Not the way her pussy felt wrapped around my cock, or the way she confidently sucked me off.

I can visualize her most intimate parts as I lie here, denying myself.

In front of Penny and our family, I can work through this and pretend it never happened. But alone in the dark, I can live with my fucked up thoughts and moral compass.

I pull my dick off and jerk off to thoughts of Penny's perfect pink lips wrapped around my cock.

❀ ❀ ❀

I TAKE THE STAIRS, attempting to avoid Penny at all costs. There's shame in the fact that I fantasized over her last night, that I'm not spiraling in the same way she is.

Part of me wants to comfort her, but it would be a lie.

We're not blood relatives, we're grown adults, we can fuck whoever we want.

If anything, there's a part of me that feels like she's blowing this way out of proportion. It was just sex, and that's all it would ever be.

Our little, dirty secret.

We're already going to need to hold on to what we did at the Key Club. What's one more thing?

I really should find a therapist.

The building is empty as I head to work, trying to leave the memories and realities of last night behind me. Yet, no matter how hard I try, thoughts of honey blonde hair and fresh tears keep popping into my mind.

TWO DAYS and no sign of Penny. Not a single peep.

Aiden hasn't mentioned her, she hasn't asked for a ride to work, and family dinner is tomorrow.

Penny never bails on seeing her parents—ever.

It's a disgusting sinking feeling I'm not familiar with settling in my stomach. I need to know that she's okay. She was already struggling before all of this, and I probably just made it worse.

I inhale deeply and leave my apartment and take the stairs. I'm standing in front of her door for a long time, contemplating if she needs her space or not. Maybe my knocking on her door will just make this all fucking worse.

Fuck it.

I tap my knuckles against the door, wondering what type of state she'll be in.

When she opens the door, I'm confused.

Her hair is piled on top of her head in a bun and her eyes are red, but not from crying, like she hasn't been sleeping.

"Hey," she says in low rasp.

I search her face, and it takes her a moment until her eyes finally meet mine. Her pretty blue eyes are bloodshot and she has slight bags under her eyes.

"Penny, are you alright?"

She walks into her apartment, not answering my question. I'm stunned for a moment, but follow her inside.

She sits on her couch, her legs pressed against her chest, as she makes herself as small as possible. I sit next to her and feel like I'm about to talk down a wounded animal.

Penny nods to her coffee table. I look at her for a few long seconds before looking at the coffee table. There's a hand-written letter along with the report.

I grab the letter first.

Penny,

I understand why you wanted to find me, why you'd want to know where you came from. I can't blame you for searching for answers, but I wish you hadn't. It's not that I don't have love for you, that I don't care about the woman you've become.

It's because no matter how much I love you, how much I want the best for you, I can never have you in my life.

It took me too long to realize I wasn't strong enough to take care of you. I was young; I was being abused, and I didn't have any other options.

I'm still on a healing journey of my own, and meeting you would disrupt that. I'm sorry, that's all I can give you.

You deserve better, and it's why you couldn't be in my life. I'm happy to hear that your adoptive family treated you well and that the cycle ends with you.

I will not tell you who your father is, and I ask that you don't go looking. I promise you will not like what you find. I have enclosed some medical family history for your private investigator.

While I doubt this was what you were hoping to find at the end of the tunnel, I hope I can bring some peace into your life as well. I had no other children. I never married again, and never plan to.

I will always carry a piece of you with me, even when it hurts.

May your life be fruitful and full of joy and may you never endure the pain you would have if I had made a different choice.

I'm sorry.

I put the handwritten note down and pick up the private investigator's file, who suggests not telling Penny her biological mother's true identity, but that she has been found and he was able to have her write a letter.

I look back at Penny, who is completely emotionless. It's unlike her.

The woman nearly wears her heart on her sleeve.

"I'm sorry, Pen," I tell her.

She rests her cheek on her knee and looks at me.

"I haven't told anyone else."

"Why?"

She shrugs and sighs. "I think because I'm so fucking mad. Between what happened..." she trails off, giving me a pointed look and sighs again. "Then this? How much can I take until I fall apart, Linc?"

I stare at her for a long moment, never having had such a vulnerable conversation with her. I've had the same thoughts and I haven't gone through something like this.

"Do you want to let some of that anger out?" I ask her.

The only thing I can do is come up with a solution for that at this point, nothing else. Everything else in her life is a fucking mess.

But rage? Anger? That's something I know how to handle.

"I don't want to go to the freaking batting cages," she says.

"Oh, I have something much better in mind."

She blinks at me a few times, and swallows.

"I'll get changed."

WE SIGN the waiver and put on the white hazmat suits and goggles. There still isn't a smile or tear written on Penny's face, but she didn't complain when she learned where I was bringing her.

She grabs a crowbar and I take a baseball bat as the kid working gives us safety protocol and unlocks the room.

When we enter, there's just a ton of shit to break; TVs, glass, bottles, printers, lamps, truly just a bunch of random old shit.

There's no music, just silence as we approach.

Penny takes in the room, but doesn't do anything right away.

I pull back and slam on the printer in front of me, causing her to startle. I put all my weight behind it, imagining the printer is everything that doesn't make sense in my life right now.

Why can't I be a better man? Why am I the way I am? Is there a point in my life where I'll actually be fucking happy? Not to mention all these mixed, confusing feelings I'm having about Penny.

The printer is fully smashed, and I look over at Penny.

"Go on, smash the TV," I tell her.

She looks skeptical, but she rears back the crowbar and hits it. The screen shatters and she looks shocked before she hits it repeatedly.

I just watch her, the way she's over exerting herself when she's already spent. The way she screams after each crunch of the old TV. Her shoulders sag after about the tenth hit.

The crowbar hits the floor with a clang and she falls apart.

Sobs rack through her body as I approach her.

Penny doesn't even hesitate as she grabs me around the waist, still fully in her hazmat suit, as she throws off the goggles and cries. The action is so reminiscent of the other night, but this time she isn't running away from me.

Her tears soak my chest as I rub her back.

"Let it all out," I tell her softly.

My chin is pressed against her hair as I hold her tight as she lets out all the built up emotion.

"She... she wants nothing to do with me. I was brought into this world under the worst circumstances, Linc. Nobody wants me," she cries.

I hold her tighter.

"You're wanted, Penny."

"I'm an obligation to my parents. I'm turning fucking thirty and I don't have my shit together. Fucked my cousin through a glory hole, and found out the base of my existence is horrific."

"You're not an obligation," I tell her.

She just cries, pouring it all out to my hazmat suit. She doesn't say any more, everything she needed to get out has already been said.

I always thought Penny was happy-go-lucky. Maybe she took the wrong turn with guys, was a little free, but always happy. To see her like this makes her feel more familiar than ever.

I understand Penny on a level I don't think anyone else does. Maybe because of our shared shame or negative thinking.

Except as I watch her crumble before me, all I can think about is how I want to take away her pain.

She cries as our time ticks down and the teenager working opens the door. He looks uncomfortable but nods his head.

"The smash room can be really cathartic," he says.

I roll my eyes, pulling off my goggles and hand them to him. Penny doesn't move, so I unzip her suit, helping her undress and giving it back to the kid. She seems like she's in a near catatonic state on the way home.

She's quiet, and her eyes are droopy by the time we get back to the apartment. I take her into her room and tuck her into her bed, not wanting to cross any boundaries with changing her clothes.

I'm about to leave as I push the blankets to her chest.

"Stay," she whispers.

I don't even have to think about it, as I climb in on the other side, fully dressed. She places her head against my chest.

It should feel uncomfortable and awkward, yet it feels fucking right.

"Don't tell anyone about the letter, please."

"Are you sure?" I ask.

"Please."

I nod and she falls asleep.

What's one more secret between us?

Penny

Disassociate

LINCOLN LEFT at some point in the morning. He didn't say goodbye or anything else. I'm glad he didn't make it awkward, yet I touch the cold spot in the bed, wishing it was warm.

What the actual fuck?

I swipe my eyes, thinking about how I hadn't slept basically since that night at Avalon. The next morning, the PI stopped by and handed everything to me with an apology.

Clearly, the universe decided my rock bottom was indeed not the actual bottom. I think my life actually dug out a piece of the earth's core to have me land at this actual bottom.

I've felt a little lost my whole life. Not that I didn't love my family or parents. It was always the why.

Why didn't my birth mother want me? Why did she wait so long to put me in the system, and this underlying feeling of not being good enough that has carried throughout my entire life?

I've searched for validation in the comforts of a romantic partner with no success. I've never been good enough for anyone, and still now it feels like I'm not good enough for my birth mother.

Her trauma is real, her pain is real, but so is mine. I'm allowed to be hurt and upset while also understanding where she's coming from—it's just not the outcome I wanted.

I turn on my phone and schedule an emergency appointment with my therapist, who can do a virtual appointment in an hour.

I kick my feet on the side of my bed and scrub my face. Working on the will to get up and shower.

Over my shoulder, I look at the spot where Lincoln slept and held me. He was there for me; he provided me comfort in a non-judgemental way that I never expected from him.

The sleepover was innocent. Yet it felt like more.

We've never been affectionate with each other as we aged and last night felt like one of the most emotionally intimate moments of my life.

Lincoln knows more about what's going on with me than my parents. Jessa is becoming a close friend, but we aren't close enough for her to know everything. I like being bubbly around people; it makes them like me.

It's easier to put on a face of happiness than to have someone ask what's wrong with you.

So that's what I do—what I do best.

I dissociate.

"IS EVERYTHING ALRIGHT, PENELOPE?" my mother asks softly next to me.

"Yeah, everything's good," I smile, and take a sip of the margaritas she made.

"Are you nervous about the event tomorrow? Aiden said you worked so hard planning it."

"No, Mom. Everything is fine. I just need to get some more sleep."

She gives me a look like she isn't fully convinced, but she leaves it alone, thankfully. There's too much going on in my life to even scrape the surface about how everything is, in fact, not fine.

"Are you planning on bringing anyone to The Bahamas?" my aunt Maggie asks, and I shake my head. "Just wanted to get an idea for head count so we can plan and see if we need to rent additional space."

"No, I'm firmly off men right now."

"Wise choice," she says glaring at her husband, who's sitting in the living room.

"What did he do?" my mom asks her sister.

"Came home at three in the morning last night. He acts like he's in his thirties, not his sixties. Grow the fuck up," she hisses and I smile.

"When the time is right, you'll find someone, Penny," my mother says, brushing down my hair.

It's so annoying when people say shit like that, but I just nod my head, not wanting to talk about it.

Especially considering the last man I was with is her nephew.

I grimace and take another sip of my margarita.

Gavin comes strutting over with a big smile on his face. "We're playing corn hole. Come join us."

I glance over at Lincoln, who is just swirling his drink and staring down at it. I take a deep breath, force a smile on my face, and nod my head.

Aiden and Lincoln are on a team against the twins as I sit in my chair and continue to drink away my problems.

"You good Pen?" Ben asks and I want to toss myself into the lake.

It's that obvious that I'm not fine. Clearly my mask is slipping.

"Yeah, just need to sleep a little better."

"My friend Brent from college brought some edibles from California, if you want some," he suggests.

I snap my fingers and point at him.

"That, I will take you up on."

"Good thing Kemper's doesn't drug test," Aiden says under his breath.

"So true, what a great boss I have," I reply and he rolls his eyes.

"What's new with you?" Ben asks Aiden. "How's Collin's daughter working out?"

"She's a hard worker, saved us from a serious disaster with The Rays," he replies.

"And she's really pretty," I chime in and Aiden glares at me.

"No. Collin's daughter? Really?" Ben replies.

"We're just co-workers, we haven't done anything."

"Yet," I supply.

Aiden glares at me and tosses the beanbag.

"I'm her boss. She's Collin's daughter."

"Oh, grow the fuck up," Lincoln says.

Aiden looks shocked as he stares at his younger brother across the yard.

"Excuse me?" Aiden replies.

"You heard me. You haven't liked a woman in forever. If you like her, who cares about all that bullshit? Be a man," he says, looking at Aiden for a long time before glancing at me.

I hide behind my margarita glass, willing this evening to be over.

It's a quick round of goodbyes, before Lincoln is driving us home. It's quiet for a short time until he breaks the uncomfortable silence.

"You didn't tell your mom?"

"Which part?" I say dryly.

"Don't be a brat. You know which part."

"I don't want to talk to her about it right now. She'll want to know how I'm feeling and talk about it until we're blue in the face. I don't want to talk about it, I don't want to think about it. I just want to not feel anything."

His hands tighten around the wheel, and he doesn't respond right away.

As we're pulling up to the apartment building, he finally turns to face me.

"You're allowed to be upset. You don't have to act happy all the time. Everyone will still love you and care about you if you aren't constantly smiling."

I blink at him and open the door and take the stairs to my apartment.

He's wrong. No one really wants to deal with my bullshit. People like me because I'm happy. I can take a joke, and I always want to please everyone.

If my smile falls, so does everything around me.

I GLANCE at the boat while we wait to board. This is exactly what I need, a distraction from real life.

"It's hot as a witch's tit out here," Sharon complains, making me and Jessa laugh.

"I don't know that me or my hair will ever get used to this humidity," Jessa says, taking the hair tie off her wrist and pulling her hair up into a ponytail. I watch Aiden stare at her with stars in his eyes. If he doesn't make a move soon, I just might shake him.

"I'm so ready for a cocktail," Sharon says and I hum in

agreement. I know I've been drinking a little too much to cope with life, but right now I don't give a shit.

"If anyone needs an Uber tonight, it's on the company," Aiden says, and I immediately know I'll be utilizing that tonight.

"Do you guys do this every year?" Jessa asks.

"Oh, we've done a tiki ride, a BBQ, and a crab feast. This is our first year going on a big boat like this," I reply.

"This is so awesome. I've never been on a boat like this," Jessa says excitedly.

"I booked it," I reply with a shrug of my shoulders.

"You did a good job, Pen," my cousin says, and a sense of pride fills me over a job well done.

It clicks for me that my favorite part of my job is the event planning. Hmm, I'll have to take a deeper dive into that once I'm feeling a little better.

We finally get on the boat. I grab a bacon wrapped scallop and Jessa by the arm.

"Come on, let's go get drinks," I say, all but hauling her over to the bar.

"What should we get?" she asks as we glance at the menu for the night's event.

"All of it, it's all on the company dime," Sharon says, and I nod my head.

"Sharon gets it."

"Oh shit, there's my ex, Hugh. I'll be right back, ladies," Sharon says, forgetting about the drinks and running off to chase her next conquest.

Jessa grimaces and I think back to the other week when I saw her upset outside of the office on the phone with her ex.

"Not chasing after your ex anytime soon?" I ask.

"Hell no, he's a bastard," she groans, leaning against the bar.

Jessa and I get our drinks and look around at the people milling about. I keep watching Jessa glance longingly at Aiden, and I sigh.

"How's the cottage coming along?" I ask her.

"Eh. I haven't done anything about all the egregious light-houses yet."

"I could come over and help you sometime."

"I'd love that."

"It's your fresh start," I tell her softly.

"What do you mean?" she says with a furrow of her brow.

"Your ex, all the bullshit you dealt with, isn't here. You can be anybody you want here, you get to start over. Take chances, be bold, reinvent yourself," I tell her, even though the pep talk is absolutely for myself.

Jessa looks back at Aiden, and I wonder if my message clicked.

The rest of the event goes on without a hitch, minus Jessa's bio brother and Tabitha making a complete ass of themselves and being rude.

I'm not drunk, but I've had more than my fair share to drink.

"Another one?" Kenny from the warehouse asks and I nod my head as he grabs us two more cocktails. "You threw a hell of a party."

"It's better than some stuffy dinner at a banquet hall, that's for sure."

He fakes shivers, and I laugh. Kenny is nice, a good guy, probably the kind of guy I should want. But when I look at him, there's no spark, no real interest there. Maybe I've always just wanted what I can't have.

"Definitely. The party was great. You're great."

I blink at him. He's cute, in the boy next store kind of way. He's a few years younger than me, and it shows.

"Thanks Kenny."

"I've always thought you were great," he says again as the captain announces it's time to disembark.

We're leaving the boat together, and he keeps rambling.

"I don't know if you'd be interested, but I'd like to take you to dinner sometime," he says.

I'm lucky that I'm headed off the ramp to dry land, giving me a few moments to come up with an excuse. But when we're finally off the boat and on the dock, I have to look at him.

"I'm sorry, Kenny, I don't think I'm in a place to date right now."

He nods and gives me a half-smile.

"If you ever are in a place where you want to date, you'll let me know?"

I'm about to answer when a familiar voice behind me startles me.

"Let's go home, Pen," Lincoln says in his dark timbre.

I inhale deeply and turn around.

"What are you doing here?"

"Aiden said you'd need a ride. I was in the neighborhood," he replies, looking Kenny up and down like he's sizing him up.

"Right, have a nice night," Kenny says behind me, and I don't even turn around.

"That was rude," I chastise him.

"He couldn't take a hint."

"I was handling it. It's none of your business."

He scoffs and looks down at me like he isn't the least bit amused.

"Whatever, Penny, get in the fucking car."

"Great to see the asshole is back."

"Never went anywhere," he says, slamming my door shut behind me and rounding the vehicle.

He's rough with his door and sits in the seat like he's super annoyed being here.

"You didn't have to come and pick me up," I say and he doesn't reply as he starts the car and drives home without a word.

The silence is pissing me off, and I snap about halfway home.

"What is your fucking problem?" I nearly shout and he pulls over behind a church parking lot violently and puts the car into park.

My heart races from the jolt as he turns around and faces me.

"You. You're my fucking problem."

"We said we would forget about it, that we'd move on," I reply, wanting to look away from him, but I can't.

"Yeah, well, I can't fucking forget about it."

I swallow, cause it's that cold hard truth slapping us both in the face.

"Linc," I sigh his name and he licks his lips.

"No one has to know," he replies.

"What?"

"We can pretend it's like Key Club. We can have our little secrets. It's just you and me."

I can't believe the words slipping out of his mouth. But then I think about how good Mr. Wayne made me feel. How after I received that note from my biological mom, all I wanted was to book the heart room and forget about all my problems.

We've already had sex, he already knows me intimately.

But if we do this?

There's no turning back.

"We shouldn't," I whisper, glancing down at his lips and then his eyes.

He's looking at me like he wants me more than he's ever wanted anything in his life. It's heady, feeling wanted.

"No one will know," he says confidently.

My heart beat is booming in my ears as I take in his words.

Can we really do this? Is this a line I'm willing to cross?

"Let me make it all go away," he says, and it feels like those words are the beginning of the end.

Best Worst Idea

IT'S NEARLY instantaneous as the words leave my mouth.

Both of us un-click our buckles and I'm sliding my seat as far back as it can go as she climbs over the center console.

It's the first time I have my hands on her waist, and it feels so fucking good.

Her hands work between us, tugging down my shorts and boxers to pull out my cock as I push her dress up to her hips, pushing her panties to the side.

It's frantic, needy, and I know it won't be enough.

She doesn't waste any time fisting me at the base and sliding the head over her slit before slowly sinking down and taking every inch of me.

Penny leans forward, and I grab a hand full of her hair and I'm gripping her underwear so tightly I know it's digging into her skin. I wish I could see it.

We don't kiss.

But her lips press against my ear. Her hair smells like coconut and jasmine. I inhale deeply, connecting the scent to her. How does she smell like fucking sunshine?

"Were you jealous?" she asks as her pussy tightens around me and her hips shift on my lap. Now is when she brings up that stupid little boy who was asking her out on a date?

I grab her hair harder, making her moan. My dick twitches inside of her at the noise.

I'd wondered what she sounded like on the other side of the wall, and now I know. She sounds perfect.

"Do you want me to be jealous, Penny?" I ask, fucking her from below. "Do you want me to tell you how I pictured him inside of you like I am now and wanted to ruin him for it?"

Her nails graze through my hair, running along my scalp as she bounces on top of me. She's breathy in my ear making my cock twitch.

"I missed this pussy," I tell her and she moans again, her body pressing closer to mine as she rides me.

I squeeze her ass roughly, moving her to the pace that I want.

"Right there," she whispers.

Her clit is rubbing against my pelvis and the only things I can hear in the cab of the car is her uneven breathing and the wet sound of her pussy taking my cock.

"You needed this, didn't you, baby?"

Her hips stutter. They shift back and forth. Her body seeking the friction she needs to get off.

"My cock makes you feel so good. Are you gonna make a mess, Penny?"

Our faces are pressed against each other when she whispers back.

"I'm going to come."

I lift my hips, fucking into her harder from below. Her grip on my shoulders and hair gets rougher as she lets out the sweetest moan I've heard in my life.

"Are you going to let me come inside of you?" I pant out and she nods her head. "Such a nasty fucking girl for me, aren't you?"

Her cunt flutters around my dick and her back arches as she falls apart, reaching her release.

I don't pause for a moment, not wanting this to end. I need more. I need everything.

She pulls back, her body still shaking as her pretty blue eyes hold mine and she watches my face as I fill her with my cum.

We're both breathing hard, staring at each other. I can feel my cum leaking out of her and onto my lap.

Yet, neither of us makes the first move.

Her face is hard to read, and I'm not sure how to describe what I'm feeling. It should be guilt. I should feel bad for her, feeling vulnerable and using it to get what I wanted. But all I feel is good. I feel better than I have in years.

Penny makes the world go quiet, and I'm not sure how to handle that information.

Her hands drag down my chest, feeling the texture of my shirt. My cock going soft inside of her, and yet, neither of us move.

I couldn't move if I wanted to.

I push her hair off her face and her eyes search mine. There's fear there, but also longing.

Fuck it.

"Give me the weekend," I nearly plead.

"What?"

"Just the weekend. I know you went to the masked event at Avalon because you were looking for more with the person who was on the other side of that wall. Give this—us—the weekend. Get it all out of our systems and then we'll go back to normal."

It will never be normal between us again, but it's all I've got.

"I don't know, Linc," she says, shifting on my lap.

"I don't have to be Linc. You can be Honey. I can make

those dirty things you've been wanting a reality. Just the weekend. There's already no going back."

She bites her lip, contemplating my words, still not shifting off my lap. Her pussy feels warm around my cock, and I'm already obsessed. Well, even more so. I was obsessed with her before I even knew who she was. But if this is all she'll give me, I'll take it.

"After the weekend, that's it. I can't lose the only family I have," she says softly.

Her blue eyes are watery, and I rub my thumb down her jaw.

Is it fucked up I'd hardly considered the family? I mean, I suppose I have thought of the repercussions somewhat. I just don't give a fuck. My parents' and my brothers' love for us is too much to let this be a wedge between us. Sure, there would be tension, it would take time to digest and maybe things would never be the same, but they'd learn to deal.

When I think about it from Penny's perspective, it feels significantly more complicated, but is it really?

"Okay, Pen."

"There need to be rules."

"No kissing," I say, and she nods.

If I kiss her... fuck, I can't even think about it.

"Good idea. We can never talk about any of this again after the weekend. Whatever happens between us dies with us."

I nod and she swallows.

"You're sure?"

"So sure. Are you ready to tell me what you want, Penny?"

She looks tense and sighs. "Take me home and I'll tell you."

Penny shifts off my cock, and I wince as she climbs back over to her seat and readjusts herself. I tuck my cock back into my shorts and restart the car, driving to the point of no-fucking-return.

PENNY LOOKS over her shoulder as we go to my apartment, like there's someone with a camera following our every move, knowing we're doing something salacious.

I don't comment, worried that she will change her mind.

Life would be easier if we walked away from this, but I can't. I've been searching for that piece that would make my life click together and I don't know how or why, but Penny's that piece.

She makes me feel like the best version of me and fuck if I don't want to do the same for her. I can't even say I wanted something that deep with Vanessa.

"Do you want a drink?" I ask as I lock the door, toss my keys on the counter, and head to the kitchen.

"Just water," she says, taking a seat on the stool. "I should go home," she says and I round the island and spin her stool so she's facing me.

"It's just the weekend, Penny," I lie. "It will be our dirty little secret. I've already filled you with my cum tonight. What's a few more times?"

Her pupils dilate.

I already knew, based on the things we did at Key Club and her bio, that we have a lot of the same interests. Penny likes the idea of this forbiddenness as much as I do. Some things feel even better when you know they're wrong or not widely accepted.

"What if—"

I cover her mouth with my palm.

"You're mine this weekend. We're not going to talk about what this means, the ramifications, any of that shit. We're not us this weekend. We're two people who met at Key Club and are exploring more. Can you do that?"

I don't move my hand from her mouth, and she nods her agreement.

"Now go to my bedroom, undress, and wait for me to come in there and eat you out."

Her eyes flash with excitement, and I smirk, leaning forward and whispering in her ear. "While you're waiting, I want you to think of all the nasty shit you want me to do to you, so you can tell me after I make you drench my face."

A muffled moan rumbles against my hand.

"Go," I say, pulling my hand away.

She stares at me for a few moments, maybe waging war in her own mind, before following directions and going to my room.

I open the fridge, grabbing a handful of grapes and grabbing a bottle of water.

My phone chimes.

AIDEN

Did Penny get home okay?

Safe and sound.

And naked in my bed, waiting for me to come take what I want. The anticipation and waiting is all a part of the game. I know she hates it as much as she loves it. I eat my fruit slowly, drinking my water and scrolling through my phone.

Part of me wants her to come out here naked and question why I'm making her wait, but Penny wants to earn praise.

It's the people pleaser inside of her.

She'd rather wait there all night naked and needy than cave and earn my disapproval. She needs to earn her orgasm. My praise isn't free, at least usually.

The car was different. It was frantic and long overdue. She needed to know how pleased I was with finally having her.

Now I just need to convince her she needs more of me after this weekend.

I answer a few emails, realizing how much time has passed and I finally give in, undressing in the kitchen and walking into my bedroom.

The sigh of relief she makes when I enter has my ego inflating alongside my cock.

"Did you touch yourself while you were waiting, Honey?"

"No," she says.

"Give me your hands," I tell her.

She shifts on the bed, her tits pushing together as she holds her hands out and I straddle her body.

I lick all of her fingertips and nip the middle one. Liking that she followed directions and didn't lie. If she's shocked from what I just did, she doesn't show it.

Her throat bobs as she looks up and down at my naked form.

"Do you like what you see?" I ask, shifting down the bed, kissing the side of her neck, breasts, and stomach. Her hand tangles in my hair and I groan with satisfaction.

"You know you're pretty," she says.

"I do. Do you?"

She shakes her head, and I lick her navel and grab her hips, nipping at her skin. "Baby, you're so pretty it fucking hurts."

I slide my tongue down to her pussy, tasting a mix of her and the remnants of me coming inside of her.

She tastes like the best worst idea I've ever had.

LINCOLN ATE me out with his cum still inside of me and then fucked me boneless. We're in the shower and I'm truly trying to push reality far, far away from my mind.

He kisses my shoulder and for that small moment it feels like nothing else matters, just this moment.

That no kissing rule sucks, but I do agree with it. If Lincoln kissed me like he ate me out, there would be no functioning after this weekend.

This weekend is my escape.

That's all it can be.

A little taste of what could have been, but then we need to face the reality of the situation.

"Are you going to tell me what things you want to do this weekend?"

I shrug, and he shakes his head, smiling as he washes the shampoo out of his hair. I've, of course, seen him in a bathing suit a million times, but it's so different now.

He's not overly ripped or anything, but he has delicious

pecks and dark hair that's scattered across the impressive expanse of his chest.

"There's nothing you could say that will make me disgusted or look at you different, Pen," he says.

God, fuck him for being perfect. So many guys that I've dated have gawked at the most tame things I wanted them to do to me. One of them acted like fuzzy handcuffs were beyond deranged.

"I like..." I clear my throat and just watch the rivulets of water travel down his body. It's just the weekend. He wants to bring my fantasies to life and then we'll forget it happened. "I like the idea of being taken, of being used for pleasure."

"That's it? What else is on that little wishlist?"

He's so casual about what I just told him and it has me relaxing tenfold.

"Well, glory holes have already been checked off."

He laughs, and damn, have I ever seen him this carefree and happy? Lincoln's smiling is addictive as a mirrored smile takes over my face.

I shrug my shoulders. "I'd like to explore more with bondage and being taken. What about you? What's on your wishlist?" I ask, stepping under the spray, washing his products out of my hair.

He grabs me by my hips, squeezing my ass and leaning down to whisper in my ear.

"You."

I shiver, knowing this is the stupidest idea, but I know I'm going to give in anyway. He's too tempting to resist, especially when he's offering me everything I want.

"So you want me to take you unexpectedly?" he confirms and I shrug.

"Yeah, I want you to be desperate for me," I say, biting my lip.

"I think we've already crossed that fucking bridge. Is there anything you don't like, and are you okay with simple color safewords?" he asks.

"Yeah, colors are fine. Mmm, I think I need to explore more to see what I really like and don't like." I bite my lip and shake my head. "Up until Key Club it's been pretty vanilla. I don't think I'll ever be much of a exhibitionist, into sharing—"

"No sharing," he reiterates.

I can't help but to smile. "I think I'd be okay with some spanking, I liked what you did at Key Club, but I don't see me as a whips and chains type of girl."

He shifts my hair and nods, taking all my words in. "You need to promise me that if you're ever truly uncomfortable or don't like something, you'll speak up."

I swallow and nod, looking up at him.

"I mean it, Pen. I don't want to accidentally hurt or upset you and you just suffer in silence because you feel like you're letting me down. I want to do this because you want it and I'm gonna enjoy the fuck out of myself, but your comfort and safety is number one, especially with something like this."

"I promise," I tell him, wrapping my arms around him.

Why does it feel like this is exactly where I belong?

I GROAN when I wake up, thankful that the curtains are closed as a tray clanks next to me.

"It's too early."

"It's nearly noon," his voice says.

"Ugh."

I shove my hand under the pillow and cradle it against my face.

"I forgot you weren't a morning person."

"There's nothing likable about mornings."

"Breakfast," he supplies easily, both as an answer about mornings and as an offering as he places the tray between us.

"You made this?" I squint as he turns on the lamp on his nightstand.

"I placed the order on my phone and had a man named Levi bring it to my doorstep. I think it counts."

I grab the breakfast sandwich and scoot up the frame of the bed. A part of me wants to bring up yet again how we shouldn't be doing this, but I don't want to ruin it. The sandwich is delicious and I eat every last bite, before crawling back into bed.

Lincoln hands me the remote.

"Put something on."

"You want to watch trashy TV with me?" I question, and he shrugs, getting comfortable.

"My dick can only get hard so many times, and I'm not letting you leave. So yeah, I want to watch trashy TV with you."

I put on the show where people fall in love with a wall between them, and he laughs.

"You've got to be shitting me."

"You said to put anything on."

"You're right, I did."

Three episodes later, he's fully invested.

"He's so ugly. Why did he think he could land someone who looks like a model?" he questions, pointing at the screen.

"Men are delusional."

"This is beyond delusion."

"I've dated guys that aren't considered attractive."

"Yeah, I know," he says bitterly. "The worst was what's his fucking name? Justin? The one who looked like his name should be rainbow bliss or some shit. I thought crickets were hiding in his beard."

I laugh so hard my stomach hurts before lightly smacking his chest.

"He wasn't that bad."

"Didn't he want to do shrooms in the woods with you to reach some sort of elevated spiritual enlightenment?"

"He did... and we did."

"No way," he says, resting his head against the pillow.

"It was actually a pretty good time. Until he started fucking Willow right in front of me," I say with a grimace and Lincoln scoffs.

"You know how to pick 'em, Pen."

"Obviously." I smack him with the pillow. He takes it and holds it next to his chest. "Maybe I should go on one of these stupid shows."

He glares at me.

"What?"

"The only men who go on these shows are ones who want to be on TV. That's not what you're looking for."

I plop down on the bed, lying on my side, looking at him.

"How would you know what I'm looking for?"

He pushes some hair out of my face and I have to contain the shiver that wants to wreck my body. After this weekend he can't touch me like this, and that feeling stings.

I shake the thought from my head; I have to enjoy now, it's all I'll get.

"You want to be someone's everything. These men with their repeated pattern button-up shirts and receding hairlines with over proportionate egos aren't for you."

"Then who is for me?" I ask.

He stares at me a long minute before he speaks. "The man who you can finally be yourself around," he says softly, turning his face to watch the stupid show.

I continue staring at the side of his head, and he doesn't call me out on it. When was the last time I felt this comfortable and safe being myself? It's not even just about the sexual stuff, it's actually being me.

I'm not afraid of making a bad joke or saying the wrong thing. I'm not lying here wondering if he finds me attractive or if he finds me annoying.

For the first time in forever, I'm lying next to a man, not wondering if I'm good enough. It's freeing and heady, but it has an expiration date.

My family is the most important thing to me. My parents have given me everything, along with my aunt Maggie and uncle Jeff. Blowing up the entire family structure because I have chemistry with Lincoln is just not possible.

I could lose everything because of what we're doing.

"Penny?" he says my name but doesn't look at me.

"What?"

"Shut up."

"I didn't say anything," I snark back.

"You're thinking so fucking loud you're giving me a headache."

"You're a real asshole, you know?" I say, and he smiles. Quickly flipping me on my back and crawling on top of me.

"I know. I think you kind of like it."

"Nobody likes an asshole."

"That's simply not true. I like yours just fine. It's too bad they don't allow phones at the Key Club or I would have taken a picture of how good you looked. Your body bent like a pretzel to please me. Your needy pussy dripping cum down to that cute little hole I'd like to see more of."

I swallow thickly. The man seriously has a way with words.

"Are you wet thinking about it, Pen?" he asks, rubbing his nose against my jaw and cheekbone. "When I ripped those naughty little stockings and took what I wanted?"

"If I say yes, are you going to do something about it?" I ask.

He pulls back and smiles. It's devastating.

His dark hair is a loose mess around his face, his blue-green eyes focused on me. I don't think I've ever seen him so relaxed—so happy.

"No. I think I'll take what I want when I want it."

Lincoln leans down, his teeth grazing against my jaw before lying back down on the bed.

"So, you've convinced me to spend this weekend with you and we're going to spend it lying in bed and watching shitty reality TV?"

"Is it so bad that I just want to spend time with you, Pen?" he asks, grabbing my waist and resting his head on my lap.

I play with his hair and realize how completely and truly fucked I am—this is more than just sex, and that's not what I bargained for.

Too late now.

LINCOLN ORDERED US DINNER, and I expected us to have sex tonight, but he didn't try anything and I'm definitely not going to be the one who brings it up.

For the first time in weeks, I've felt like a whole person, and it's all because of Lincoln. We joked, laughed, and just talked all day. It felt so natural and easy. None of my relationships have ever felt like this, not even close.

We haven't had a single sip of alcohol either. All of this is clear-headed and consensual. It's just hard to grapple with the idea that this is all I can have, this is all I get.

The universe truly is a cunt.

I look over to my left, and Lincoln is passed out. He looks so much less stressed and unbothered when he sleeps. A sick part of me wonders if it's because he's sleeping next to me. A rabbit hole I definitely don't need to be digging into.

Eventually, I close my eyes and dream of a reality I know I can never have.

A LARGE WEIGHT is pressed against my back, and I try to gasp as a hand wraps around and covers my mouth.

My heart races as panic fills my entire body, and my lungs expand, searching for air. I'm dazed and confused from waking up in the middle of the night in an unfamiliar room. I blink a few times to adjust my vision.

"I'm taking what I want. Red if you want me to stop," the dark voice next to my ear whispers.

Immediately I know it's Lincoln. Yet, I don't stop struggling.

I try to shift and turn around, but he's far stronger than me. I mumble against his hand and he laughs while still restraining me.

It makes me wet.

It's wrong, it's fucked up, it's... what I always fantasized about.

"You think you're going anywhere?" He grinds his hard dick against my ass roughly. I'm only wearing one of his shirts, so it's just the soft material of his boxer briefs rubbing against my skin.

"Yell when I take my hand off your mouth and I'll give you something to really yell about," he says.

His hand drops from my mouth and grips the base of my throat, squeezing lightly.

"That's it," he says, accentuating every word with a thrust of his hips. "You want my cock, don't you?"

"No," I say, trying to be convincing.

His nose is pressed against my hair and his lips against my cheek. "We'll see about that," he says.

Lincoln grabs my hip roughly, his body still on top of mine as he slides his hand over my stomach and attempts to finger me. I squeeze my thighs together and I can feel him smiling against my face.

"Are you trying to hide how wet your pussy is right now? Are you embarrassed how bad you want it, baby?"

A little whimper escapes me and he laughs again.

"So needy for a stranger who broke into your apartment in the middle of the night, aren't you?"

"No," I say. It comes out breathy no matter how hard I try.

His weight feels perfect on top of me and as badly as I want to turn around and have him fuck me, I also don't want this role play to end.

"Such a little fucking liar," he says, pushing my thighs apart and cupping my wet pussy. "I could slide into you right now and you'd be gushing around my cock."

"Stop."

His hand pauses, a moment broken, but only briefly.

"I didn't say red," I whisper and his hold on me tightens again.

"Don't lie to me. Be a good girl and maybe I'll let you come too."

I try to move from under his hold, but it's no use. He's so much bigger and stronger than me. I like that even if he can overpower me, if I said red, he would be off of me in a second. It's a game, one where I'm completely safe but can also fully express my desires.

"Get off of me," I say and he just pushes harder against my body, his palm rubbing against my clit.

"That's not what you want, is it? You want me to take this

pretty pussy? Make you beg for more?" he asks and I moan. "That's what I thought."

There's a brief moment when I'm able to move as he unsheathes his cock from his boxers, but I don't get far before he's pushing my body back against the bed with a hand between my shoulders.

"Where do you think you're going? I haven't gotten what I want yet."

He slides his cock inside of me with so much ease it's borderline embarrassing how wet I am.

My body is flat against the bed as he lies on top of me, his pelvis hitting my ass with each thrust and his chest arched against my back. He tightens his hold on my throat as he kisses the side of my face.

I think about turning my head and stealing a kiss from him, but it would break the scene and our rules.

"Are you going to come?" he asks menacingly.

"No," I hiss out and he shifts my body so that one of my legs is bent out to the side, which has my clit flush with the sheets.

Each thrust of his hips has my sensitive clit dragging over his over-indulgent sheets.

"What about now, little liar?"

"Fuck," I hiss out.

His hand slides from my neck to the back of my head, holding it still against the bed while he fucks me.

His thrusts are hard, unrelenting. He takes what he wants from my body, wringing me dry in the process.

"I'm going to fill your pussy up with my cum whether you finish or not," he says.

"Please," I rasp out.

"Please what? Fill this pussy? Let you come?"

I fist the sheets in front of me, panting and taking every

thrust of his hips. His fingers graze my scalp in a rough controlling way, but not too tight to truly cause pain.

"I...I..."

"I know what you need. Just lie there and take it, we both know you want it."

It throws me over the edge, my clit rocking against the sheets, his heavy body on top of mine, and how deep and hard his cock is situated inside of me.

I fall apart, moaning into the sheets as his hips slap against my ass. He just keeps taking what he wants from my body and I shiver and shake as the crest of my orgasm reaches me.

He fists my hair, more of his weight falling on me as he whimpers into my ear and fills me with his come.

"Look at you coming all over a stranger's cock. Can't lie and say you don't want it now," he says in a euphoric way against my face.

I'm catching my breath, which is still hard to do with him still being on top of me, but he doesn't move right away either.

Lincoln kisses the side of my face before sliding his cock out of me and giving me some relief of him not being on top of me.

I'm about to turn around and get up when he grabs my hips.

"Wait," he says, adjusting me so that I'm on all fours. "Let me watch it drip out of you."

It should be humiliating, mortifying even. For me, it makes me want to do it all over again.

He doesn't push it back in, but I can feel his release drip down my thighs as he watches my pussy with rapt focus.

"Let's go shower," he says, once he's seen everything he wanted.

We're quiet for a moment as he turns on the spray and we both step into the foggy glass capsule.

"Was that all okay?" he asks me, his face searching mine and his hands cupping the sides of my face.

He looks serious, like he does when he talks about work.

I approach him, wrapping my arms around his waist and resting my head on his chest.

"It was more than okay, Linc," I say.

"What do you need?" he asks.

"Just hold me," I reply, and he does just that, the warm water spraying against our backs as he holds the back of my head with one hand and holds me close with another.

Too bad this weekend was also way more than I ever imagined it would be. I hold on to him tightly, not knowing how I'm supposed to let go come tomorrow night.

Lincoln

Remember Your Promise

PENNY IS NOT A MORNING PERSON, and I don't wake her. I just stare at the pool of blonde hair taking up a significant amount of real estate on my pillows and think of ways to convince her to give me more time.

I've been so good with order, liking my life organized and clean for so long. But right now I want to find long blonde hairs clinging to my suit jacket before going to work. I want every shower to be with her; I want to watch more stupid shows and get drunk and sing karaoke at Calamity with *her*.

It all boils down to Penny.

The woman who's always been in front of me, but never a second thought in my mind. But then Avalon happened and everything changed.

I wish I could just let this weekend pass and all these memories fall away with her, but I can't.

Is it because she's what I can't have?

No, it's definitely more than that. Penny's the first person to make me smile and feel so carefree in such a long time. I didn't even feel a fraction of this with Vanessa and I thought I was going to marry her.

She wouldn't be a fraction of the wife or mother that Penny would be.

I groan and rub my face just thinking about it. My life could always be how this weekend was. Maybe I fucked up, convincing her that we just needed to get it out of our system, because the fact is Penny's embedded in my fucking veins now. Whether she wants to be or not.

"Stop staring at me, you freak," she groans, and I grab her by the waist, holding her tight against my chest.

"I wasn't staring. I was admiring."

"Then continue," she sighs, nestling in against my body with her eyes still closed.

"What if I said I didn't want to go back to real life after the weekend?" I ask.

Her body stiffens, but she doesn't leave my embrace.

"That's not what we agreed on, Linc."

"I know."

She can clearly hear how dejected I feel, and she pulls away. She uses my large shirt and tucks it over her knees as she holds her legs close to herself and looks at me.

"I've put my parents through a lot, Linc. This family is all I have."

"You can't deny what we have, Penny," I try to reason with her.

"I'm not denying anything. This weekend has been amazing, more than amazing. But we can't, Linc. As much as I loved this weekend and I care about you, I can't lose my family."

"You're not losing your family, Penny."

She glares at me, standing up and pacing in front of my bed.

"You don't get it."

"Tell me what I don't get," I say, crossing my arms over my bare chest and leaning against the headboard.

"They would choose you, Lincoln. If we did this and told them everything and then things fall apart between us? They would choose you. I'd be Holly and Tim's once-adopted daughter that's been disgraced from the family."

"You're being dramatic," I say, and she stops her pacing to stare at me.

Her blue eyes fill with tears and I suddenly want to swallow the words back down my throat.

"I know they'd choose you, because I'd choose you too, Lincoln. It's why I need to go."

She grabs her dress from the corner and I finally stand up to stop her from leaving the bedroom.

"Sunday isn't even over yet," I say.

She comes to stand before me, dress clutched against her chest.

"I need to leave," she whispers.

"But you don't want to."

"I know, that's the worst part," she says, throwing the dress on and pushing past me through the living room and kitchen toward the front door.

"Penny, come back. We can talk about this."

Her hand is on the door handle and she breathes, resting her forehead against the door for a short moment.

"I always change myself for the guy I'm with, you know that?" she says and I furrow my brow, wondering where the fuck this conversation is going.

"Whatever hobbies they have, I take up. Whenever they thought something was funny, I'd laugh even though I hated it. Their favorite food became my favorite food. I was always willing to toss these small pieces of me away for them—they were small pieces. What was the big deal? But recently, I figured out that too many pieces of me are gone. I don't know who I am."

She's crying now, and I go to approach her, but she waves me off.

"As much as you made me feel like one whole piece this weekend, without my family, I'll be just as lost."

"Penny, just stay. We can talk about this."

"Thank you for the weekend, Linc. Remember your promise," she says, opening the door and leaving me behind like she didn't just take a piece of me.

I sit on the couch, my head between my hands, and contemplate all of her words. Of course, all my first thoughts are selfish ones, like telling the family and having her see that she's wrong.

Not that there wouldn't be discontentment if we were to publicly come out as a couple. There would be a serious adjustment period. They wouldn't be happy, but they'd get over it.

But she's thinking this all under the guise of it being some fling, something that will eventually fizzle out.

I need to prove to her that I'm serious and that I want it all.

I'M ALREADY HATING life because it's Monday, I haven't seen Penny, and the amount of bullshit that's on my desk is abhorrent.

Marie comes in and drops off my coffee with a contemplative look on her face.

"What has you in such a shitty mood?" she asks.

I glare at her, and she glares right back.

"Your brother called," she says.

"Which one?"

"Gavin. He wanted to make sure that you all were still planning on going to Sarasota this weekend."

I groan and tap my head on top of the table.

"This is all very dramatic, even for you, Lincoln."

"Yes, I'll call him and confirm. Why didn't he text me?" I ask and Marie looks around and I roll my eyes. "He's checking up on me?"

She shrugs her shoulders. "I don't know. I just answer the phones. We're ordering lunch from Hugo's. Do you want anything?"

"The usual, thanks."

"You got it," she says, though I know she wants to say more. I just don't have the patience for that today.

I open a browser and pathetically search for ways to make a woman fall in love with you, romantic gestures, and therapists' offices near me.

All I find is bullshit.

I'm not good at this. At sharing my feelings, and being overly sweet and kind. But for Penny, I'll do it. I just don't know how to do that when she's put her foot down on the whole situation.

Maybe instead of pursuing this so heavily, despite my wishes, I need to give her some room to breathe and realize it on her own.

Way easier said than done.

IT'S BEEN two days of my self-talk of leaving Penny alone, to stop hyperfixating and giving her room to breathe.

Well, it's not going well.

I'm standing outside of her apartment door holding an iced latte that's freezing my hand and a breakfast burrito in another.

She opens the door, clicking the button to lock it before spinning around and gasping.

She drops her purse and clutches her chest.

"You fucking scared me," she complains, grabbing her purse and looking up at me. "What's that?"

"Breakfast," I say plainly, and she glares at me.

"Why are you standing in front of my front door holding breakfast?" she asks.

"Because I wanted to. Everyone needs breakfast."

"Lincoln," she sighs my name, walking toward the elevator and pushing the button, not taking the coffee or breakfast.

"Let me drive you to work."

She goes to open her mouth and I shove the straw of the latte in between her parted lips before she can speak.

"I drive you to work all the time."

"That was before."

"Before what?" I ask, wanting her to admit she's been thinking about me, too.

She sighs, grabbing the burrito out of my hands. "Never-mind," she groans as we both enter the elevator.

She's quiet, and I hate it. I like when she doesn't shut up and babbles on about shit. When we leave the building and are smacked with the Florida heat, she concedes.

"Fine, I could use a ride."

I repress a smile as we head over to my car and get in, blasting the AC immediately, and I drive slowly to Kemper's.

"Are you going with your brothers to the beach house this weekend?" she asks.

"Yes, I'm sure Gavin and Ben have some ridiculous shit planned."

She smiles and nods. "I wouldn't expect anything less."

"What are you doing this weekend?" I ask her.

Penny takes an extremely long sip of her latte and shrugs her shoulders.

"I'd cancel, you know?" I tell her as I pull into the parking lot. She thankfully doesn't get out right away and turns her head to face me.

I wonder if she's thinking about how she climbed the console the other night to ride my dick.

"If you wanted to spend the weekend together, I'd cancel."

"Lincoln, I can't do this," she whispers.

"I'd choose you, Penny."

Her eyes well with tears and she shakes her head, opening the door and leaving me behind in the dust. I sit in the parking lot for far too long, my brother coming over and tapping the roof of the car and I roll down my window.

"Everything good?" he asks.

"Yeah, what's up?"

"Penny just looked a little upset, and you've been parked in my lot for a good ten minutes."

"Had a phone call," I lie.

"And Penny?"

"She won't tell me what's up with her." A lie, but not really. I promised I wouldn't bring up her birth mother, and I won't.

"She's been off lately. I'll see if I can get her to talk to me," Aiden says. Forever the pragmatic sweetheart of the Carlson brothers.

"Good luck with that," I say.

Aiden furrows his brows and looks at me.

"And you, is everything okay with you?"

"Just fucking dandy. Can one of you assholes drive this weekend?"

"Yeah, sure," he says, searching my face.

I roll up the window before any additional conversation can be had and head to the office.

I don't want to make Penny cry, I don't want to make her life harder than it already is. But the lengths I'm willing to go to get her to understand how we should be together is concerning.

It's been a long time since I've been fixated on anything, let alone a person.

But here I am, daydreaming about loose blonde curls, pretty blue eyes, that just so happen to belong to my adopted cousin who's adamant there can be nothing between us.

When did my life get so fucking complicated?

I DON'T KNOW how I manage to get through the morning at work. All I can think about are Lincoln's soft eyes telling me he chooses me.

That's all I've ever wanted, to be someone's choice and priority, yet he's the one person I can't have. It would ruin everything. Men don't stick around long enough once they truly get to know me.

Lincoln wants me now because it's exciting and new, but eventually he would leave. I'd be left broken hearted with no family, and then who would I be.

I do my best to try and keep a pep in my step and not let my happy-go-lucky facade break as I head to Jessa's cubicle.

"Hey, got some time to grab lunch?" I ask.

"Sure," she says with a smile, grabbing her purse and following me outside. I'm not sure how to fill the silence, because I think if she asks me what's wrong, I might just fall apart. "Penny, are you okay?"

I blink at her, and as I suspected, the floodgates burst open as I cry into my hand. Jessa drags me out of the food truck line and we sit at one of the wooden picnic tables. She rubs my back in a soothing manner as I try to get my shit together. "This is so fucking stupid. I can't believe I'm just breaking down like this." I wipe my eyes, trying to collect myself while Jessa keeps rubbing my back assuredly.

"We can talk about it if you want, or if you just want to sit here. Whatever you need," Jessa says, and I give her what I'm sure is a pathetic smile.

"Have you ever loved someone you couldn't have?" It's a broad thing to say. I'm not romantically in love with Lincoln, but I know I could be. There's already a love for him in my heart, but deep down, I know it could be devastating.

She shakes her head, but doesn't stop rubbing my back.

"Why can't you be with them?" she asks. Probably wondering why I've never brought up my dating life before.

"Because it's so stupidly complicated I can't even get into it." I scoff. The last thing I need is her realizing how fucked up I am and that she should run far, far away.

"But you both want to be together?" she asks and I nod my head. "Then I'm sure you can figure out a way to make it work."

God, I wish it was that easy. I wish I could give into him and just see what life could be like between us.

I start crying again, and Jessa, being the amazing friend she is, doesn't stop with the soothing back rubs. When I'm finally done sobbing like an asshole, she wraps her arms around me and squeezes me into an affectionate hug that I desperately needed.

How I got so lucky with her entering my life when she did, I'm not sure. But I'm not letting her go.

"I'm so sorry for ruining lunch."

"Hey, you didn't ruin anything," Jessa says, pulling back and rubbing my arms. "Do you want to go home early? I'll cover for you at the office."

"Really?" I ask, with a small smile.

"Of course. What are girlfriends for?"

"Thanks, Jessa."

We hug and I make my way to my apartment, where I plan on being a mess until my dreaded appointment with my therapist this afternoon.

I FIDGET with the side of the couch as Deb grabs a new pen and looks at me.

As soon as her inquisitive brown eyes meet mine, I fall apart and spill my guts out. I tell her everything; Key Club, the letter, the weekend.

She doesn't speak as I spew it all out and tell her far too many details about what's going on in my ridiculous life.

I don't even know how much time passes when I get the whole story out and finally meet her eyes.

"Well, that's a lot," she says, taking a moment to gather her thoughts. "Let's start with the letter," she says, and I grimace.

"Do we have to?"

"You pay me, Penny. You wanted to get this all off your chest and work through it, and that's what I'm here for."

"It set me back," I reply, wrapping my arms around myself.

"In what way?"

"You know that I've been wanting to get to the bottom of who I am and what I want. When I read that letter, I felt like I didn't matter, that I shouldn't even be here. She didn't go into detail in her letter, but it's not hard to guess what happened. I guess it kind of makes sense."

Deb's brows furrow. "What do you mean by that?"

"My beginnings were fucked up. Why wouldn't the rest of my life?"

"Why do you think your life is so bad, Penny? You have a

job, you have a family who loves you. You're working on your-self to be the best you can be, so that you can have a healthy, happy life. Where is all this negative self talk coming from?"

"I don't know," I say, looking away from her. "But in case you missed the other half of my story, I also have romantic feel-ings for my cousin beyond all the sexual stuff I didn't get too graphic with."

"What does he want?" she asks.

"He wants to be together."

"And you don't want to lose your family?" she asks, knowing what I feel right off the bat. I nod and she jots down some notes. I think my case file grew by multiple pages after this session. "Are you worried that it's just some torrid affair and that nothing would come out of it besides devastation?"

"That's how all my other relationships have gone. I get so sucked into the moment and the haze of it all that I don't see the signs before it's too late."

"But you've done a lot of work, Penny. A year ago you didn't recognize this about yourself, now you do."

"Are you seriously suggesting that I go figure things out with Lincoln?"

"No, I'm not suggesting anything. I'm just saying that you're being too mean to yourself. You're intelligent, caring, and kind, Penny. You deserve peace and happiness. This choice is solely yours, and it comes with a lot of potential consequences. It's not something you should take lightly. The fact that you didn't just agree to be with him shows how much you've grown."

I swallow and nod my head.

"Let's get back to the letter," she says and I groan at Deb. "You can be angry and mad at her. You're allowed to feel however you need. It's separate from her trauma."

"I know. I went to a rage room with Linc," I say. I swear her lip tilts in a half smile before it quickly disappears.

"That's one way to get those feelings out. I'd like for you to write a letter of your own back. It's not something you'd send. But I'd like you to write it, get it all out and then burn it."

"I can do that."

"We will move to weekly sessions for the foreseeable future to work through everything else as it comes," she says.

My face falls, and she shakes her head. "Needing to see me more is not a backslide, Penny. It's understanding yourself."

I nod and leave the building, contemplating what to write into the letter.

IT TOOK me three hours to get down the words I wanted to say, what I needed to get off of my chest. But the words are on paper and clutched in my hand as I sit on the rooftop deck.

It's late and humid as the small fire pit lights up before me. I twiddle the paper between my fingers, considering keeping it. As cathartic as the words were to put on paper, something still feels off about the whole process.

The door to the rooftop slams and I jolt in my seat, immediately relaxing when I see it's Lincoln approaching.

"Are you stalking me now?" I ask, as he rounds the patio furniture and takes a seat next to me. He holds out his beer and I scrunch my nose and shake my head.

"I'd say you're stalking me. I come up here all the time," he jokes, searching my face.

Neither of us mention this morning, the weekend, or anything between us. Thank God. I really don't feel like crying anymore than I already have today.

"What's that?"

I sigh and unfold it. "A letter to my biological mom, my therapist's idea."

"You aren't going to give it to her?"

"No, Deb said I should write it and burn it. But I don't know if that's what I want to do."

"What did you say in it?" he asks. His posture is relaxed as he leans back on the couch and searches my face.

I open up the letter and sigh. Reading it out loud feels real, raw, and terrible, but I do it anyway.

"I want you to know that I don't blame you for putting me up for adoption. I can't imagine what you went through or what your life was like. But I do know how my life went. I was blessed to be adopted by a good family who gave me the world. Not only a place to live and food to eat, but pure genuine love. So I want to thank you for that. I know life could have been wholly different if you didn't make the choices you did."

Lincoln's palm reaches out and squeezes my thigh. I know I should shove him off, but I don't. His touch is too comforting.

"But I'm still angry. I'm angry that you don't want to meet me, that I built up what it would be like meeting my biological mom only to find out I was the product of abuse. I've spent a lot of my life feeling lost, like something was missing. I thought maybe once I knew where I came from, why I wasn't wanted, maybe it would all make more sense. But now, I just feel more confused than ever. I know it's not fair to put this anger and pain solely on you. You did what you had to. But I'm lost."

I wipe a tear from my eye and breathe as I continue, not daring to look over at Lincoln.

"I realize I can't push you for a relationship and I have to live with the unknown. It's a hard pill to swallow, but I'm going to accept your boundaries. I'm not really sure what else to put in this letter besides my hopes. I hope that you find happiness and peace. I wish the same for myself. I'm going to hold my family tight, and one day when I have children of my own, I'll tell them about you, even if it is this little piece of you. Because even though you couldn't take care of me, and you probably didn't want me to be brought into the world, you did, and you did the best you could. So I guess all that's left to say is thank you and I'm going to work on moving on with my life."

I don't even second guess it. Once the words are out, I toss the letter into the fire and watch it burn.

Lincoln doesn't speak, but he pulls me close into his chest and I rest my head on his shoulder as we watch the letter burn together. I don't know how it helped, but it did, saying everything I felt out loud.

"You did good," Lincoln says softly.

I stay in his embrace for far longer than I should. He just feels too good and when he isn't talking, it makes things easier.

"I should go," I whisper.

He places a wordless kiss on the top of my head and I leave the rooftop feeling lighter than I did before I came up here, but just as confused.

Lincoln

Batman's Calling

I SHOULD HAVE CANCELED, stayed home and made sure that Penny was alright. But I knew if I didn't leave the fucking apartment, I'd just sit there and constantly think about her all the time.

It's not healthy, I'm more than well aware.

My obsession with Penny is only getting worse with each passing day. When she read that letter, though? More of me understood why she feels like she can't be with me, why our family is the crucible of who she is.

Doesn't mean I'm not pissed about it.

It's been a series of stupid games the twins have come up with and Aiden looking like he's floating on cloud nine thinking about his new girlfriend. At least I know Penny is over at her new friend's house tonight. That's good. She needs a close friend.

The twins are wasted, singing and dancing acting like the happiest bunch of assholes I've ever seen and I can't take it anymore. I've had too much to drink, but not in a way that makes me feel good. I feel hopeless and somewhat depressed as I look over at Aiden.

"Cigar?" I ask Aiden.

We head outside to the back deck, listening to the roar of the ocean as we sit in a moment of silence before I look over at Aiden, smiling at his phone.

"I'm happy for you, ya know?" I tell him and I mean it. I might be slightly fucking jealous that my love life isn't as complicated. But I'm happy that Aiden has found someone. Even if it's still somewhat of a secret to the general public.

"I know."

"You deserve to be happy. I'm excited to meet her. You know, outside of Avalon." I smirk and he rolls his eyes. He, in fact, did not kick my ass after that encounter. What a softie.

"You deserve to be happy too, Lincoln."

"I'm not sure the rest of the family would agree," I reply, and he clearly doesn't get the connotation of what I'm saying and I wave him off. "You should invite her to The Bahamas. I know it's a while away, but that just gives you more time to be together."

His relationship is new, and hard launching her into the Carlson household is honestly just rude. But if they last the next couple of weeks, I know our mother would be thrilled.

"I'll ask her."

"I'm going to go for a walk," I say, grabbing another drink and waving off my brother as I walk down the beach.

The beach is nice as it always is as I walk in the sand, letting the lights from the ocean front houses guide me.

I pull out my phone and scroll through to Penny's name.

Are you awake?

PENNY
Jessa's couch is uncomfortable as fuck.

I smile and decide to call her instead of texting.

"Who's this?" she says with a little slur in her words.

"Batman," I say in a deep gravelly voice and she laughs.

"How is Gotham faring without you?" she asks.

"I'm pretty sure Aiden is talking to Jessa and the twins are probably passed out somewhere in the house."

"Jessa is sound asleep," she replies, which means Aiden is also very likely passed out.

"Did you have a good day?" I ask her.

I swear I can feel her smile over the phone. "I really did. It's been so long since I've had a girlfriend to hang out with. It's nice. Her and Aiden are going to be perfect for each other."

"He seems happy."

"They deserve to be happy," she replies.

"So do we."

There's a soft silence for a moment over the phone and she sighs. "Can we be different people tonight?" she asks.

"I already told you I'm Batman."

She laughs and sighs before she speaks again. "I wish you were just Batman."

"Me too," I reply, looking out at the waves.

I grab a shell and toss it into the water, both of us still on the phone, just wanting some amount of closeness.

"We've got to stop doing this, Linc."

"I know," I groan.

"Maybe some distance?"

"Okay," I reply, hating the thought entirely.

"Goodnight, Linc."

"Night."

I hang up the phone and stare at the dark, inky ocean in front of me. I either need to work on this obsession and give Penny up, or I need to convince her that this isn't some fleeting feeling.

IT'S BEEN a week and a half and I haven't seen Penny. I consider going to Avalon. Hell, even going to Key Club and meeting someone new. But every time I think about doing it, I immediately shut it down. I'm trying so fucking hard to move on, but no matter what I do, I can't.

I always thought the phrase when you know, you know, was bullshit. Especially since Penny has been in my face this whole time. But after everything we shared, I know she's my person. She's the one I'm supposed to be with.

I'm working obscenely late when Aiden walks through my office.

He rounds the chair in front of my desk and sits on it.

"Are you going to tell me what's going on?"

"What do you mean?" I ask, not even looking away from my computer.

"Even for you, this is a bit much," he says, waving a hand in my direction.

"I like my job."

"No, you're fucking burying yourself in this job. What's going on Linc? I mean, I knew things after Vanessa were bad, but lately you just seem—"

"I'm fine, just have a lot of work to do."

"You haven't been going to Avalon."

"I didn't even really like Avalon," I say, and my brother glares at me.

"You're so full of fucking shit. Is this about some woman?"

No, it's about the woman I should be with right now, but we just so happen to have a complicated family tree.

"I'm fine, Aiden."

"No, you're not. I know a thing or two about not being okay, Lincoln."

I look away from my computer and over at him. He's basically handing me a life preserver, but I'm in too deep. I'm drowning in this need and there's nothing Aiden or anyone else can do to prevent me from drowning.

"I promise. I'm good."

He sighs and stands up from his chair.

"When you decide you're not fine, I'll be there."

He leaves my office and I go back to work, trying to drown out all these feelings I wish would go away.

ANOTHER SATURDAY without Penny in my bed feels like a fucking crime. I feel like shit as I leave to go grab my food for the evening, which I will be eating alone, like some crotchety old man with no friends.

Penny makes me want to be better. Fuck, I'll buy a pair of Reeboks and learn to be nicer to people if that's what she wants.

I'm leaving the apartment building and I see Penny standing in the lot. She's wearing a dark blue sundress with her hair in a messy bun.

Fuck, she's so beautiful.

Wait? Why does she look so nice and where the fuck is she going?

A black SUV rolls around the lot, a handsome man rolling down the window and smiling at her before she gets in.

You've gotta be fucking kidding me.

Instead of going and getting take out, I drive down to the bar we all used to get wasted at when we were all home from college.

A date? Could she seriously be going on a date right now?

I'm not an idiot. I know Penny could land any guy she wanted. She's my person. It wouldn't make sense for me to be hers. Doesn't make me any less selfish, wanting to hoard her away for myself.

But she told me that I needed to move on, that we couldn't do this.

How the fuck am I supposed to move on? I hadn't even moved on from my last fucked-up relationship; I don't think there's any working past this.

I order drink after drink, wanting to feel numb.

Deep down I know I use alcohol too much, so I don't have to feel, but right now I truly don't even fucking care.

The idea of Penny laughing with some asshole on a date makes my stomach churn.

"Seat taken?" A woman asks and I wave at the seat. "Party for one, I guess?" she jokes.

I laugh sardonically and roll my eyes.

"What an asshole," she says to her friend and I order another drink.

My phone buzzes in my pocket and I groan, digging it out and seeing my brother's name.

Ignore.

He calls three more times until I finally give up and answer the fucking thing.

"What?"

"Why is Jasper calling me and telling me that my brother is acting like a drunken asshole at the bar?"

"I don't know. You have three brothers."

"Do you want me to call you a ride?" Aiden asks.

"I'm fine, Aiden."

He sighs over the phone. "Fuck it. I'm coming to pick you up."

"You don't need to do that."

"You sound like you're fucking wasted. I'll be there in a half-hour."

"Fine," I say, before hanging up and ordering more drinks. Wondering how much more I can get down my gullet until Aiden arrives.

Aiden gets to the bar way before his thirty minute ETA.

"Let's go," Aiden says, handling my tab and tipping the bartender graciously.

"I'm a whole ass man, I can get myself home."

"You're coming with me," he says, grabbing his phone and making a call, stepping away. I keep sipping my drink and he rolls his eyes and snatches it away.

"I'm not done drinking, asshole," I tell him.

"Shut the fuck up," Aiden says back to me before sighing and talking to the person over the phone. "Sorry, I'll be there in fifteen."

He puts an arm around my waist and supports my weight, lugging me into the car.

I press my face against the glass, it feels great against my skin.

"This isn't the way to my house," I say, looking out the window as we cross a bridge.

"I've gotta go pick up Jessa first."

"Your girlfriend."

"Yes, my girlfriend."

I make a noise of understanding and close my eyes as Aiden drives us wherever the fuck we're going to pick up his girlfriend.

I'm tired and groggy by the time we get there and he looks over at me before we get out of the car.

"Whatever this is, you've gotta work through it man. This isn't you," Aiden says, looking me up and down as he gets out of the car.

Whiskey Joe's is on the bay so you have to walk through sand to get to tables, the bar, and chairs. It honestly feels pretty fucking unsanitary when I think about it. My feet sink in with each step, the music is loud and there's a bunch of rowdy assholes who have pulled their boats up to drink and eat.

Why the fuck is Aiden's girlfriend at Whiskey Joe's by herself? And why the hell couldn't he have just dropped me off at home instead of making me suffer this unending trek to get to a shitty wooden table plopped in the sand.

Aiden groans, grabbing my arm and I follow suit, hating the bright glare of the sun and how miserable I feel.

It's then as we finally are approaching the tables that I realize Penny is with Jessa. I want to pull her into my lap and drown her in the ocean at the same time—it's very confusing. I got wasted and made a complete asshole out of myself while she's just been at this shithole of a beach bar with her friend the whole time?

"You've got to be fucking kidding me," I mumble as we approach

"What is your problem, Lincoln?" my brother asks.

Our pretty, unobtainable cousin. That's my problem.

Penny

Whiskey Joe's

JESSA AND I ARE LAUGHING, drinking too many margaritas and enjoying the outside bar when Aiden calls her phone and I ignore it, looking around at the people dancing in the sand, swaying in my seat to the beat of the music the live band is playing.

Maybe we did go a little hard and heavy on the margaritas with too little food. But fuck it, this has been the best I've felt since the last night Jessa and I hung out. If only I could tell her everything, it would be a relief to have a friend's point of view on this, not just my therapist's.

But I'm too scared of what she might think. I'm too scared of what everyone would think if they found out what Lincoln and I did. I've finally got a good friend. The last thing I want is to be judged for what I did by accident... and then on purpose.

God. I take a deep swig of my margarita in an attempt for the tequila to disrupt my nerve endings and make all these feelings go away.

Why are longing and regret at the forefront of my mind? I miss Lincoln, and I hate that I do. It's not even just sex, I miss his smiles, his jokes, his touch. I miss everything about him and I wish I didn't.

Jessa nearly shakes me, in order to get my attention. "Penny, Aiden is trying to decide whether to drop Lincoln off first or come and get us."

I blink at her a few times. "He's with Lincoln?" she nods and fuck, I know I shouldn't see him. But the part of me that still desperately wants him doesn't agree. It's probably the margaritas making the decisions but oh well. "Tell him to pick us up first."

"Did you hear that?" she says down the phone, while Aiden replies "Okay. See you soon."

I start biting my nails. Oh fuck. Why did I tell him to bring Lincoln? I can't see him like this. I'll cave.

"Everything good, Pen?" Jessa asks.

"Yeah, maybe too many margaritas?"

"Let's get some water and wait till Aiden gets here."

I nod and Jessa grabs us some water and we sit by the bay and wait for Aiden and Lincoln to get here.

"So tell me more about the family. I haven't met a partner's family before," Jessa says nervously.

"You have no reason to be nervous. They'll all love you."

"How can you be so sure?"

"Because Aiden adores you, I adore you. That's all you need," I say with a smile.

"It's just new, you know. I'm not used to how easy and fast this is all going."

"When you know, you know," I tell her and she smiles.

"Oh, there they are," Jessa says, pointing to where Aiden and Lincoln are headed towards us. Lincoln looks pissed as hell. *Perfect.*

"Oh fuck," I whisper as Aiden takes a seat next to Jessa, and Lincoln sits next to me.

"Water?" Lincoln asks me and I give him a look that I'm sobering up. "Good."

Lincoln stares as Aiden kisses Jessa on the head and I know it's longing. It makes my gut churn with guilt.

Because I understand that longing more than I'd like to admit. I shouldn't want to kiss Lincoln right now, but I do. I want him in every way I know that I possibly can't.

Why is it so fucking hard wanting what you can't have?

"Jessa, you've met my brother," Aiden says, and I can hear how annoyed he is with his brother's behavior. I'm even more frustrated because I know I'm the reason he's been drinking.

I hate it.

"Hey," he says, tilting his head, and I make an exacerbated noise in the back of my throat. He's mad at me. He shouldn't be rude to Jessa. He glances over at me like he's done nothing wrong. "What?" he asks, and I glare at him.

"You can be a little nicer to Aiden's girlfriend, considering he hasn't had one in forever."

Lincoln laughs at his brother's expense and shakes his head, going back to glaring at me.

"How much have you had to drink?" Lincoln asks me, like he isn't completely wasted himself.

"A few rounds, but one of them was free?"

"What?" Jessa asks and I shrug at her.

"This older dude wanted to buy us a round. I might not be the brightest, but I don't turn down free drinks."

Everyone looks at me like I'm insane for taking a free drink, and I shrug it off.

"Can I please drive you two degenerates home now?" Aiden asks, looking at me and Lincoln.

Lincoln's hand lands on my thigh and he rubs his hand back and forth under the table. My heart rate immediately picks up as I glance over at Aiden and Jessa who seem like they're in their own little romance bubble. I should stop him. I know I should fling his hand off and tell him we promised not to pursue this any longer. But it feels too good, and I missed him way too much.

I know there's a sick part of me that likes the wrongness, the fear of getting caught. Though I don't truly want that, not really. I try to grab his hand, and he swats me away.

"I need to eat something," Lincoln complains and I nod in agreement.

"I swear, if you fucking throw up in my car," Aiden warns him.

Lincoln rolls his eyes but picks up the menu. He orders some food and never stops touching my leg under the table. Of course Jessa drops her phone at that time and bends under the table to grab it. Lincoln isn't paying attention and I'm too slow to move his hand.

Fucking stupid slip up.

When she pops back up, she blinks at me, clearly confused by what she just saw. I shake my head and she just waves it off. I'm nervous she's going to tell Aiden what she saw, but I don't think she would do that to me.

"Aiden?" she says, looking over at him.

"Yeah, baby?"

"Do you want to dance with me?"

"Sure," he agrees, and they stroll off to the dance floor.

It's official, Jessa Peters is the best friend a girl could ask for as she distracts my cousin and moves him far away from our table.

Lincoln's hand slides further up my dress and I grab his wrist.

"What are you doing? Jessa just saw your hand on my thigh," I hiss at him.

"Good."

I pull his hand off, and he plants it right back on.

"Stop being so fucking difficult," he complains, like I'm being unreasonable.

"Fuck you. I'm not being difficult. We decided that we wouldn't do this, it was the weekend only. We can't be anything beyond that."

"No, Penny. You decided," he says, his gaze boring into mine. "I know you miss me just as much as I miss you. Tell me you didn't miss me and I'll leave you alone."

"Linc," I sigh his name and he squeezes my thigh hard and I look up at him. Usually I'm a pretty good liar, but right now as much as I know I should lie, I don't.

"That's what I thought," he says and I sigh.

"I'm thinking I should move," I tell him softly. I've been debating it for the last few weeks, him living on the floor beneath me only creates a deeper tension. Maybe if I'm out of the complex and only see him for family functions, it will make things easier.

"No."

"No?"

"No, you're not moving. No, you're not denying us what we both want. Just give me a chance, Penny."

I scrub my face, wishing I hadn't had so many margaritas and that he hadn't drunk so much of whatever it was that he was drinking.

"Tell me it was just sex," he says, his handsome drunken face pleading with me. "Tell me it was just about that and I'll stop, Penny."

I swallow. "You know it wasn't."

I try to pull away from his hand, but he holds me there.

"You knew I was with Aiden. You wanted me here," he says. *Well, he's fucking got me there.*

I'm not sure what lie I can possibly say, but he doesn't let me get one out. "You've missed me just as much as I've fucking missed you. Did you tell Aiden to come pick you up because you wanted to see me?"

He squeezes my thigh tighter.

"Yes," I grate out.

"I want you in my bed. I want to finish that stupid fucking show with you and feed you breakfast and fuck you into my mattress," he says.

He presses his nose against my cheek and I want to give in. I want to tell him I want all the same things. That I'd happily go home with him right now if the circumstances were different.

"What happens when you realize that you like the idea of me, not really me, Linc? What happens when you get bored or decide you don't want the same things as me? You'll be okay, you'll be forgiven. I'll have nothing."

"How could I ever get tired of this, of you?" he asks and I swallow, his words linger against my ear as I look over his shoulder and see that Jessa and Aiden are about to turn around and I pull away in shame.

Lincoln's eye's meet mine and he looks behind him, realizing that they are headed in our direction.

He rolls his eyes as the server brings our food.

"Who gives a fuck what anyone else thinks?"

"Me, Lincoln. I care, and you acting like I'm being ridiculous just pisses me off." He grumbles something and starts eating his food like he's a starving man as Jessa and Aiden take their seats next to us.

"Christ, Linc. Slow down," Aiden scolds him.

Jessa's eyes dart between the two of us, trying to figure this all out. Making two of us, because I don't know what I'm doing. We can't keep playing this tug of war where he tries to convince me this can be a real thing and I'm the clear-headed one.

Lincoln eats with one hand, and places the other back on

my thigh. The worst part is? I love it. I love that he always wants to touch me, that he's so into me, and he would scream it from the rooftops if he could.

His hand slides up, nearly touching my pussy and I jump slightly.

"You good?" Aiden asks, giving me an odd look.

"Yeah, Penny? You seem tense?" Linc says, his hand gripping my hip.

I'm not sure who misses Lincoln more, me or my vagina.

"I'm fine," I lie and Lincoln nearly cups me from the outside of my clothes. We're in public, Jessa and Aiden across from us, I should feel ashamed, I should be scared that we're going to get caught... yet, I'm wet and wish everything around us would disappear and we could be alone again. I clear my throat and shake my head. "I'm going to run to the bathroom real quick," I say, grabbing his hand and squeezing it before walking across the sand to the restrooms.

I knock and enter the single stall. I'm about to shut the door when a large hand swipes out and stops me from shutting it. Lincoln forces his way in, shutting the bathroom door and locking it behind him.

He fists the front of my dress, pulling me closer.

"Linc, stop it," I say, pushing at his chest with no real effort. Because I want it, it's what I wanted at the table, no matter how frustrated I am with him, I always want him, especially like this.

He holds my dress in one hand, his other sliding down my body and cupping my pussy. Lincoln's eyes bore into mine, but he doesn't kiss me as he pushes my panties to the side, sliding his fingers through my embarrassingly wet slit.

"Tell me to stop," he says.

"We should stop," I say breathlessly.

His fingers rub tormenting, delicious circles around my clit.

His stare is magnetizing, and I don't look away. I could get lost in his cerulean eyes, even though I know I shouldn't.

"Tell me I don't make you feel good, Penny. I know how much you like to fucking lie."

"Lincoln," I rasp out his name.

His fingers are basically the eighth wonder of the world as he works me over. The amount of cocktails I've had has me feeling the right amount of buzz and I'm nearly over the edge and he hasn't even put his fingers inside of me.

"This is a bad idea," I whisper.

"You're not moving out of the building," he says, sliding two fingers inside of me. His grip on my dress is tight, nearly holding me up as he uses his palm to rub my clit.

"We need to stop this, Linc," I say, moaning the lie right between my teeth.

He presses his face against mine, still not kissing, but his lips brush against my jaw.

"That's the fucking problem. I can't stop," he says, his palm rubbing me in just the right spot as his fingers curl inside of me. "I can't stop thinking about you, wanting you, needing you. It's all your fucking fault, so you have to deal with it."

It's fucked up, it's wrong.

But his words make me come on the spot.

No one has ever been as intense about me as the intense that Lincoln is. It's addictive. Not only the way he's seemingly obsessed with me, but I know part of the allure is the wrongness.

We're not meant to be together.

But despite everything, I want him, I need him just as bad.

He fucks me harder with his fingers, my pussy clenching around his hand as he breathes into my ear. I moan loudly, not able to control how good it feels, not giving a single shit if someone is outside of the door listening. Or the fact that Aiden and Jessa are probably wondering where the both of us are.

I just let myself feel good for a moment. Like nothing except Lincoln and I existing.

My legs are shaky and he pulls his hand away from my wet, traitorous vagina and lets go of my dress.

I go to open my mouth to speak, to say we can't keep doing this, and he pushes his two wet fingers inside of my mouth and grabs my jaw.

His gaze is serious as he stares at me, holding my jaw and forcing me to taste my release on his fingers.

"You're not moving and this isn't fucking over," he says before turning around, unlocking the door, and leaving me behind.

I lock the door behind him and sit on the toilet, taking care of myself and trying to regulate my breathing. Why am I so fucking weak when it comes to him? And why do I like when he tells me what to do?

Every time I tell him no, he just pushes me harder and I like it.

I like that he's filthy, that he says and does the right things. I like it even more that he's so into me.

But I can't do this.

I can't get swept away in Lincoln and lose everything.

I picture the look on my mom and dad's face when I tell them I'm fucking their nephew and my heart sinks. What's even worse is when I think of Lincoln's brothers. How disgusted they would all be to find out what we've been doing behind closed doors.

We've known each other our whole lives as a familial unit. Am I really willing to risk this infatuation, this sexual awakening, when it could all come crumbling down?

Even if we risked it, fooled around more, eventually we would get caught. Lincoln thinks he wants me because I'm the one person he's not supposed to want. He's in a similar crisis that I am. Two lost people looking for solace in the depths of hell.

No matter how good he feels, it's only temporary. Everything is.

I groan, wash my hands, and open the bathroom door. Jessa is standing there and I nearly take a step back from running into her.

"Are you okay?" she asks sweetly.

"Yeah, I'm fine."

"He isn't—"

I cut her off immediately. "No, it's not like that, it's complicated."

She nods her head, probably thinking back to my mental breakdown earlier in the week and clicking all the pieces together.

"I'm ready to go home," I say, not wanting to talk about it.

What can I say out loud that I haven't already said in my head? Maybe I should talk to someone besides my therapist about this, but it all comes down to the fact that it's not a good idea.

"Are you sure, Penny? I could have Aiden drop us off at the cottage if you don't want to ride with him."

I give her a soft smile. "No, I'm good, I promise."

When did I become such a good liar?

Lincoln

Cleaning Out My Closet

PENNY AVOIDS ME, not that I'm surprised.

I'm trying to understand while also... just not giving a fuck.

If the family doesn't like it, I can be her family. Though, I have more faith in the Myers and the Carlsons than she does. But then again, I wasn't adopted. I don't have the same hangups and insecurities as she does.

I'm trying to be patient and failing miserably.

I put the passcode into Aiden's house and enter.

"What's up, asshole?" I yell, walking through the kitchen, where I'm greeted by his tiny girlfriend, who is holding a rolling pin over her shoulder. She sighs with relief when she realizes it's me.

"Jesus Christ," she says, dropping the rolling pin on the counter and folding her arms over her chest.

"Is my brother here?"

"He went to grab dinner. He'll be back soon."

"Are you cool if I wait?" I ask her and she nods her head.

I pull out the barstool and take a seat. She looks at me cautiously and my brows furrow.

"What?"

"Um. Nothing," she says too quickly.

"She told you?" I ask, not wanting to give myself away, but needing to know. The idea of Penny telling her new friend about me is beyond pleasing.

"No, I saw you at Whiskey Joe's."

I click my tongue and nod my head.

"If you hurt her," she starts, and I smile.

"To be honest, I think I'm the one who needs to worry about being hurt here."

Her brow furrows as she looks at me.

"What do you mean?"

"Nothing. So, Aiden invited you to The Bahamas?"

She clears her throat and nods. I sigh dramatically. "You have nothing to worry about. My mom will be thrilled that at least one of her sons turned out semi-normal."

"Are the other brothers like you?" she asks and I laugh.

"No, Ben and Gavin are the happiest assholes you'll ever meet. It will be fine, we're all happy for Aiden."

She blushes. "I really like him."

"Good. He's been different since you two started dating, happier. Still up my ass, though."

"He has a big heart," she says dreamily, and I want to roll my eyes, but hold it back.

It's not like I'm jealous or anything. Like I wish Penny was in my kitchen and I was getting us takeout food and we were talking about how happy we are—definitely not.

The garage door sounds and a few moments later, Aiden is walking through the door and looking back and forth between me and his girlfriend.

He kisses her head and places the food on the table.

"Didn't know you were coming over," he says, looking at me cautiously. "I brought plenty of food if you're hungry."

I knew he wouldn't toss me out. He's too worried about me being in the deep end or some shit. It's obvious I'm intruding on a date, and I should go home, but I don't.

The fact is, maybe I'm in too deep.

I've always liked my life in little boxes. It's easier to function when you know what to expect and have most aspects controlled in your life.

Penny has been the biggest destruction in my life, and I just genuinely don't know what to do.

I can't tell Aiden the truth, not until Penny agrees to be with me.

But fuck, I feel so alone.

We eat and watch the game on TV. His girlfriend is kind and sweet, the perfect match for him. It's a sick longing feeling watching them on the couch together.

How did I ever think that domesticity wasn't something I wanted?

Maybe it's because I never wanted it before Penny.

"I'm going to head up to bed. Good seeing you again, Linc." She waves and heads to Aiden's bedroom as the game continues on.

Eventually, my brother turns to me.

"You ready to talk about it?"

I shake my head, and he sighs.

"Are you at least done drinking like you want to drown yourself?"

"That's yet to be determined."

He rubs his jaw, looks at the TV and then back at me.

"Is it a woman?" he asks.

I don't deny or confirm, and he just nods, like he fucking gets it. And I suppose he does, now anyway.

"What's the issue?"

"It's too much to go into. It's complicated."

"You love her?" he asks.

It's an even more complicated answer. So I don't even respond, and Aiden sighs.

"Whatever the hang-up is, figure it out. I've never seen you like this. Not even when you broke up with Vanessa, which you also bottled up and kept to yourself. This isn't healthy, Linc. I just want to see you happy, man."

I swallow the emotion I feel at his words. Does Penny feel like she doesn't have this unconditional love like I do?

No matter how disgusted or pissed Aiden might be if he found out, when I look at him, I know that he would eventually get over it. Me being his brother is more important than anything.

"What if it was someone you didn't think was a good fit for me?" I ask him.

"I mean, I didn't like Vanessa," he says with a shrug.

"You never said anything."

"You never asked for my opinion, and you seemed happy enough."

"Why didn't you like her?"

"She always seemed to have one foot out the door, always looking at her phone during family events. I don't know. She seemed like she was convenient for you, not that you were totally into her."

I rest my head on the back of the couch and look at the ceiling.

"She had a husband and two kids," I admit.

"You knew?" he asks, shocked.

"No, I didn't fucking know. When I found out, I broke up with her."

"How do I feel like I know you so well but don't know you at all?" he asks.

He couldn't be closer to the truth if he tried.

"I'm gonna head home," I tell him standing up, he gets up too, clearly eager to get back to his girlfriend.

"Whatever it is, you'll figure it out. You're like the most stubborn asshole I know," he says.

"Thanks," I reply with a few slow blinks before leaving and heading home, with only one destination in mind.

I STAND in front of Penny's door, debating on knocking or going back to my own lonely bedroom.

Knowing I need to at least see her, I knock.

When she answers the door with red-rimmed eyes, wearing my t-shirt from the weekend we spent together, I nearly fall apart.

"What's wrong?" I ask, and she wipes her face and shakes her head. "Penny," I sigh her name and she takes a step back.

I don't care. As I enter her apartment, she backs up against the wall and wraps her arms around herself.

"Why were you crying?" I ask softly, shutting her front door and giving her space, making sure not to touch her.

She wipes her face again and takes a deep breath.

"The PI called me today."

"Did your birth mom change her mind?"

Her face scrunches up, and she shakes her head.

"She died," she barely gets the words out.

It doesn't matter what I want, or feel in that moment as I wrap her up in my arms and hug her. She grips on to me like I'm a life line.

I'm the only person she told about getting in contact with her birth mother. There's no one else she could confide in.

I rub her back, just letting her cry.

"Do they know what happened?"

"He said it was a car accident. I thought... I thought maybe one day she'd change her mind, you know? It was stupid, I know that. But I had hoped, despite her letter, that one day she would come around, but now I'm just stuck wondering forever. He sent me her picture," she says, breaking our hug and heading to the kitchen to grab her phone.

She uses the collar of the shirt to scrub her face and scrolls through some pictures before landing on one and handing me the phone.

"She was a nurse," she says.

"You look alike," I reply, looking at the woman in her early fifties in her scrubs, smiling. They have the same blonde hair and smile.

"You think?"

I nod and hand her back the phone. She stares down at the picture.

"I don't mean to keep crying on you," she says.

I enter her space again and wrap my arms around her.

"Let me stay." It's nearly pathetic how much control she has over me.

"You shouldn't."

"I know, but let me stay anyway."

Penny rubs her face against my shirt and nods, grabbing my hand and bringing me to her bedroom.

She turns on the TV and starts the stupid fucking reality show from the same episode we started from.

I pull her close against my chest, and she doesn't protest and I take that for the win it is.

"I'm sorry about your birth mom," I whisper against her hair.

"Me too."

Now's not the time to convince her of anything. I just have to be there for her.

I kiss her head and she sighs dreamily. Before we both fall asleep, I feel more contentment than I have since the last time I shared a bed with her.

THERE'S a loud knock on the door that startles Penny and I awake.

"Oh fuck," she grumbles.

"Who the fuck is knocking on your door like that?" I ask, halfway off the bed and Penny grabs me by the shirt and opens her closet door.

"It's my mom," she says with wide eyes and shoving me in the closet.

"Penelope," I hear my aunt Holly yelling from the kitchen.

"Fuck," Penny hisses. "Stay in here and be quiet," she whispers.

Holly's footsteps get closer, and I hear Penny's bedroom door open.

"Sweetheart, didn't you hear me calling your name?" Holly asks.

I'm in pitch darkness, a hanger poking my back and I'm pretty sure I'm standing on top of a high heel, but I don't move.

"Sorry, I was just getting out of bed."

"We're still on for lunch, right?" Holly asks, and I can hear her walking around the room. "Do you have that dress I got you from Valentino?"

The knob of the door turns and the closet partially opens, before slamming shut.

"Yeah, I'm sure I do."

"You're acting strange," her mother replies. The closet partially opens again.

"Mom, why don't you go make a cup of coffee and I'll get dressed really quick and we can get going."

There's a long pause.

"Sweetheart, have you been crying? And what on earth are you wearing to bed?"

"I'll tell you everything at lunch, I promise. Just let me get dressed, okay?"

"Alright," Holly says, though I can tell she isn't convinced, but the bedroom door clicks shut.

Penny opens the closet door with a frantic expression on her face.

"As soon as I leave with her, you can sneak out," she whispers.

"You're going to tell her?" I ask.

"About my birth mother," Penny says, looking away.

"Right," I say in a shitty tone, and louder than Penny likes. She pinches my arm and I let out an even louder noise.

"I swear to fucking God I will kill you right now, Lincoln Rowan Carlson."

"Full name, huh? Say it a little louder so your mother can hear and we can get this all over with."

She rubs her face. "I knew this was a bad idea."

"Yeah, you sure do like to say that a lot, but keep ending up in my arms, Pen." I know I'm being unfair, that I'm the one who sought her out and insisted I stay, that I wanted her in my arms. But being constantly pushed away at every turn is eating at me. If I knew she truly didn't want this, maybe it would be easier, but I know she does and she's just hurting us both.

She blinks at me and her face falls.

"I—"

"Save it. I'll leave once you and your mom leave. Here's the dress she wants you to wear," I say, grabbing the little black dress and handing it to her.

She looks like she wants to say more, but keeps looking at her bedroom door.

Penny grabs my shirt at the hem, tossing it off and throwing her dress on no bra, and shimming her panties off to exchange it for another pair in her drawer. She works quickly. Redoing her hair in the mirror and trying to apply some makeup on her face.

I sit in the closet like the dirty little secret I am and for the first time since we started whatever this is, I find myself resenting her for it.

She gives me one last sad look before leaving the room, and I decide that maybe I'm fucking done chasing a woman who doesn't want me.

MY MOTHER and I sit down at her favorite waterfront restaurant and she taps her nails against the table.

"Please tell me you're not seeing that man who has the reptiles again," she says, referring to Johnathon.

I grimace, remembering how I had to pretend to like snakes, so he thought I was interesting. But he had a nice house and wasn't an animal abuser, quite the opposite. God, my bar is seriously in the pits of Hell.

"Ew, no."

"Oh, good. He was probably my least favorite," she says.

I know she doesn't mean it as a dig, but it feels that way. My face must look dejected as she reaches across the table and grabs my hand.

"I didn't mean it like that, Pen. You're just my beautiful, brilliant daughter. I want to see you with someone who knows that as well as I do. You're my most treasured person. I love you so much."

I grab the napkin, totally over being a cry baby lately, but life has seriously been kicking my ass. Crying in a public place is extra sickening, and I try to rein it in.

My mom's eyes widen as she looks at me blot the corner of my eyes.

"This isn't like you, sweetheart. Tell me what's going on."

I look across the table at my beautiful mother, who's never asked for anything, who only gives. Part of me doesn't want to tell her anything because I don't want her to have to shoulder the burden. Hasn't she done enough already?

"You're scaring me," she says and I shake my head.

I spill my guts and tell her everything about the PI, my birth mother's letter, my letter to her, and what happened last night.

She rounds the table and gives me a hug so motherly I nearly combust. If I lost this? If she didn't look at me the same anymore, I don't know that I'd survive.

"I'm so sorry, Penelope," she whispers in my hair, holding me tight. "I wish you would have told me at your place. We didn't have to come here," she says, retaking her seat and blotting her eyes with a napkin. "I always hoped I would get to thank her one day for giving me you." I try to rein in my emotions as my phone buzzes.

> **LINCOLN**
>
> I'm out of your apartment. I won't bother you anymore.

I stare down at the phone and re-read the words. It's what I wanted, right? For this thing between us to end and clear my conscience? Yet, why does it feel like the deepest heartbreak I've ever felt?

"Penny," my mother says my name. She must have said it a few times as I look up at her. "Please tell me there isn't something else?" she asks.

"No mom, there's nothing else," I lie, my heart breaking over mid-day mimosas and a turkey club sandwich.

* * *

A WHOLE MONTH without Lincoln and my heart aches. I thought that distance would help, but it's only made me miss him more.

I thought Lincoln was full of shit, that he would come knocking on my door in the middle of the night telling me we belong together, but he hasn't. He's kept his promise of staying away, and I feel guilty that I wish he hadn't.

He's actually done and I hate it. The distance between us is palpable and I wish I could have him back without risking everything else. But that's not how life works, I made this choice for the both of us and I have to see it through.

Jessa is over as I toss shit in a suitcase for The Bahamas.

"You're rage packing," she says as I throw multiple bathing suits into the suitcase.

"Well, I have a lot of rage."

"You know, if you keep all these feelings bottled up they're bound to explode."

I glare at her, and she holds her hands up.

"I'm just saying, we've been friends for months now and I still feel you're keeping secrets. Big, massive, cousin-sized secrets."

I wave her off.

She sighs, grabbing a few dresses for me out of my closet and putting them on the bed for me to pack.

"I'm just saying you didn't judge me when you found out what I'm into. I wouldn't judge you either."

She says that now, but it feels like a lie.

Everyone always says they won't judge you or they can keep

a secret. They never can. Sure, she hasn't told Aiden what she saw, but Jessa doesn't know everything.

"Well, it might come up on vacation, so I'll give you a heads up. I found my birth mom."

"Oh my gosh, how exciting."

"She's dead," I reply and her poor eyes widen and her mouth parts.

I wave her off again.

"Don't worry, I'm doing a significant amount of therapy to work through all my shit."

"Do you think it helps?"

"Therapy?" I reply, grabbing my cosmetics and tossing them into a bag. "Yeah, I mean, I think I'd be way more fucked up if I didn't go."

"You're not fucked up," she replies, and I give her a small smile.

"Thanks."

"You're not, Penny. When no one else was kind to me at Kemper's, you made me feel seen. You might not share much, which is fine, but I've never had such a fun friend. I love being around you," she says.

I stop in my tracks, looking at where she's sitting on my bed.

"If my cousin doesn't marry you, I will."

She grins. "As pretty as you are, I think I'm in too deep with Aiden."

I toss a shirt at her, and she laughs. "You two are sickeningly cute."

"We are, aren't we?"

"Are you sure you guys don't want to fly down with us?"

"No, Aiden said that would be too much. Meeting the family trapped in the sky."

I shrug. "Fair."

"I'll meet you there," she says as I zip up my suitcase, and I give her a hug as we both head out for the long weekend.

I'M last to the airport since I had to get a ride share. So I'm sweaty and handing my belongings to the attendant before grabbing my seat next to Gavin. Ben and Lincoln sit next to each other, facing us. I grew up with this luxury, but I'm not sure the fact our family owns a plane will ever truly sink in.

"Thought we were going to have to leave you," Gavin jokes.

Probably would have been for the best, but there was no way I was leaving Jessa alone with this pack of wolves.

I look at Lincoln, but he just stares out the window.

"Well, I made it."

"So, what's his new girlfriend like?" Ben asks, wiggling his eyebrows.

"She's a literal fucking angel. So if any of you are mean to her, I'll stab you in your sleep."

Lincoln glances at me for a second, but then goes back to being gloomy and looking out the window. I fucking hate it.

I miss his smiles, his hugs, the way we would joke together. I look around the plane at where my parents and aunt and uncle are sitting and taking a breath. I'm protecting all of this. I'm keeping the family together.

It doesn't matter what I want.

"I mean, she's gotta be able to hang," Gavin jokes next to me.

I roll my eyes at him and he just stares right back.

"She can hang, just don't scare her off. She's sweet and Aiden really cares about her."

"Must be nice," Lincoln grumbles, his palm against his chin, still looking out the window.

"Hopefully this asshole turns his frown upside down soon," Ben says, grabbing Lincoln by the neck and squeezing his face, trying to make him smile.

"Get the hell off of me."

"You need a cocktail or something?" Ben asks, pulling away.

"No," Lincoln replies sharply.

I swallow back the bile filling up in the back of my throat. This wasn't what I wanted. None of this was. The only thing I can do is give him distance and hope that maybe after some time passes these feelings will slowly dissipate.

"There's mold in the extra bedroom. So unfortunately we're going to have to double up in rooms," my aunt Maggie says. She leans forward looking past Gavin. "Penny, honey, you don't mind sharing with Lincoln do you?"

My eyes widen with the use of honey, but I just shake my head.

"Great. The twins can sleep on the top bunk of the double and Aiden and his girlfriend can share the bottom. Lincoln and Penny can sleep in the smaller room with the twin bed and futon."

I swallow and look over at Lincoln.

He doesn't even react to the conversation. But what was I supposed to say? No, please put me somewhere else because I'm sort of in love with Lincoln but also pushing him away because I know this will all end so fucking badly.

Nothing good can come out of us sharing a room together. *Nothing.*

LINCOLN and I are putting our things in our room. I'm waiting for Jessa to get here so there isn't as much tension.

He doesn't speak as he throws his suitcase on the futon, giving me the bed.

"Lincoln," I whisper his name.

"Don't," he says back, not even looking at me.

"We have to talk, to be in the same space as one another," I say.

His beautiful eyes flick up to mine. He hasn't shaved in a few days and for being so miserable, he still looks so handsome.

"If you told me yes right now, I'd go out into the living room and tell them all that we're together and they can fucking deal with it. I'd shoulder it all. But I wasn't worth it to you. Do you know how that makes me feel?"

"It's not—"

"I don't want to talk about it anymore. I'm exhausted trying to make you see what I already know."

"That's not fair, Lincoln. It's not that simple."

"God, you're gonna make me fucking drink this weekend. Just... just enjoy the vacation, Penny," he says, leaving the bedroom and going to God knows where.

I sigh and sit on the bed. The mattress sucks. We used this room a lot as kids, and usually someone sleeps in this room when we visit, but right now, it feels like a prison cell.

I rub my hands over my eyes as my dad walks by and knocks on the doorframe.

"Hey kiddo, mind helping me stock the boat?" he asks.

"Sure thing, Dad."

He throws an arm around my shoulder as we head out back and onto the patio to start gathering supplies for their fishing trip tomorrow.

"You sure you don't want to go fishing tomorrow?" he asks.

I usually enjoy it. Growing up with three boy cousins, I did whatever the majority wanted.

"Yeah, I think a girls' day is much needed while you all go fishing."

Plus, being trapped in the middle of the ocean with Lincoln sounds like a good way for him to throw me overboard.

"I've missed you lately," he says.

"I haven't been anywhere," I say, and he shakes his head.

"You haven't been the same. I just want to make sure my little girl is alright."

"I'm not little anymore, Dad."

"You always will be to me. My little miracle," he says. I nudge his side and he hugs me. "I know things have been heavy for you lately, but if there's anything else that's weighing on you, you know me and your mom are always there for you. We love you no matter what."

"No matter what?"

"No matter what," he says, with another squeeze of my arm.

I just wish I could believe that was true.

Lincoln

I Don't Hate You

I SHOULDN'T HAVE COME on this fucking trip.

Not only is Penny around every goddamn corner I turn, but she keeps giving me this sad look like I'm the one who broke her heart.

I was the one who wanted this; I was willing to risk it all, but she's acting like I'm being unreasonable.

Ben and I are setting up the bonfire for the night. We do this every year.

"You sure you're not drinking?" he asks me.

"Changed my mind about that," I say.

"My man. Help me get the cooler?"

I nod, helping him fill it up and carrying it down to the beach where the rest of my brothers, Penny, and Jessa, are wait-ing. Penny glances at me, the sunset and fire hitting her face in just the right light.

Why'd she have to be so devastatingly beautiful?

I take my seat, sipping on my beer. I promise myself only two. I can't keep self-medicating.

"Who would have thought that big bro would bring a girl on

vacation? I thought you were going to become a cat lady, Aiden," Ben jokes, and Aiden rolls his eyes.

"True, I thought his social security would be on auto-pay to Avalon," I reply, feeling like a dick, but I can't help it. Watching my brother with his girl on his lap has me feeling jealous. It's a disgusting trait, but I can't take it back now.

Aiden narrows his eyes at me, and his girlfriend sticks up for him.

"It will be, except it will be a couples membership." Ben and Gavin start cackling and I can't help but to tip my beer and metaphorical hat in her direction. My brother beams at her, happier than a pig in shit, and I'm back to feeling like a lonely asshole.

"Can we talk about something else besides Avalon?" Penny says, looking at me and I shrug my shoulders. "It's so nice to have another girl. Don't you fuckers ruin this for me," Penny says, pointing at each of us. The twins hold up their hands in mock surrender, and she glares at them a little before turning and smiling at Jessa.

"So, what did our precious brother have to do to nab you? It surely wasn't his ugly mug," Gavin says to Jessa.

"I did have to look past his face. You're right." My twin brothers and Penny laugh as she leans closer to me. "But if I had to pinpoint a moment, it was probably when he took a splinter out of my finger and kissed it."

Penny makes an aww sound while the twins make noises of revulsion. I look over at Penny and wonder if there was a moment she fell for me too, or if it was all just sex for her. God, when did I become such a loser?

"Disgusting," Gavin says, verbalizing my own thoughts.

"One day, you two will eventually stop acting like children," Penny says.

"We're planning on being single forever," Ben says for the both of them, and Gavin nods in agreement.

"Single by choice or because no one wants to date you assholes?" Penny asks, and I have to hold back a laugh.

"We can't all date a bunch of winners like you, Penny," Gavin says, and Penny glares at my brothers. Feeling particularly called out by that statement, I step in.

"Will you two shut the fuck up, already?" I sneer.

"What about you, Lincoln, hmm? You can't seem to hold down a girlfriend either," Ben says, doing what he does best, getting under my skin.

"I'm going to head in for the night," Penny says, giving her friend a wave and walking back to the house.

"Yeah, I'm done too. Make sure you put the fire out," I tell the twins and they wave me off as I follow Penny back to the house.

It's truly pathetic, the way I'm like a lost puppy following her around.

No matter how many times she kicks me, I still want her to want me.

I groan, tossing my beer bottle in the trash and head up to the shit hole room we're staying in together.

She's lying on the bed with her arms crossed over her torso as she looks at the ceiling fan cycle.

"Scoot over," I tell her.

The twin bed is pressed against a wall, so she turns to the side, her back to the wall. I lie on my side and stare at her for a few moments.

"I'm sorry," she whispers.

"Me too."

We don't go into what we're sorry for, because we both already know. I'm sorry for being a dick and she's sorry she can't give me what I want.

"What are we going to do, Linc?"

"Maybe you should move out," I say, hating the words falling out of my mouth.

She nods, even though she looks like she hates the idea as well.

"I don't want you to hate me."

"I don't hate you. That's the complete opposite of how I feel about you."

"I don't hate you either," she says, and I fear it's the closest thing I'll ever get to how she really feels.

My hand automatically reaches out and pushes her hair off of her face. She presses her face against my palm and closes her eyes.

"Let me kiss you, just this once," I ask.

Her eyes open, her face nuzzling my hand as she licks her lips and nods in agreement. My hand slides behind her neck and cradles her head as I lean forward and press my lips against hers.

It's everything I thought it would be.

Penny kisses with her whole body. Her one hand gripping my hair and the other resting on my chest, that slides up and cups my jaw.

I grip her hair harder, keeping her lips pressed to mine. I can't get enough.

She moans against my mouth and shifts her body closer to mine, which has my hand sliding down her frame and gripping her ass, tugging her body flush against mine.

I'm supposed to be getting her out of my system, but here we are, her claws digging even deeper.

She parts the kiss only to grab my face and look at me for a long moment.

"Fuck it," she whispers, before bringing her lips back to mine.

The kiss gets even deeper and all the resentment completely fades away. I didn't want to give her space; I didn't want to be an asshole. This is what I wanted all along. Knowing she wants me back in the same way sends a wave of need through my body.

My cock aches, and Penny immediately slides her hand down and cups it through my shorts.

I moan against her mouth and I'm about to shift my hand and slide it up her dress when the bedroom door flies open.

"Hey, do you have—"

Penny and I part to see Gavin standing there slack jawed staring at the both of us. Penny is quick to adjust her dress, and I just stay put.

I roll my eyes and get off the bed.

"Just keep your fucking mouth shut, yeah?" I tell him and he just blinks, his gaze shifting between me and Penny.

"Um, what the fuck did my poor little eyes just witness?" he says.

"Nothing," Penny replies.

I want to roll my eyes again, but don't. I give my brother a glare and he goes back to staring at each of us.

"Am I just really fucking high... or were you two making out?"

"Jesus Christ, Gavin, get out," I tell him.

He shrugs his shoulders, holding the doorknob. His eyes are bloodshot red and he stinks as he sighs.

"You know, you two kind of make sense."

Penny gets off the bed and approaches the door.

"Please don't tell anyone, Gavin. Please," she pleads with him.

"This was a one time thing?" he questions.

Penny, being the amazing liar she is, nods her head. "We drank too much. We weren't thinking. It was just a kiss."

Gavin looks over her shoulder at me, and then back at Penny.

"Your Alabama secret is safe with me," he says.

"Gavin, get the fuck out," I nearly yell and he smiles, grabbing the door handle and shutting it behind him.

As soon as he shuts it, Penny begins to spiral. She's pacing back and forth and I just lie on my futon.

"Gavin has the biggest mouth of all of you," she complains, and I nod in agreement. "You know he's going to tell Ben. He tells Ben everything."

"Yeah," I mumble.

"Did you plan this?"

I sit up on my elbows and glare at her. "Yes, Penny. I planned to kiss you at the exact fucking moment that my stoner brother came barging in asking for God knows what. You caught me."

"Sorry," she hisses, while she continues her pacing.

"You really think Jessa isn't going to crack and tell Aiden, anyway?" I ask her.

"She said she wouldn't."

"Two people know, Pen."

"I know that," she snaps. Her pacing picks up.

I stand up and get into her space, grabbing her face.

"Take a deep breath."

She listens to my directions, and her eyes meet mine.

"I'm going to give you time to think. I didn't intend for tonight to happen, but I'd be lying if I said I'm not glad it did. I've tried to stop thinking about you, to stop wanting you. I know you feel the same way. You kissed me back. Despite everything, you want this too."

She nods her head slightly, confirming that at least I'm not deluded and dealing with a completely fucked up unrequited love situation.

"My brother just saw us and really didn't give a fuck. Jessa doesn't care either. Do you think maybe you're underestimating our family?"

She blinks at me, taking in my words before closing her eyes and resting her forehead against my chest.

I rub her back, and she pulls away.

"I don't want another life lesson, Lincoln. I want a life partner. If you really want me. This," she says, pointing between the two of us. "Then I need to know it's for keeps."

I can't help the smile that takes over my face.

"You're really going to give this a shot?" I confirm.

She bites her lip.

"We need to make sure we work before we can't take it back."

"Penny, you already know we're in too deep."

She groans, resting her head back on my chest and her hands coming back to my waist.

"Please don't break my heart or take away my family," she says, looking down.

I tug at the base of her hair, forcing her to look at me.

"Your family isn't going anywhere and out of the two of us, you're the one who could break us."

I lean down, kissing her again.

Hating that this is still a secret, but loving that she's no longer resisting me.

"Lincoln!" I hear my name screamed from down stairs and Penny and I part.

"I'm going to kill my brothers," I say softly against her face.

"Go," she says, rubbing her hands across my chest.

"This weekend is going to be long as fuck," I groan.

Despite everything, I still smile and kiss her one last time. This weekend just changed everything in a way I couldn't imagine.

Penny

Orange Juice

MY HAIR SHIFTS and I swat at whatever dared to wake me up. I desperately need more sleep.

"Go away," I grumble.

"I'm going fishing. I'll see you later," Lincoln says.

"Bye," I groan again, turning on my side and wrapping myself tighter into the blanket. He kisses the side of my head before leaving with his brothers and our fathers for a day out on the ocean.

I try to go back to sleep, but this hard mattress and everything that happened last night is weighing on my mind.

I truly completely agreed to give me and Lincoln a shot.

That doesn't mean I want anyone else in the family to know, honestly, I don't ever want to cross that bridge. But... I have to see where this goes.

I need to know for sure that this isn't about forbidden feelings or wanting what you can't have. What if my person has been in front of me my whole life and I'm just now seeing it? It would be the biggest regret of my life if I didn't at least give it a shot—a real shot.

No more tension so thick I want to choke on it and die. It will still be our dirty little secret, but we're really going to try this. We're going to be a real couple within the privacy of our own homes, but what exactly does that mean?

All I know is I can't stop thinking about that kiss, or about how much Lincoln wants me. I smile like a fucking idiot into my pillow as there's a knock on my door and my mom comes in.

"Hey, sweetie. Are you ready to get up and go shopping?"

I grumble, even though I'm awake, I don't actually want to be.

My mom and aunt love shopping, and I suppose I do too, but all I want to do is get off this island and go back home with Lincoln and figure this all out. What's the next step? What does dating each other but not telling our family or friends look like? Well, at least the ones who don't already know.

My cheeks heat when I think about Gavin walking in on us last night. But Gavin isn't like the rest of our family, he's forward thinking and easygoing, my mother on the other hand is not.

She proves her point as she taps impatiently on the door frame.

"Jessa and Maggie are already up," she says, coming to sit on my bed and rub my back like she always did when I was a kid.

"Why are we going so early?"

"We don't want to waste any time we have together as a family," she says sweetly.

"We see each other all the time."

She makes a frustrated noise and grabs my blanket, snatching it off of me.

"I'm pretty sure Maggie is in the dining room telling Jessa she wants her to marry Aiden. You can't leave your friend out there with that fate," she says, and I groan.

"Fine," I reply, getting out of bed and following my mother

into the dining room, where my aunt Maggie and Jessa are waiting for us.

Jessa looks relieved, yet skeptical of me as I sit down.

"How'd you sleep?" Jessa asks, and I pin her with a look.

"We need to replace that bed," I reply, adding some fruit and pancakes to my plate.

"Bed isn't big enough?" Jessa says when I'm bringing a strawberry up to my mouth.

"Part of it, I am a grown woman," I reply and I give her a tight smile that I hope indicates I don't find her inside joke funny.

"As soon as we're done remodeling the other room, we'll fix that one. I think we could fit a queen in there," my aunt Maggie says.

"The house is really lovely," Jessa says.

"I'm just so sorry you and Aiden have to share a room with the twins," Maggie says.

"Probably smelled like a dispensary in there," I mumble and my mom knocks my foot under the table.

"Yes, well. My youngest boys seem to have a little bit of Peter Pan syndrome."

"A little bit?" I grumble and my mom hits me harder under the table. "Ouch," I groan and she smiles at me.

"They'll figure it out," Maggie says, sipping her coffee.

I want to whisper *doubt it*, but I really don't feel like getting kicked under the table again. Gavin and Benjamin live life on their own terms. They don't really give a shit what other people think and I don't see them settling down anytime soon.

"Once you finish eating, go freshen up and we'll head out," my mother says.

Jessa smiles at me across the table, and I smile back. My new best friend is more of a menace than I realized.

MY MOM and aunt Maggie are spending money like it's their job, while Jessa and I are trying on different sandals.

"So, what happened last night?" she asks.

I look over at where my mother and aunt are at the store across the street looking at jewelry.

"I think we're dating," I say, looking back at her, and sliding the sandal that's just a tad too small off my foot.

"Shut the fuck up. But what does that even mean?"

"I don't know. We didn't get to talk about it. Gavin kind of saw us last night."

Jessa's jaw drops, and she blinks at me.

"He saw you fucking?"

"Ew, no. Just kissing. And then Lincoln kicked Gavin out of our room and the twins called Lincoln downstairs. I fell asleep before Lincoln came back for the night and they left early for fishing."

"What did Gavin say?" she asks, riveted by my drama.

"He was shockingly okay with it."

"Does that mean you're going to tell everyone else? On this trip?" she asks, her eyes widening.

"Hell no. I need to make sure that this isn't just us wanting what we can't have, you know? I don't want to blow the family up for no reason. So, we'll continue being a secret, but no more holding back."

"Your family seems understanding," she says with a small smile.

"Forward thinking and realizing your kids who grew up together are fucking are two different things."

She snorts a laugh and grabs a new pair of sandals to try on.

"You know, he came to Aiden's a few nights ago, was real mopey."

"He's so dramatic," I say with an eye roll.

"So are you," Jessa says, and I gasp in shock.

"I'm not dramatic."

She gives me a look like I'm being unreasonable and I wave her off. "If you could keep this between us still, I'd appreciate it. I need to hunt down Gavin later."

"Of course," she says with a tight nod.

I stare at her a little longer and she lets out a breath.

"Okay, fine. I haven't told Aiden anything. I'll keep your secret."

"That's right, chicks before dicks."

"I don't think I've ever met anyone quite like you, Penny."

I grin. "And you never will. You can have other friends, but you can't like them more than you like me, okay?"

She shakes her head at me as we put the shoes back and head over to the jewelry and crystal store my mother and aunt are shopping at.

"Oh my God, Penny, come look at this," my mom says, and I head over to my mother while Maggie and Jessa talk at the register.

"What is it?" I ask, and she points to the case.

"You've got to get it," she says, pointing down at the necklace.

I can't help the laugh that belts out of me, not that my mother would get it. It's a silver chain, with a rounded backing with a fucking penny in front of it with the word *lucky* stamped over Abraham *Lincoln's* face.

The saleswoman comes over and takes the necklace out of the display case.

"I'm getting it for you. I don't care what you say," my mom says, instructing the woman to add it to her order.

"Thanks, Mom."

"Maybe I should get one too," she says, and I shake my head.

"You're right, I already have my lucky Penny," she says, squeezing my shoulders.

"You know, I think you're turning into a bigger sap the older I get."

"One day you'll have a daughter, if you're lucky one as amazing as mine, and you'll understand," she says, squeezing my arm.

It's weird. I'd never pictured my future children before, but now I am, with messy brown hair and blue-green eyes. Lincoln Carlson has single handedly changed my brain chemistry and I'm trying to not let anything damper that.

I glance over at my smiling mother and my heart sinks a bit when I think about her reaction. I shake it from my thoughts, pushing that conversation to the side, if it ever even happens.

I put the necklace on during the car ride home, Jessa seems a little out of it and I wonder if Maggie said something to offend her. I love my aunt Maggie, but the woman can be intrusive as hell.

When we get back to the beach house, Jessa says she's taking a walk on the beach and I go to follow her, but she clearly needs a moment to clear her head, so I stay back at the house, waiting for the guys to get back from fishing.

MY DAD and Uncle Jeff are grilling up the fish they caught today while my mom and aunt nap.

Aiden and Jessa are MIA, and the twins are probably up to no good somewhere around here.

I'm prepping some sliced potatoes and vegetables in the kitchen as Lincoln walks toward the fridge, looking around, before opening the fridge and glancing around.

I can't help but glance over at him as I continue food prepping. His skin has some redness from being out under the sun today, but other than that he looks absolutely perfect. It's truly unfair how ridiculously good looking he is, and it hits that he's completely mine. I smile to myself as I attempt to slice and ogle him at the same time.

He grabs the orange juice from the fridge before grabbing a glass from the cabinet. He looks around one last time before placing a chaste kiss against my lips, before resting his hip against the counter.

"How was your day?"

"Fine, it would have been better if you came. How was shopping?" he asks.

He turns, pouring the juice into the simple glass with palm trees imprinted all over it.

"I got something today you might like," I say with a smile, putting down the knife from chopping the potatoes into thin slices.

"What's that?" he asks with a devastating smile.

He tilts his head at me and I can tell that if we weren't on this trip with family around we would be doing a hell of a lot more than chatting in the kitchen.

His demeanor from when this vacation started to now are like opposites and I can't deny liking that it's because of me. Lincoln makes me feel like the most important person in the world and I wonder how I can do the same when we can't be ourselves in the presence of our family.

I grab the charm on the necklace between my fingers and show him. He leans in close, the juice in one hand as he gently touches the necklace, his thumb grazing over the words.

He laughs and tenderly puts it back against my collarbone.

"That's cute, Pen."

"I thought so," I reply. He's so close to me that all I'd have to do is lean forward ever so slightly to steal another kiss, but he pulls back ever so slightly.

He takes a sip of the orange juice, a rivulet traveling down the side of his mouth, which he cleans up with his thumb. I track the motion and lick my lips as he pulls his thumb away, sickly I wish he'd push the juice-covered thumb between my lips just like he did that night at Key Club.

"You thirsty, baby?" he asks.

I know he means it in more ways than one; I nod my head for both cases. I'm both parched and in desperate need of him. He smiles, fuck I missed his smile. I can't even be upset about him being a cocky bastard, because he always delivers, his cockiness is completely deserved.

"Open your mouth," he commands.

I don't even question him as I part my lips. He presses his thumb against my chin as he brings the cool glass to his lips, putting the juice in his mouth.

It's nearly in slow motion the way he tilts the glass back, holding the liquid in his mouth, before putting the glass on the counter, it clinks against the countertop and shivers erupt over my skin.

He holds the back of my head with one hand, keeping his thumb on my chin. His lips meet mine as he transfers the sweet citrus into my mouth.

The citrus flavor splashes against my tongue as I swallow.

Some of it leaks out of the corner of my lips as I press a kiss against his lips, that taste like oranges and sin. His tongue lashes out, licking up the sweetness off my skin and I can't repress the moan I was holding in.

His hand tightens in my hair as he steps closer to me, his tongue sliding down the side of my throat, before his teeth graze my pulse point.

"I need you," he rasps out.

The hand that was on my chin slides down my body and grips my waist pulling me closer.

My hands are sliding up his shirt, feeling the hard expanse of his body and sliding further up against his chest hair.

"I need you too," I whisper back and I mean it with every fiber of my being.

With the taste of him on my tongue I'm feeling greedy and all I want is more. Lincoln dips his fingers in the orange juice and drags the sticky drink along my throat and down the valley of my breasts in the loose shirt I'm wearing.

My flesh breaks out in eagerness and desire as his tongue starts between my breasts and he licks it up all the way behind my ear.

"I want to lick every inch of you," he whispers against the shell of my ear. "So fucking sweet, baby."

I sigh, wetness pooling in my panties over his words and touch. He pulls back and leans down to kiss me again. My breath hitches as I await the soft press of his lips and another hit of his tangy tongue, as the backdoor begins to slide open.

We pull apart immediately, Lincoln taking a step back as my heart races in my chest and I grab the knife.

I'm so frantic that when I attempt to cut the next potato, I slice the tip of my finger.

"Fuck," I hiss.

"What's wrong?" I hear my dad's voice behind us.

He's approaching, the only feature on his face is concern for my finger. He doesn't look pissed or like he saw me and Lincoln together, so I swallow back some of that fear.

Lincoln grabs a paper towel and holds it against my cut. When I look at his face, all I can see is hidden sadness, that he hates being a secret. I swallow thickly and wince at my finger.

"You need to be more careful, Penny," Lincoln says, a small smirk on his face.

I somehow want to kiss it and slap it off his face at the same time.

"I'll go get the first aid kit," my dad says with a nod before wandering off.

"No more messing around while we're here," I tell him.

"You started it."

My mouth parts, and he swallows, leaning down and kissing my bottom lip.

"I just said—"

"I know what you said," he replies, kissing my cheek and applying pressure as my dad comes back with the kit.

Lincoln pulls back the towel and my dad looks at the cut.

"Doesn't look like you'll need stitches," my dad says, using disinfectant and putting a bandage on it. "Now what the hell did I come in here for?" he questions and looks around the kitchen. "Ah, that's right," he says, grabbing some lemons out of the fridge. "Be more careful, yeah?" My dad gives me a cautionary glance as he leaves the kitchen.

I'll need to be more careful indeed.

"See you for dinner," Lincoln says, grabbing his glass of juice and hums after he swallows. "Delicious."

Someone please make this torturous vacation hurry the hell up.

PENNY WANTS us to be good little cousins and keep our hands to ourselves the rest of the trip. Meanwhile, the idea of getting caught and ripping off this elephant-sized band aid seems like a great solution to me.

Honestly, it's only a matter of time, Gavin already asked me a million fucking questions last night about what's going on between us. I told him the highlights, not wanting to upset Penny, but also needing to get it off my chest. He promised he would keep our secret, but I already know that little prick told Ben. Both of them kept making little jokes while fishing today.

I can handle them though, especially since they don't seem to care. Why would they? It's not like they aren't into their own weird shit.

It would be a relief for the family to know and to no longer carry this secret. I want to take Penny places, be a real couple— something completely foreign to me. But when it comes to Penny? I selfishly want everything.

Part of me knows Penny won't tell the family until we're

forced to, and while I don't want to fuck this up, it wouldn't be the worst thing in the world if it *accidentally* happened.

"The futon is nice," I lie. The futon sucks, but I would like Penny to climb over here and ride my dick.

She's facing me while she lies on her bed only a few feet away.

"I bet it is."

"You know how nice it is?" I smirk, fisting my cock outside of my boxers.

"You're really the worst, you know that?" she says, shifting on the mattress, trying to look anywhere besides where my hand is.

"I'm the best, and it's why you couldn't stay away."

She rolls her eyes, and I pull my length from my boxers and stroke myself.

"This could be all yours. You just need to travel the short distance between us, *honey*." I draw out honey like an inside joke instead of a pet name.

"We need to be more careful."

"Lock the door then," I tell her.

"No. No more seducing me while we're here with our family."

"It's been so long, Penny," I complain, stroking my cock, my eyes not leaving her face for a second. "I miss your pussy."

"You're extremely romantic," she says, even while glancing down at where I'm jerking myself off.

"Come over here and I can tell you all the other things I miss about you," I whisper.

"You are truly the most unfair person I've ever met," she complains.

"I know you want to come over here. I know you want it," I say, slowly stroking my shaft and she tracks the motion.

She shakes her head, and I groan.

"The payback for the weeks of denying me is going to be severe, Penny."

Her eyes widen, and she licks her lips, liking the idea. It's part of why I can't get enough of Penny. We're constantly on the same page without even trying.

But now there's more, there are feelings. Ones that couldn't be shoved down or ignored even if I tried.

There's a promise of this being what I always wanted it to be, beyond exploring each other's bodies. Though, right now, all I can think about is my aching cock and how badly I wish she was bouncing on top of it.

"You know what I've been jerking off to?" I ask her, my strokes increasing and her chest rising and falling with her heart rate rising.

She likes watching, and I like having her full attention.

"What?" she asks in a breathy tone.

"That night in the car," I tell her and her brows furrow. Of all the things we've done, that was one of the most tame. There were no walls between us, no playing, just us fucking and desperate for each other.

"Me too," she replies.

"Are you going to touch yourself? Let me see what I'm missing?" I ask.

She shakes her head, and I groan in frustration.

"You're killing me, baby."

"Do you really think about me when you touch yourself?" she asks, her hand sliding dangerously close to the apex of her thighs.

"Everytime."

"Show me," she says, and I grip my cock harder.

My hand shifts up and down as my wrist twists every time I reach the head.

"The things I want to do to you right now, fuck."

She looks at the door of our bedroom, and then back at me, sliding her hand down her sleep shorts.

I'm pissed I can't see, but it's more than I was getting a moment ago.

"Do you think of me when you play with that sweet little cunt of yours?" I ask and she shakes her head, her lips parting as she plays with herself.

"You're so lucky I don't just come over there and take what I want," I say, my pace quickening.

"Oh God," she moans, watching me fuck my fist.

Her hand moves more quickly under her shorts and the idea of her getting off to thoughts of me is what sends me over the edge.

I moan as I squeeze my cock, cum dripping out of the tip while Penny watches.

Her mouth parts and her gaze rotates between my face and the mess I'm making of myself.

I stay like that, just holding my length while my release covers my fist and Penny increases her pace and finishes. Her mouth parts and her eyes close as she brings herself to orgasm and the only thing I wish is that it was by my hand and not her own.

She slides her hand out of her shorts, not touching the bed as she looks at me.

"We shouldn't have done that," she whispers, shaking her head.

"You're right, you should have been over here riding your boyfriend's dick."

"Boyfriend?" she says, blinking at me.

"Yeah, you might not be willing to tell our family yet, but I'm your boyfriend. We're exclusive, even if I am your little secret."

She smiles, getting up from the bed.

"I can agree to those terms."

Penny stands and I grab her wrist, bringing her cum-covered fingers to my mouth. Kissing the tips and sucking them into my mouth, before releasing them, still holding her hand.

"When we get back home, this is a real thing. We'll keep the family out of it, but real dates, a real relationship. I really do want this."

Her pretty blue eyes search mine and I swear they're about to well up with tears, but she blinks them away. She grabs my chin and kisses me softly.

"Be patient with me."

She pulls away and I nod my head in understanding. She glances down at my softening cock.

"You might want to clean yourself up, boyfriend," she says, turning to leave the room.

I swat her ass as she leaves, and for the first time in a very long time I feel hopeful.

*   *   *

"CAN YOU GET MY BACK?" Penny asks while we wait for the owner of the jet ski place to take us out onto the dock.

Gavin and Ben look over at us and it takes every ounce of me to not toss them into the water with rocks in their pockets.

"Yeah," I reply, rubbing the lotion against her skin.

The plans I have to pay her back after all this torture is the only thing keeping me going.

She turns around putting more lotion on her hands and rubbing on her face, she has a patch on the bridge of her nose and I automatically reach out and rub it in. Her smile is casual and light and I just want it to be like this all the time.

"We only have three available for today. We could get some paddle boards out," the owner says, and Gavin shakes his head.

"Penny can share with Linc, and Ben and I will take turns," Gavin says, maybe I should poison him instead.

Penny clears her throat as we get our life jackets on and I get on the jet ski first, holding out a hand so she can get on the back.

Her arms wrap around my waist tightly before we take off.

She laughs behind me during the ride as we zip through the water. Aiden is letting Jessa drive and she surprisingly drives like a maniac.

I slow down and put it in neutral when we're further out.

"Do you want to drive?"

She shakes her head, just resting it on my shoulder.

"Gavin doesn't care, you know? I think if anything he's encouraging it."

"Can we please not talk about this right now?" she says and I grunt.

"At some point—"

Penny reaches over cranking the accelerator and I have to grab on quickly and begin steering.

I know I'm being demanding, that I constantly want more. I remind myself that I need to be patient. But I've never been the type of man who enjoys waiting.

We eventually finish up jet skiing, my mood feeling shitty and I know I'm not good at hiding it.

We load off at the dock, returning the water sports and Aiden takes Jessa's hand.

"We'll see you guys back at the house," Aiden says, escaping with his girlfriend.

"Are you two going to sneak off and fuck somewhere or do you want to go to the bar with us?" Gavin asks.

Penny gasps next to me and Ben shrugs his shoulders.

"So much for keeping a secret, Gavin," I shout out to him.

"How you expected me not to tell my twin, the person I

share DNA with, the gossip of the century is truly your own fault. God, Mom is going to—"

I smack Gavin's chest. "Shut up."

"Ouch, dick," he hisses, rubbing his chest.

"So are you all coming or what?" Ben asks, completely unfazed.

"We'll go with you, but I'm leaving if either of you brings this up," Penny says, her cheeks hot from embarrassment.

Ben holds his hands up in surrender.

I grab Penny's hand and she nearly pulls it away. "They already know, they're okay with it. Please give me this," I ask her.

She takes a deep breath and eventually laces her fingers with mine. I squeeze her hand, enjoying the domesticity of it all as Gavin orders a car and we make our way over to the beach bar.

We order food and drinks, though for me at least, I will stick to only a few. My brothers on the other hand have different thoughts as they throw them back—it is vacation.

"Bachelorette party, ten o'clock," Ben says to Gavin nodding his head.

Ben grins and Penny scrunches her nose.

"Which one are you interested in?"

"Whichever one wants to go to Paris," Ben says plainly.

Penny's mouth drops as she stares at my brothers and I shake my head. Ben looks over at her shocked expression and shrugs.

"It truly can't be that shocking."

"Um, yes it is. Is this a common thing with you two?" she asks and Gavin and Ben both pick up their drinks at the same time chugging them back.

"I think it's best if we keep some secrets between us,

wouldn't you agree?" Gavin says pointing between me and Penny.

"Yes, please," Penny says, grabbing her margarita and sipping it.

"Well, you two do whatever it is you do, we may or may not be back tonight," Ben says as they get off their stools and head over to the bachelorette party.

"I don't think I've ever wanted a vacation to be over so badly," Penny says.

I grab her chair and spin her so she's facing me.

"They already know, we're two random people at this bar in The Bahamas, we can be whoever we want tonight," I tell her, hoping she plays along.

I want my free, happy Penny. Not the one who's constantly looking over her shoulder worried about what people will think about her.

"Is that so, Mr. Wayne?"

"Damn right it is, Honey."

Penny
Forget Your Morals

IT'S different being out with Lincoln like this.

Not being a secret. It feels more real than any other date I've been on, and I somehow feel at peace.

His hand is freely roaming literally anywhere it can touch; my hair, my thighs, my waist, while we drink and eat.

"What's the first thing you want to do when we get home?" I ask him.

"After I fuck you senseless?" he jokes and I nod, sipping on my margarita. "I want to take you out on a proper date. Go see some stupid movie and talk about it over dinner and then take you home and wake up next to you."

"I do like sleeping next to you," I say. My heart flutters over his answer.

"My bed misses you," he says.

"You know, I never knew you were this smooth."

"You just haven't been paying attention."

I laugh, and he leans forward, peppering my face with kisses. My cheeks hurt from smiling.

"What about you? What do you want, Penny?"

"I want to spend time with you and work on figuring my shit out more."

"What shit?"

"I'm still working through everything. With you know," I wave my hand in the air and he nods in understanding over all my birth mom's trauma. "But before the Key Club and everything after, I was kind of on a mission to figure out who I am."

His brows furrow.

"What do you mean?"

"I just feel like I've always catered to what I thought other people wanted me to be like and never really worked to figure out what I like."

He grabs my stool and scoots me even closer to him, like there can't even be a breath's width between us.

"You're Penelope Abigail Myers, the most gorgeous, selfless, funniest woman I know. You hate mornings, love pets and babies, watch shitty tv shows, and you can't sing for shit."

My mouth gapes open and he smiles.

"You love the sun and it loves you back. You hate overly loud noises and rude people." He pushes my hair behind my ear. "You're strong, stronger than anyone gives you credit for, and you're the best fuck of my life."

I throw my head back and laugh.

"You really had to go and ruin it."

"I am the most romantic person you know," he throws my words from last night back at me .

"It wasn't a lie," I whisper, meaning it.

Lincoln might be crass, a total fucking baby when he doesn't get his way. But he wants me in a way I didn't think was possible. It's the type of romance I've always read and dreamed about. The thought of this all crashing down is terrifying.

But I'm falling so hard and so fast, I just hope he's still around to break my fall.

It's pouring rain outside as the band continues going through their set list, the white noise of the rain fall just adding to the melody.

"Dance with me?" he asks.

He gets off his stool and holds out his hand, which I grab before getting off my own. He smells like coconut sunscreen and sunshine as we join the dance floor. It's a slower number, and he rests his hands on my hips as I hold his shoulders.

The strumming melody has me leaning forward, resting my head on his chest as he holds me tight. Lincoln presses a small kiss to the top of my head and it's at that moment I know I'm completely in love with him.

I love his sarcasm, his humor, and how thoughtful he is. Not once has he tried to make me into someone I'm not. He's never told me to stop crying or that my feelings aren't valid. Even with all this business with our family and how frustrated he's been, he's never truly tried to change me, just make me understand.

With his arms wrapped around me, I feel secure and cared for in a way I haven't felt in a really long time, and never by a romantic partner.

Lincoln has chosen me repeatedly and all he's asked for is the same in return. I hope he can sense what I feel, that I'm willing to risk it all for him too.

I tug on his shirt to tell him just that as he curses and pulls out his phone.

"Hey Dad," he answers the phone, not taking his hands off of me. "Uh," he says, looking around the bar for his brothers. "They aren't here."

There's a long pause, and he looks down at me and sighs.

"Yeah, we'll meet you out front," and he hangs up the phone. "He's picked up Aiden and Jessa and wanted to pick us up before the storm gets any worse."

I nod, hating that this bubble is being burst, but it's like reality tossing ice cold water over me again.

"Hey," he says, cupping my face. "We'll figure this out."

I nod, wishing I could get over this, that I could give him everything he wants and deserves. Because, to be honest, he deserves the entire world.

I wrap my arms around his waist, resting my head against his chest, my chin on his sternum to look up at him.

"You're the sweetest man I've ever met, though most other people wouldn't know it. You'd give the shirt off your back to anyone who needed it. I've never laughed or smiled more around anyone else in my life. You're too hard on yourself, but it's what made you so successful. And… you're the best fuck I've ever had in my life," I say.

He grins down at me, his smile making my stomach do a flip.

It wasn't a love confession, but it sure felt like one.

Lincoln wraps his arms around me and picks me up, kissing me roughly.

"One more day," he whispers against my lips.

One more day and we won't be surrounded by family constantly and we can really see if this is going to work.

"One more day," I repeat as he closes our tab and we go outside and wait for my uncle Jeff to pick us up.

TONIGHT'S DINNER is catered and there's no fear of slicing a finger or Lincoln seducing me in the kitchen. Though I can only imagine what other sexy things he could do with other food and drink.

I'm sitting in between Jessa and Lincoln at the dinner table as the first course is served. It's a Caribbean ceviche, and it nearly melts on my tongue.

"How have things been going at Carlson's?" My dad asks Lincoln.

"Good, we've got the trade show and awards coming up next month," he replies easily.

"Those things always were a headache," Lincoln's father says.

"What's worse is Krystal, the event planner, is out on maternity leave earlier than expected," Lincoln says.

"You should take Penny if you need someone to help with events," Aiden says easily, and Jessa squeaks a little next to me. "You good, baby?" he asks her, and she nods her head.

"Yeah, must have just swallowed wrong," she replies.

"You know, I really could use someone to keep us on track," Lincoln says with an easy smile, clearly loving the idea.

"What about Kemper's?" I ask Aiden.

"It's just a few days. We'll be fine. Maybe Tabitha will do some of her own fucking work for a change," Aiden says, and both Jessa and I snort a little at that.

"It would be great for you, Penny. You love event planning," my mother says enthusiastically.

"Plus, Lincoln can just get a hotel room with two queens. He doesn't even need to get you your own room," my aunt Maggie suggests.

"That truly is so convenient," Gavin suggests.

"Weren't you supposed to be with a bachelorette party?" I say as he directs his shit-eating grin at me, changing the subject about Lincoln's upcoming event.

"And miss time with my lovely family? Never," he replies.

"I'm so sorry about them. I'm hoping one day they all find girlfriends to help make them a little less feral," Maggie says to Jessa.

"Don't hold your breath," Ben whispers.

"There's hope for Lincoln at least," Maggie says with a smile. "Vanessa was nice. Whatever happened to her?" she asks.

I still in my seat and Lincoln pauses in his. He takes a deep breath and shakes his head. "Considering she was already married with kids unbeknownst to me, I'd say I could do better."

My jaw drops, and everyone is silent for a few moments. It clicks for me then, why he was so detached for so long, why that breakup changed him.

Maggie clears her throat. "Well, on second thought, she's a bitch and if I ever see her—"

Ben laughs and interrupts her. "You'll what, mom?"

"I don't know. Have very colorful words for what a terrible person she is."

Lincoln smiles and shakes his head. "I appreciate it, Mom, but looking back, it wasn't as serious as I thought."

"You deserve a good girl," Maggie says and Gavin chokes on his food across the table.

"You really do, Lincoln," Gavin says, and I truly want to grab the butter knife and poke his eye out.

"I'm sure it will happen for me eventually," Lincoln says, discreetly sliding his hand under the table and squeezing my thigh.

I couldn't stop the heat traveling up my neck if I tried.

"Penny, are you okay?" My mother asks and I nod.

"Yeah, I think I had a bit too much sun today."

"That Caribbean sun will get you, alright," Gavin says.

Maggie furrows her brow and looks at Gavin. "Is there something we're missing here?"

"No, just fucking with Lincoln."

"Leave your poor brother alone," she says. "You're going to scare Jessa away."

"It's nice seeing a family like this. I'm not planning on going anywhere," Jessa says. Aiden wraps his arm around her shoulder, squeezing it like he couldn't be prouder to be with her.

It hits me then that I want that open, easy affection.

I want it with Lincoln.

His hand is still on my thigh, soothing as ever, even though I feel like I might combust with the tension and our secret hanging over our head.

There's a piece of me that just wants to stand up and blurt it out, and deal with the fallout. But I don't. I stay seated in my chair, yet I don't remove his hand.

Maybe there's a piece of me that wants this secret to be unfolded for us, but I also want to keep him to myself. What if telling them ruins everything and creates a wedge between us?

It's so much easier to forget about the consequences when I'm not surrounded by my family every waking second.

"What about you, Penny? Are you seeing anyone?" Maggie asks.

This woman is out to kill me. Why yes, Aunt Maggie, I'm falling in love with your son, who has his bare hand on my thigh right now. Lincoln squeezes my leg.

"There's someone I like, but I'm not sure yet."

Maggie and my mom both perk up wanting to know more, and I know I fucked up. I should have lied. But lying about having feelings for someone seemed like too big of a lie. Haven't I hurt Lincoln enough?

"What's the issue?"

"It's complicated," I say, grabbing my glass of water and willing myself to disappear.

"What's so complicated about it?" Maggie asks.

"It's a moral issue," I reply.

Her brows furrow. "He's of age?"

I gasp, Gavin and Ben laugh, and Jessa covers her mouth next to me.

"Ew, yes, he's of age. What the fuck?" I whisper the last line.

"You said morality," Maggie says, waving her hands.

"Nothing that deplorable, Jesus."

"Then forget your morals. Go get the guy you want," she says.

Lincoln squeezes my thigh again, and I smile at my aunt Maggie softly. The woman has no idea that she just inadvertently gave me the green light to fall for her son.

Lincoln

Delicious Payback

"THAT WAS the longest three-day weekend of my life," I complain, my hand on Penny's thigh as I drive us back to our building from the small airport.

She squeezes her thighs together and her hand rests on top of mine.

It feels like I can finally breathe. I can finally have Penny in the way that I want—in a way we both desperately need.

"I'm glad to be home," she says.

It's later than I'd wanted it to be when we got home, but all that matters is we're off that island, far enough away from our family, and we can finally just be us.

There's clear anticipation thick in the cab of the car as we drive home.

We haven't had sex since that one weekend, and it's different now. We might not be fully out in the way I want, but it's in the right direction. There's no more *we should stop, or this is a bad idea.*

Though I'm not opposed to reverting back to that to play at some point. Right now, I want Penny in a visceral way I can't even explain. I feel like a fucking caveman with the way I want to drag her by her hair to my apartment and have my way with her.

She traces the tendons and veins on my hands, and doesn't say much.

We both know the moment we step out of this car and go to one of our apartments this is real. This is us agreeing to give it a real shot, and neither of us wants to fuck it up.

There's also so much pent-up want and desire I'm trying to decide what exactly I want to do with her. Do I want to fuck her quick or slow? Do I want to toy with her like she's been doing to me for weeks on end, or do I want to give into this need immediately?

I squeeze her thigh before releasing her leg and putting both hands on the wheel to park the car and we head into the building. I grab my duffle and her suitcase and bring them into the building.

She seems shy, maybe nervous.

I like it more than I should. I didn't know how desperately I needed her to be all in. Maybe I'm more needy than I ever realized.

The elevator opens, and I automatically hit her floor, bypassing my own. Penny doesn't comment as the doors close and it travels up.

When the doors open on her level, I grab her by the waist and use my arm to keep the elevator from shutting.

"You're going to go and get ready for bed. You need a goodnight's sleep for work tomorrow," I whisper in her ear.

"What?" she says, confused, and I know she can feel the smile I press against her hair.

"Our building is so safe, isn't it? You can sleep soundly with the door unlocked, can't you, Pen?"

Her swallow is audible, as she looks over her shoulder to glance at me and searches my face.

"You're right, it is late, and we both have work tomorrow," she says, playing along.

I grip the back of her dress as she goes to step out onto her floor, tugging her against my chest.

"Wear my shirt," I reply. "And don't forget your bag."

I push the handle of her suitcase into her hand and release her dress. She steps out of the elevator, giving me a smirk before the elevator doors shut and I go back to my apartment.

It's nearly ten and I contemplate just how long I'm going to make my pretty Penny wait for her payback... not that she won't enjoy it immensely.

I MAKE her wait two hours. I spend the time scrolling on my phone and answering work emails so that if I'm a little late tomorrow, it won't be a big deal.

Unfortunately, I have to take the stairs up one floor so I wear shorts and a t-shirt. The last thing I need is to be scaring the shit out of one of our neighbors. I did ditch shoes, only wearing socks to help me be quiet. It's not like I've done a staged breaking and entering before.

I shake my head, thinking about the ridiculousness of it, but loving it all the same. The fact that Penny trusts me with her desires means everything to me. I'm the only one who can give her this, and she's about to fucking learn that tonight.

When I place my hand on her front door knob, I'm worried that maybe she got tired of waiting and locked me out. When the handle gives and the door silently opens, I smile with satisfaction. I lock it behind me as I stroll through her space. Only the oven light is on, but the rest of the apartment is silent.

I wonder if she fell asleep or if she's been sitting in her bed impatiently waiting for me to 'break in' and have my way with her.

Her bedroom door is open, none of the side lamps are on, and the door is cracked just wide enough for me to enter without having to part the door any further.

Penny rests on her side, her blonde hair spilling against her lavender sheets. My shirt is large on her, pooling around her frame, and a white knitted blanket covers her from the waist down.

I look at her in awe, knowing that she's really truly mine now.

Her room is messier than usual. Her suitcase cracked open, with her clothes and shoes spilling out onto the floor.

I remove the small length of bondage rope from my pocket, happy that her headboard is made of brass and the intricate designs are the perfect place to tie her up.

She doesn't shift in her bed, and her chest is rising and falling at an even pace. She truly must not have slept well on that shitty twin mattress. It's not like I slept well either, not with her next to me or the lumpiness of that fucking futon.

The angel on my shoulder is telling me to just crawl into bed with her and let her sleep. But my aching cock has other plans.

I've been patient. She can deal with some exhaustion.

I make my way over to her side of the bed to see if she moves, and she doesn't. I loop the rope around the bars of her bed, making two quick knots. There's a creak of the headboard, but she doesn't stir. I could tie her up right now, with her passed out, but that would ruin the fun.

There are so many ways I could do this, and I think about what she would want. What she likes and would get her off the most.

It's not the fear that she likes, it's being used for my pleasure. So it's this delicious circle of us both getting and taking what we want.

This isn't something I've done with someone else before, or something I'd really considered, but with Penny, it's different. There's a significant amount of trust and understanding when it comes to this type of roleplay. Both of us put each other's safety and comfort above all.

If I ever felt like she was uncomfortable, I'd stop immediately.

But I kind of enjoy taking what I want. It's long overdue.

I fist her hair and cover her mouth in the same motion. Her eyes widening and her hands reaching up to claw at my wrists. There's a moment of pure panic before she stills. Instead of swatting at my wrists, she holds them tightly.

Her eyes are still wide, and her breathing labored through her nose as I hold her mouth shut.

"Did you leave your door unlocked for me, pretty girl? Did you know I was watching?" I ask her.

She tries to pull away from my hand, and I just grip her hair even tighter in my fist.

"You wanted me to break in and take you, didn't you?"

She shakes her head against my mouth, and I smile.

"Don't lie to me."

I climb onto the bed, my hand sliding out of her hair as I straddle her waist. I keep my hand against her mouth, keeping her head pressed against her pillow.

Her hands are pulling at my wrist, trying to tug my hand away. She's actually using a decent amount of strength, so I remove my hand.

As soon as I do, she's trying to push me off.

"Get off of me," she says, her chest rising and falling as she tries to shove me away from her.

"I thought you might fight me," I say, grabbing the ends of the rope that I've already tied to her headboard.

Her eyes go wide and she's nearly stunned for a moment, not fighting me as I grab her wrists.

"The more you fight, the more I like it," I tell her.

The boy scouts pay off as I make a handcuff knot and tighten it around her wrists. There's enough slack in the rope that she can rest her hands above her head with no tension.

"Please, just take whatever you want and go," she says, while trying to hide her eagerness.

"I am taking what I want. I might not leave, though."

I slide my hands up and down her torso, cupping her breasts from the outside of her shirt, my thumbs rubbing circles around her nipples.

"Do you have any panties on, or were you just waiting for me?" I ask her, scooting down to her calves.

She tries to shimmy, but the effort she's putting in is diminishing. She wants it too fucking bad.

I grip the hem of the shirt, tugging it up to her collarbone so I can see her beautiful body.

She tries to hold her thighs together, but gives in with little effort as I grab her by the knee, spreading her wide.

"You're fucking dripping for it. I knew you'd have a pretty, needy pussy."

An eager moan slips between her lips, and she tugs against the restraints.

"My boyfriend will be home any minute," she says.

I can't help but laugh, and slide two fingers along her clit, dragging down to her aching entrance.

"What will he think? Seeing how much wetter you get because I can give you what you want?"

"I don't want this," she says, bucking her hips against my

hand, her body begging me for more while lies seep out of her mouth.

"Little liar," I whisper, pushing two fingers inside of her pussy.

Her walls grip my fingers as I curl them, hitting that soft spot that has her back arching off the bed.

"Are you going to come before I even take your pussy?" I say, holding her leg against the bed.

"No," she rasps out, her lips parting and her eyes closing in ecstasy as I rip her first orgasm out of her.

I use my thumb to strum her clit, my fingers never slowing as she clenches around me and she falls apart, moaning as her thigh shakes against my palm.

She pants and I slide my fingers out of her cunt, my hand covered in a sheen of her release.

"Would you look at that?" I say, spreading my fingers as her cum separates between two fingers.

I shift my shorts down with my other hand and grab my length with my wet fingers, stroking my cock.

Penny breathes frantically.

"Maybe you should taste what a mess I made of you," I tell her.

She shakes her head as I move up her body and grab her jaw. She holds her mouth shut.

"I did just make you come," I try to reason with her. She still doesn't part her lips. "Open those pretty lips or I'll do it for you."

Her eyes flash with desire as I press against her cheeks, parting her mouth and pushing the tip of my cock in.

She sucks on the tip, her blue eyes never leaving mine. The imagery of her lips wrapped around my cock and her hands tied above her head is almost too much as I slide in and out of her mouth.

"This mouth was made to be fucked," I groan, fisting the top metal of the headboard. She sucks harder and I tsk at her. "Look at you so greedy to swallow my cum. Too bad I have other plans for you."

She groans as I slide out of her mouth. I fist the neck of my shirt, throwing it off and I'm frantic to get my shorts off.

Penny parts her legs for me as I grab her thigh with one hand and my length in another, pushing inside of her.

We moan at the same time as I slide into her. I let go of her thigh and rest my forearms on each side of her face, grabbing her tied hands and lacing our fingers.

"Fuck," I hiss against the side of her face.

She moans, shifting her legs around my hips so I can get deeper.

"Kiss me," she whispers and I let go of one of her hands, grabbing her jaw and bringing her lips against mine.

We kiss passionately, her tongue dancing with mine as I devour her.

Her cunt is perfectly wrapped around my cock, and I know I'm not going to last much longer.

"Give me another one," I say against her parted lips as I use my knees for balance and fuck her harder. "Come on, Penny. Let me feel that pussy milking my cock."

She moans, her hands tugging against the restraints like she wants to tangle her hands in my hair. There's a huff of frustration when she can't move, and that must turn her on even more as she lifts her head to kiss me again.

My cock is deep inside of her and her lips are soft and sweet against mine as I swallow her sounds of pleasure and her cunt grips me like a vice. My hips stutter as I put more weight on her. My hands cradling the back of her head as I fuck her and fill her with my come.

I'm not even sure what noises she rips out of me, but I know I sound desperate as I finish inside of her.

Our bare chests are touching, both of us breathing heavily as I loosen the rope just enough for her to release her hands.

They immediately come around my neck, her nails dragging along my back.

"It took you long enough to break in," she says with a smile and I laugh, my dick jerking inside of her.

"I told you payback would be steep," I reply, pushing her hair off of her face.

She pushes her head up, kissing me again.

Being with Penny is as easy as breathing.

"I missed you," she whispers, her fingers sliding from my back, to my neck, to my face. "We're really doing this?"

"Yeah, baby, we really are."

I kiss her again before pulling out and collapsing on my side of the bed, the closest to the door. You know, in case there ever is a real ass intruder.

I tug her close to my chest, kissing the top of her head, and groan before getting up and going to the bathroom. I clean myself off before running a washcloth under warm water and wringing it out before coming back to the bed.

She's pliant in my arms as I drag the warm cloth over her messy pussy, cleaning her up.

"Was that okay?" I ask.

"Yeah, more than okay. I think we both needed it," she whispers in a sleepy voice.

I toss the rag on the floor and hold her close to my body, inhaling the scent of her hair and enjoying the warmth of her body against mine.

"My bed missed you too," she says softly.

I fall asleep feeling lighter than I have in weeks.

I ABSOLUTELY DID NOT WANT to wake up this morning. The urge to call out and lie in bed with Lincoln all day was so tempting.

But the man grabbed me by the ankle and pulled me down the bed and all but tossed me in the shower with him.

Mornings aren't so bad when I get to stare at my hot *boyfriend* in the shower.

I'm not sure that term fits what me and Lincoln are, but he seems dead-ass set on holding the title, and well, I like that he wants a label on it—even if it's loose as hell. While I'm absolutely not looking to be with anyone else, it's still weird since the people closest to us don't know.

I know he hates it. That he wants to rip the band-aid off and just deal with how our families react. But my insecurities are still holding me back.

I get these glimpses of what our lives look like with one another when we're alone and it has me ready to take that jump, but then we get around our family, I want to disappear and act like this is all some twisted dream I'm just not waking up from. Which is ridiculous, because not even my wildest imagination could have cooked this up.

"My place tonight? I can pick you up after work and we can go out to eat or just pick something up?" he asks while he washes my shampoo out of his hair.

The idea of him smelling like my lavender shampoo has a smile spreading across my face.

"Yeah, I'd like that."

"How are you feeling after last night?" he asks.

He's rubbing his jaw, and that's when I see it. I'm not the only one with insecurities in this relationship. Lincoln is always so confident, sure of himself and what he wants. But deep down, he's scared too.

There's a deep sinking feeling in my stomach over the fact that I made him feel that way. That I made him think he was unwanted and I hate it.

I wrap my arms around his waist, holding him tight, the warm water spraying against my back.

I think about saying I love you, but fear still holds me back. A piece of my heart has always belonged to Lincoln, but now the whole thing is his. Yet, I still can't let the words fall off my tongue.

I rest my chin on his chest, looking up at him. His hands are casually resting on my hips, giving me a soft squeeze as he looks down at me.

"Amazing. You're amazing, Linc," I say, pressing my cheek against his chest.

One of his hands slides up and cradles the back of my head.

"It took you long enough to figure it out."

I pull back, my mouth falling open as he gives me one of his wide smiles. "You're pretty amazing too," he says, leaning down and peppering my face with kisses, making me laugh.

The promise of my mornings being filled with Lincoln's smiles and sarcasm has more of my reservations about this relationship slipping away. Letting myself love Lincoln might be the biggest risk I've ever taken—but I know it's too late to turn back now.

LINCOLN DRIVES me to work and, for whatever reason, gets out of the car when I do.

"What are you doing?" I hiss as we approach the office building.

"Walking my girlfriend to work," he replies lazily, and clearly not going back to his car.

He trails behind me and when we reach the glass office building, there are hundreds of papers taped to the office front.

They're all pictures of Jessa and Aiden kissing at a Rays game they went to. Completely outing them to the entire office.

"Fuck," I hiss, grabbing one of the papers and ripping it off the wall.

"Who would do this?" Lincoln asks, furrowing his brow and looking at me.

There are already cars in the lot, which means most of the employees saw this shit and did nothing about it.

What a bunch of bitches.

"That's what I'd like to find out," I say, swinging the front doors open and stomping into the lobby.

The cubicles are to my right, and I hold up the paper.

"Who the hell put these up front?" I say.

A bunch of cowards—including Sharon—tuck behind their cubicle walls in shame. Meanwhile, Zach comes strolling toward me. Lincoln's at my back and I swear I feel him inch closer as Zach leans against my desk, grabbing the paper out of my hand and sneering down at it.

"Serves him fucking right. Honestly, I thought he was better than this," he says. He's had it out for Jessa ever since their father gifted her the shares in the will. He's been cruel, but this goes beyond what a dick he's been.

"Did you fucking do this?" I question him.

Zach looks me up and down, like I'm something stuck under the bottom of his shoe.

"Please. Like I have time for something as petty when it comes to that bitch."

"Your father left her those shares, and this company is rightfully Aiden's," I say, trying to watch my language. Technically, Zach is a part owner and I unfortunately need to keep this job.

Zach rolls his eyes, not even acknowledging Lincoln's menacing presence behind me.

"Do what you do best and sit behind a desk, look pretty, and keep your mouth shut," he says.

"The fuck did you just say?" Lincoln says, grabbing my arm and tugging me behind him. Lincoln is older than Zach by a good six years, but definitely more built and slightly taller.

"Lincoln, it's fine." I try to calm the situation and grab his arm.

"Is this what you do, Penny? Have your family handle all your problems? It's why you have this job. It's not like we'd ever actually—"

Lincoln grabs a fist full of Zach's shirt and I gasp, grabbing his arm tighter.

"You wanna finish that fucking sentence?" Lincoln says, getting in Zach's face.

"Lincoln, it's okay. Let's go outside."

The two men stare at each other for a long time, and Lincoln lets go of his shirt, slightly pushing him away. Zach acts like he's dusting himself off and turns around to see everyone in the office watching the altercation.

"Get back to work," he sneers, storming back to his office and slamming the door.

My heart rate is through the roof and everyone in the office is still staring, so I grab Lincoln by the sleeve and drag him outside as I angrily start ripping off the flyers.

"You shouldn't have done that," I say.

"He shouldn't have spoken to you like that."

"No, he shouldn't, but you can't just put your hands on people when they're mean to me," I say, gripping the papers with Jessa and Aiden's cute faces on them. It almost feels wrong crinkling up their happy moment. But I really don't want her to get to work and deal with this. She's already had to deal with enough shit from Zach. Jessa and Aiden are in such a good place after the trip. This will just sour it.

"I just grabbed his shirt." He waves a hand in the air like it isn't a big deal.

"He's still my boss."

"Well, he shouldn't be," he snaps back.

"It's not like I have many other options."

He invades my space, in that way he always does—constantly pushing me.

"Penny, you know damn well you could do anything you put your mind to. The only thing you like about this position is the event planning. I could talk to Krystal and see if her service is hiring with her baby on the way. I'm sure she'd be looking for extra help."

I blink at him, a sinking weight hitting my stomach. It always feels like people are helping me and I can't ever do things myself.

"I don't want you to use your connections to get me a job," I say, hastily grabbing more papers.

"It would be an interview, and you and I know you're more than capable."

I pause, trying to swallow back all the insecure mean things I want to say.

"You really think she would want to hire me?"

He grabs a few of the papers that are taller than I can reach and hands them to me.

"Yes. It's not a handout. It's me knowing Krystal's company needs help and knowing the perfect fit. You aren't happy here, and I don't like how that fucking dickhead spoke to you. But beyond that, you should be following your dreams. You said you were working on finding yourself. Don't let your pride get in the way of a good thing," he says.

I sigh and look up at him, it's still too hot outside, but the sun brings out the different shades of his hair and God, he's fucking handsome.

"Why are you so good to me?"

"You know why," he says softly before cursing and pulling his phone out of his pocket. "Shit. I have a meeting in ten minutes. Are you okay handling this?" he says, waving at the wall.

"Yeah, I got it."

"If he talks to you like that again, you tell Aiden right away," he says sternly. I nod and he leans forward to kiss me, but stops and sighs. "The next time I drop you off at work, I'd really like to kiss you goodbye."

I realize I want that too; I give him a smile as he walks away. I go back into the office and call the security company asking them to send the footage from last night and grab my trash can. It feels like the employees of Kemper's Sports Supply are a bunch of traitors as I go to remove the flyers by myself. But I know it's because Zach is acting this way and no one wants to upset a partial owner.

I'm taking more of the signs down and mulling over the potential of switching jobs. If I could work solely planning on events? It would truly be my dream job, and he promised that it wasn't a handout, that he truly thinks I'm built for this.

Lincoln believes in me and suddenly I feel like maybe I can believe in myself.

The sun is hot against my back as Aiden and Jessa walk together from the back of the building towards my direction. I pluck the papers off at an unnatural speed. Like I could actually get them all down in time.

"Fuck, I thought I'd be able to get them all down by the time you got here," I say, yanking another flyer.

Jessa looks dejected but resolved over the situation.

"Okay, so everyone knows we kissed," Jessa says calmly, but it's clear she's pissed.

I grimace, knowing that everyone knows it's more than that. "Zach is on a bit of a tirade inside."

"Who put these up?" Aiden asks, taking Jessa's hand and I shake my head.

"I called our security company and asked for the footage," I tell him.

"Thank you," Aiden says, pulling Jessa off to the side as I keep tugging down the papers.

They're chatting in low tones as I keep taking them down. Aiden and Jessa go inside as I get every last disgusting piece of paper.

Who would do this?

My trashcan is full and I head back to my desk and eavesdrop on the entire altercation and listen to Jessa tell her half-brother to go fuck himself and that she quits. I act like I'm working when I'm really listening to everything and wondering if I can be more like her.

Kemper's is a secure job, one that isn't overly difficult. Can I really just branch out and try something new? It's terrifying, and I'm wondering if I'm brave enough to leave a sure thing?

The office quiets, and eventually Jessa comes around the corner with a box full of her shit. As much as I'm considering taking up Lincoln's offer, it doesn't mean I'm happy about her leaving me here with these assholes.

"This doesn't change anything between us, you know?"

"I know, but now who am I supposed to get lunch with? Sharon?" I make a face, feeling like she completely betrayed me today. Jessa is the best work friend I've had ever. I mean, we're more than that now, but it still sucks.

"Who knows, maybe this will take off and I could use some help." I love that she'd be willing to hire me, but I hate the idea of someone else feeling like I need a pity job.

"What exactly are you going to do now?"

"I think a mixture of freelance design and finally putting my designs on apparel. That's always been something I wanted to do, but just never moved forward on. I think it's time I start following my dreams, and working here with Zach breathing down my neck isn't it."

"But Aiden," I say softly, wondering what it's going to be like for him without Jessa here.

"He understands, and we're going to be okay. More than okay, actually."

"No kidding. The family loved you, by the way, if you didn't pick up on that. I've never seen Aiden this happy, and of course he wants you to follow your dreams, but who is he going to stare at all day?" I joke, trying to swallow down my fear that Jessa and I won't be as close as we are with her getting a new job.

Just add it to my very long list of shit I need to talk to my therapist about.

She laughs and waves me off. "I'll come by for lunch next week, okay?"

"Okay," I sigh, standing up and walking around my desk to wrap my arms around her to squeeze tightly. "Don't be a stranger," I tell her and she hugs me back.

Maybe I'm naive, but I think this friendship might survive just about anything.

Lincoln

Support System

PENNY OPENS the passenger door roughly and slams it behind her when I pick her up.

"Bad day?"

"Jessa quit," she says, crossing her arms over her chest.

"Because of her relationship with Aiden?" I question, hoping that this doesn't set us two steps back.

"No, she just didn't feel like dealing with the bullshit anymore. Zach was a real dick to her."

"Color me surprised," I say under my breath.

"I really don't feel like going out to eat tonight."

"Takeout and rotting in bed, it is."

She turns towards me and gives me a small smile. "You just get it," she replies.

I reverse the car and head to my favorite Chinese spot with my hand on her thigh the entire ride.

※ ※ ※

WE'RE LYING in my bed, watching a show that Penny has seen a million times, when Penny's phone buzzes on the night-stand. She grabs it and she gasps when she sees the text.

"What is it?" I ask.

"The papers weren't Zach or someone from the office. It was Jessa's ex. He tried to attack her and Aiden."

"Are they okay?" I ask, fear for my brother racing through me grabbing my phone, attempting to call Aiden, he sends me to voicemail.

She stares at her phone and nods her head.

"Aiden says he'll tell me more details later. They are both safe and at his house, Jessa is really shaken up. I'm going to try and go see her tomorrow for lunch to get a gauge on how she's handling things. Her ex is in custody."

Penny stares at her phone a little longer and mine buzzes with a text from Aiden letting me know what happened and to not worry and that they are safe.

"They could have been seriously hurt," she breathes out, clutching her chest.

"But they're not, they're safe."

She nods her head, sending one last message to Aiden before putting her phone away.

"They're safe." She sighs and rests her head against the pillow. "I really hope Jessa is okay. I can't imagine how scared she must have been."

"She's with Aiden. He'll make sure she's okay."

"You're sure?"

"It's the same thing I would do for you."

She bites her lip and nods. Something about that clicks with her and calms her nerves. But it's true. Aiden is protective and strong. She's in good hands. He will make sure that she's safe and they can work through this together.

"He wants you to visit tomorrow?" I reiterate and she nods.

"Do you think you could take me over there tomorrow? I know you're probably—"

"I'll take you, it isn't a big deal."

"I really should start driving again," she sighs.

I realize then that I never asked her why she didn't drive places. I kind of just always liked that she depended on me in that way.

"Why don't you drive?"

"Promise not to laugh?"

"I promise."

"I watched the most fucked-up documentary about this woman driving on the wrong side of the road and everyone she killed in the crash and ever since then I just... I don't know, I can't stomach driving. It didn't hurt that Kemper's is right down the street. Everyone is close, and you were always willing to give me a ride. I think I got comfortable in this little bubble of my life."

"I can just continue driving you everywhere," I suggest, and she snuggles up against my chest.

"Or I could work on being braver. Knowing what Jessa went through today, and how strong she is, I want to be more like her."

"You don't need to compare yourself to her," I tell her honestly.

"She's been through so much and—"

"So have you. You're brave. Look at where you are right now, in my bed. That's brave. Taking the interview with Krystal would be brave, too."

"Did you talk to her?"

I nod and grab her hand, interlacing our fingers and kissing the back of her hand. "She has a proposition for you."

"What is it?"

"I think I'll leave that to Krystal," I say, knowing it will drive her crazy. She glares at me, but there's no heat to it.

"Pretty sure you were put on this earth to torture me, Lincoln Carlson."

"You're not wrong," I reply and pull her tighter to my chest.

I can't imagine what Aiden is going through right now. The only reason I'm not panicking is because he specifically said that they were okay. But the idea of Penny being in that type of danger makes my stomach sink.

"I'll check in on Aiden while you meet with Jessa tomorrow," I say against her hair.

"I think he'd like that. I wonder how serious everything got. I mean, I knew her ex was a controlling asshole, but to break into her cottage?"

"They're okay," I repeat.

She rests her hand against my chest as we lie on my bed and I send up a prayer that this is the way I spend the rest of my life. In my bed, knowing my family is safe, with the girl I love in my arms.

PENNY TAKES her and Jessa's food upstairs to Aiden's room while I hang out with him in the kitchen.

"How bad was it?" I ask. He looks like shit. His green eyes are weary and heavy with bags from lack of sleep.

He scrubs his chin, and the scratch against his scruff is audible.

"The bastard had a fucking gun," he says, gripping the edge of the counter. "I thought..." He shakes his head, and the intrusive thought away. "I've never been so fucking scared in my life."

I rest a hand on his shoulder and squeeze for comfort.

"You're okay, she's okay."

Aiden looks up at the ceiling like he's able to see what she and Penny are talking about right now.

"Physically, yeah. Everything else?" He lets out a groan of frustration and sits on the bar stool and rests his chin in his hands. "I love her more than anything. He almost took her from me."

"But he didn't. You took care of her, you're taking care of her. You need to take care of yourself, too."

He glances up at me and then back down at the table.

"I know, I will."

"Delegate more at the office, work from home. Put you and Jessa first. Fuck the rest."

"You're right," he agrees.

He looks at me skeptically. "Since when do you give sound advice?"

Since I also met the person who means the most to me, but I don't say that, at least not yet. Now that I have Penny in the capacity I want, we'll take it at her speed to tell the family. As much as I've pushed and pushed over the last few months, it's time to let her run the show.

"I'm very wise. You just never noticed."

Penny comes down the stairs looking a little downtrodden, she barely spent any time up there.

"Jessa wanted to lie down for a bit," she says with a sigh and scrolls through her phone. "She really wasn't in the mood for talking, but my therapist's office does virtual appointments. Maybe you'd like to mention it to her?"

Aiden gives Penny a warm smile. "Thanks, Pen. We didn't get much sleep last night. This was probably too much too soon. I'll let you know when she's ready for you to visit again."

Penny smiles at him and looks like she's contemplating something. "Whatever you need at the office, just let me know."

I wince, feeling guilty over the plans I have for Penny and how that might affect Aiden. But my brother remembers fucking everything and just gives me a look, knowing I wanted her to come to Vegas with my company.

"Thanks, Penny. Working from home shouldn't be much different. It's time for Zach to step up if he still wants to have a part in the company, anyway."

Just the mention of that asshole's name has me wanting to drive to Kemper's and kick his ass. But, hopefully, Penny won't be working there much longer, anyway.

"Thanks for coming by, I appreciate it."

"We'd do anything for you, Aiden," Penny says, hugging my brother.

"I'd do the same for you two."

Let's hope that's true when the time comes to tell our family that we're in a relationship.

"We'll plan something soon," he assures Penny and we leave Aiden's house.

As soon as we get into the car Penny huffs in frustration.

"She looked terrible."

"Remember how brave you said she was yesterday? She'll get through this, especially with Aiden at her side."

"You're right," she agrees, grabbing my hand and kissing my knuckles before placing it on my lap.

I drive her to work, kissing her in the car goodbye and just enjoy the normalcy and domesticity of how our day started and how I hope it ends.

PENNY HAS BEEN a mess over Jessa over the last few days, but Aiden assures her that she's doing better and that she can come over soon.

She's even more fidgety knowing we're meeting with Krystal this morning.

"The blue or the black?" she says, holding up two dresses.

"The blue," I reply.

"Are you sure?"

"Yes, go get dressed, baby. It will be great. You have nothing to worry about."

"I haven't had an interview in years. What if I say something stupid or embarrass you?"

"One, you could never embarrass me, second, I say stupid shit all the time. Krystal will be used to it."

"Not helpful," she huffs, getting dressed and displaying her back to me. "Can you zip me up?"

I kiss her shoulder blades and zip up the dress, and she lets her pretty blonde hair fall down her back.

"Hey, you have no reason to be nervous."

"I guess I didn't realize how bad I wanted it, especially with Aiden and Jessa out of the office. It makes working there unbearable."

"You'll do great, you're a perfect fit," I tell her, placing a quick kiss on her lips. "Let's get going."

I drive to my office, Penny tapping her leg the whole drive. I lead her to the conference room, where Krystal is waiting.

"Meet me in my office later. You got this."

She takes a deep breath, entering the glass office and shaking Krystal's hand, while I head over to my office and get myself organized for the day. Time ticks by, and I take it as a good sign that Penny is still speaking to her.

I like that I was able to help with this; it's even better knowing she would be perfect for the job.

Nearly an hour later, a grinning Penny comes into my office, shutting the door behind her.

"She's amazing," she says dreamily.

"What did she say?"

"That she wants me to help you in Vegas to see how I do and then we can discuss a part-time position which could very quickly turn into full time. She wants to expand her client list, but with a baby on the way, that's a big undertaking. Krystal thinks I'd be a good fit."

"I told you that you would be."

She rounds my desk, resting her butt on the edge, and I swivel my chair to face her.

"Did you suggest the Vegas thing?" she asks.

I shrug, and she shakes her head.

"I have to prove myself on that trip. I'm not there to be your personal bed warmer," she chastises me.

"I'm fairly sure you're capable of doing both."

She rolls her eyes and sighs. "I feel guilty, though. What about Aiden?"

"Aiden will understand, I promise."

Her gaze narrows on me. "You already told him, didn't you?"

"Only about the Vegas trip. He already agreed to it while we were in The Bahamas. He knew it was coming."

"That was before everything went down."

"Penny."

She looks at me softly and I grab the back of her thighs. "You're earning this, you deserve this. Don't worry about the rest."

Her hands tangle in my hair and she leans in for a kiss. It's a soft press of her lips against mine as my office door opens.

"Oh, oh," Marie says in shock. "Hi Penny."

Penny's cheeks are red as she lifts herself off my desk.

"Hi Marie. See you around," she says, scurrying out of my office. I groan in annoyance as Marie's wide gaze meets mine.

"That's why you've been in a good mood?" she asks. "Oh, my God. Does your dad know?"

"Not currently, and I'd appreciate your discretion."

"Your secret is safe with me. I mean, wow, holy shit. But also… she makes sense for you," she says with a shrug.

"Thank you for your seal of approval. Is that all you needed?"

"Krystal wanted me to ask if we needed to book another room for the conference, but I'm going to go out on a limb and say that's a no."

I blink at her with a straight face. "Is that all?"

"That's all," she says with a smile that says she can't wait to go home and tell her husband everything.

I just hope getting spotted didn't set me back with Penny.

When will people learn to not enter through doors unless they are invited in?

Penny

Viva Las Vegas

I'LL BE out of the office for three days and the weekend to make sure everything goes smoothly and report back to Krystal.

Before I leave, I'm having dinner with Jessa at her house. Well, her and Aiden's house. She's still been a little out of it, but every time I come and visit, she seems to be getting better and better.

I knock on Aiden's door, and Jessa greets me with a smile. I don't know why I don't mention Vegas, the new job, or how amazing spending time with Lincoln has been; it doesn't feel right to talk about what's going on with me when she's been through so much.

But I suppose that's a bit of a problem I have, isn't it? Letting everything build up inside because I'm too busy acting happy and not telling people what's truly going on with me. Even though, right now, I'm happier than I've ever been.

Talking about it brings some of the harsh realities to light though, ones I'm not quite ready to face.

Lincoln has been patient and loving, and the fact that he is a secret makes me sick to my stomach, he deserves more than that.

He deserves everything and more. These past few weeks of just coming home after work to be with one another have been the best I've ever had. Lincoln makes me a better person, and I think I do the same for him.

So why am I still so afraid of telling our families? Why can't I make that extra push? I keep telling myself that I'll be ready soon, but then when I think about telling them, I retreat and feel like an anxious mess. Our little bubble is a happy one, and I don't want it to pop.

"Hey, Penny. Thanks for coming," she says.

I hold up the food with a smile. "Of course. How have you been?"

She smiles, and it's a true one. Not the forced ones she's given previously.

"Actually, really good."

We head into their kitchen and divide the food.

"I'm working myself up to leave the house. I promise we can go somewhere and eat soon."

"There's no rush, Jessa."

"I know that. Everyone has been so kind and patient with me. Especially Aiden, God. I don't know where that man came from, but he's a literal angel."

"The Carlson men will do that to you."

"Do you want to—"

I shake my head. I don't want to burden Jessa with the details of my life. She reaches out and squeezes my wrist.

"We're friends, Penny. Best friends, if I remember correctly, from a drunken conversation. Just because I have my own stuff going on doesn't mean you can't share yours."

I give her a smile.

"You're right, I know you're right. Can I ask you something?" She nods and I clear my throat. "When you found out that Collin was dead, did you feel a lot of regret?"

"Yeah, of course. I still wish I had more time with him, even my mom too. But I can't change anything. There's nothing to be done about the situation. So I had two choices. I could hate Collin and hang on to this resentment I felt, or I could move forward and try to not let it bother me. Some days are better than others."

"I found out my biological mom passed away, and well, before that, she wanted nothing to do with me," I sigh.

"You never said anything," she says, her eyes going soft as she grabs my hand.

"I think I like the idea that everyone thinks I'm fun and exciting. Not sharing things about myself makes that easier. I'm working on it."

"You have so many people who love you, you don't have to do this alone anymore," she says.

"I know. I think I'm starting to truly understand that now," I reply, and truly mean it.

There have been so many times I've pulled away from my family and fallen in the arms of unsuited boyfriends because it was easier to be who they wanted than myself. Sometimes the reality of being who I am is hard, but I'm slowly realizing there's no one else I'd rather be.

I've completely fallen for Lincoln. And in the process of that, I think he's helped me fall in love with myself.

"LET'S GO," I usher Lincoln to the car.

"We don't need to be at the airport this early," he complains, rolling both of our suitcases out to the car.

"Yes, we do. I'm in charge of making sure everyone gets to where they need to be."

"Very serious," he jokes, and I roll my eyes.

"I want to do a good job. Krystal needs to know that I can keep people in line and make sure things run smoothly under pressure."

"You're going to do great, baby," he says, leaning over and giving me a quick peck on the lips before loading the car and driving to the airport. On the way, I make sure I know every detail of the long weekend, like I haven't memorized it backwards and forwards.

Lincoln reaches over, his reassuring hand on my thigh, squeezing. He doesn't joke about it again, knowing I'm a little anxious.

It's not that I don't think I can handle the work, I just really truly want to prove myself. I've never wanted a job so bad, working for Krystal would be the opportunity of a lifetime. She doesn't care about my education; she cares about my work ethic and dependability and I plan on proving myself worthy in both aspects during this trip.

Lincoln and I park in long-term parking and head toward check-in as I gather everyone's tickets. I'm inputting our information and scrunch my brows at the screen.

"You put us in first class?" I ask, glancing over and Lincoln.

"I was flying first class, anyway. You think I'm going to let my girlfriend sit in the back?"

"They can't see you giving me special treatment."

"Why? You're not an employee. You're working for our subcontractor. They won't even notice. They'll assume Krystal put you there."

I push the button with more force than needed, not wanting to argue with him, mostly because it's a longer flight and the idea of coach doesn't sound great.

"Is there anything else you've upgraded or have planned that I don't know about?"

"Where's the fun in that?" He grins at me as we check our bags and wait for his employees to arrive.

Lincoln must run a tight ship, because they're all on time and I don't have to hunt a single person down to make sure they don't miss this trip.

Phase one complete.

There's a weight off my chest as we go through security, grab breakfast, and wait at our gate.

I go through the schedule again.

"Seriously, Pen. I know you have it memorized."

I nod and close out of the schedule on my phone.

"How do you want to celebrate if you win Commercial Design of the year?" I ask him.

He's hardly even mentioned the award, like it's not a big deal. He's put plenty of his salespeople and marketing up for awards, but this would be the big one.

"We won't. There are too many nominees, but they expect you to submit for tons of shit. Milking me fucking dry, if you ask me. How many tables did we purchase?" he asks.

"Two," I reply, not knowing the cost.

"Ten grand a table."

"Seriously?"

I start doing all the math in my head: the event, the flights, the hotel, and food. Lincoln has taken a significant chunk of money to fund this trip for his employees.

"Why spend all of this money?"

"It's good for morale, everyone loves Vegas. Plus, the convention beforehand is informative."

"I don't know what I'm going to do with myself for those two days."

He taps my thigh twice, and I know he'd love to just rest his hand there, but he doesn't.

I think I'm getting tired of being in the dark when I want nothing more than to fully embrace Lincoln in the light of day.

Our gate boards and I'm very thankful for the upgrade as we make our way to Vegas. I don't know why, but this trip feels like a turning point in my life.

THE FIRST TWO days were easy, beyond easy. As I sat on my ass, accepted overpriced spa treatments from Lincoln while everyone was at the conference.

The only thing I truly had to do was handle dinner in the evenings, and those weren't even mandatory, though most employees take advantage of drinking and eating on the company's dime.

It's been nice seeing Lincoln with his employees. They clearly respect him and find some joy working here. I wonder if it's a Carlson brother trait to be so good at managing people.

But today is the big night. Tomorrow we have some team-building exercises and then the rest of the day is free for everyone to enjoy the last bit of their trip.

I straighten Lincoln's tie, and he glances down at me.

"You look too good in a suit," I say and he shakes his head.

"How can someone look too good in something?"

"I don't know, but you've managed it."

"Can you tie the laces on my back?" I ask, throwing my hair over my shoulder as Lincoln ties the straps to the rose-gold sequin dress that I blessedly got on sale. I know Lincoln would have bought me a dress for the event, but I didn't want to ask, not when he's already done so much.

"I think I know what you mean about looking too good," he says, kissing my bare shoulder.

"Are you excited?" I ask, turning back around and straightening his already straight suit jacket.

"I've been coming to this thing for over a decade," he says. "But this one is special, because you're here." He kisses my cheek, not messing up my gloss. "Everyone has said how lovely you are, and how smoothly everything has gone."

"Lincoln Carlson, are you inflating my ego?"

"Will it get me laid tonight?" He smirks.

"Most definitely. Now, let's go get your employees and rack up those awards," I say, grabbing the camera that Krystal gave me to take better pictures of the event and the employees. She stressed that posting about this on the company website and social media would look good for clients.

Lincoln blessedly carries my ID, lip gloss, and credit card in his pockets, so all I have to worry about is the hefty camera.

We head down to the lobby, waiting for all the employees to arrive. One by one they trickle in, looking like a million bucks. I take headshots and pictures of them smiling and mingling.

"Where's Jacob?" I ask, looking around.

He's up for an award based on his volume of sales and if he's not there to accept the award, that will look bad on the company, on Lincoln, on Krystal. I'll get a key to his room and drag him down here by his hair if I need to.

He comes running around the corner with windswept hair and his suit out of place.

"I'm here. Sorry, lost track of time," he says, catching his breath.

"You look a fucking mess," Paula says, helping him fix his hair and Lincoln leans into me.

"I saw the look of murder in your eyes."

"You saw no such thing. Alright, the cars are here," I say, leading everyone to the underground garage. The ride is only a few minutes, but we make our way through the hotel to their banquet hall.

I can tell Lincoln wants to stay at my side, but I push him away as I take pictures of everything and watch as an observer.

I take more pictures of Lincoln than I should... I'll just save some for myself and delete the others before I return the camera to Krystal. He just looks so good, so in his element. He commands respect and just has a swagger to him that I find too enticing.

When I look at Lincoln, I realize that I've never actually been in love before. Maybe my heart was always reserved for him and I just didn't know it.

Lincoln

Double Down

THE WHOLE TIME my team is drinking champagne and downing canapés and I mingle around with the same assholes I've known my whole career, I can't help but glance at Penny.

She's fucking beautiful in her sparkly champagne-colored dress and a beaming smile on her face.

When I shake hands with Carter Salvo and greet his wife, Valerie, all I can think about is how Penny should be on my arm. I should be flaunting around my gorgeous girl to all these stuck-up assholes.

I'm petulant, but I'm working on it. Penny wants to do a good job for Krystal and the last thing I need to do is push her any further. Slowly but surely, I think it's sinking in that this is real, that we're in this for the long haul. The more she under-stands just how serious we are, the more prepared she'll be to go fully public.

"You know, Lincoln, my cousin Cecelia is here. I think you two would hit it off," Valerie says, looking around the room. Carter seems used to his wife's antics and shrugs.

"I'm actually seeing someone."

Valerie gasps. "You didn't bring her?"

"Unlike your husband, I don't plan on torturing her," I joke, they laugh, it feels gross and of course at that moment Penny comes up to us taking a picture.

"They want us to take our seats," she says softly, waving hello to Carter and Valerie.

"I'll see you later," I tell Carter, though I won't. I'll see him next year at this event like I do every year.

I picture what next year will look like. Would Penny be working for Krystal, doing the same grunt work of keeping us all on track, or will she be on my arm as my girlfriend, or possibly something more?

Penny squeezes my biceps and Valerie tracks the movement with a twitch of her lips as we head to the reception hall.

"You probably want to sit next to Jacob and Paula since they're both up for awards," she says.

"No, I want to sit next to you."

She glances up at me with a small, shy smile on her face as she nods. Everything around us disappears, the fancy decor, the clattering of drinking glasses, and loud chatter.

"You're not going to fight me on this, are you?"

"No, I'm not," she says as we take our seats.

It's clear that all my employees note who I'm sitting next to. I'm not sure how inconspicuous we've been, because I truly don't care. Part of me feels like Penny doesn't either.

I place my hand on her thigh, where it belongs, and she doesn't move my hand as the ceremony begins.

It's long, tedious, and fucking boring.

Paula and Jacob both win their awards and Penny is frantic with getting up and down, taking photographs of them and their awards.

The award for best commercial design comes up, and it's a project that took years. It meant a lot to me and my dad. It was the first project he had no part of and he handed me over the company. It took years to get it off the ground with all the site development issues we had, but I'm proud of it. Even if it doesn't win, I have that.

"Goes to the Optic Center by Carlson Commercial Enterprises."

My jaw goes slack as I look around the table. It happens so fast as Penny grabs my face, kissing me publicly for the first time. It's not scandalous, but it's significant. As she pulls back, her eyes water as she beams at me.

"I'm proud of you. Go get your award."

It takes a moment for me to pull away from her. If anyone is shocked at our table, I don't notice as I go up to the podium and accept the award. Penny takes a ridiculous amount of pictures as I head back to our group, placing my award on the table.

My employees congratulate me and Penny looks at me like I hung the moon.

"Well, now we need to really celebrate," she says.

"What did you have in mind?"

"Just wait and see," she grins.

Is this what it feels like to be on top of the world?

PENNY INSISTS on taking all the awards back to our room before the after party, stating she would cry endlessly if someone lost theirs and we didn't bring it back home. As soon as they're on the table in our suite, I grip her hips.

"We could just stay up here."

"No way, mister. You just won the award. We're celebrating."

"I can think of better ways of celebrating," I reply, kissing the column of her throat.

"Good things come to those who wait," she says, grabbing my chin and placing a small kiss on my lips.

"You kissed me in front of everyone," I remind her.

"I did."

"You're not worried?" I ask, sounding like an insecure asshole.

She smiles and shakes her head. "You're too bright to be hidden away, Lincoln Carlson."

I grip her hips harder. "Now I really just want to stay in the room with you."

"Too bad we're celebrating. Tuck in your dick and let's go."

I grumble, but grab her hand, feeling lighter as we enter the party holding hands.

The space has bright lights while still being opulent. The music is loud as people dance and drink. Penny drags me to the bar where my employees are waiting. She holds out her hand and I give her the company card as she starts a tab for everyone.

A bunch of industry members are here, and I glance over at her as she shrugs. "I sent out an email to see who would be interested in an after party. We didn't have to book the space as it's open to the public. Everyone just has to open their own tabs."

I smile at her and she blushes.

Everyone starts to branch off, doing their own thing and hanging out with people they usually only see once a year.

"Dance with me?" Penny asks, after we both get our drinks.

We head to the dance floor, some pop song loudly playing and it hits me then, with her body pressed against mine. I'm at the peak of my career. I was okay with life before Penny, but I realize now I was just going through the motions of staying alive.

Being with Penny is like seeing colors for the first time, and I can't hold it back anymore.

"I love you," I whisper into her ear, and she whips around, spilling some of her drink over her knuckles.

She blinks at me a few times before a smile takes over her face. Without a care in the world, she wraps an arm around the back of my neck and pushes me down so we're face to face.

"I love you too," she replies, her eyes locked in with mine before we kiss.

It's not the chaste kiss from earlier. This is *the* kiss.

My heart is racing in my chest and I just want to repeat how much I love her repeatedly. I'm all fucking in and Penny isn't going anywhere.

I pull back my lips a few inches from hers.

"Let's get married."

She pulls back further, but doesn't move her arm from my neck. "What?"

"I'm all fucking in, Penny. We're in Vegas, we could do it tonight. You wanted to know that this was real, that I wasn't going anywhere. Marry me. Our family can learn to deal with it."

She blinks at me rapidly. "How much have you had to drink?"

"This is my third since the event."

"You're being impulsive."

"No, I'm not," I tell her sternly, and her eyes search mine.

"You'd really want to marry me?"

"I want everything with you. I'm sick of not showing you off, of not being with you in the way I want to be. Be my wife, be my everything."

She thinks for a long moment, and I wonder what Penny always pictured her wedding looking like. Did she want something big and extravagant and I'm crushing her dreams?

"Why do you want me to be your wife?"

I fist her hair, holding her face close to mine. Everything and everyone around us is irrelevant.

"Because I've never been this happy. You make life worth living, Penny, and I want to spend the rest of mine with you proudly on my arm, my ring on your finger, our kids running around. I want everything and I want it with you."

She wraps her other arm around my neck, squeezing me tight.

"You are actually the most romantic person I've ever met."

"Is that a yes?"

She pulls back, smiling. "Yes, it's a yes."

Her lips crash against mine. The music blares in the space as relief fills my chest. Fuck the repercussions, what anyone thinks. I'm marrying her before she has a chance to change her mind.

WE END up in Downtown Las Vegas. There's a woman in a motorized scooter with duct tape over her nipples, a man contorting his body, and another dressed as a politician dancing.

Penny tugs on my hand as we head to the small wedding chapel. It's not classy by any means.

"It's a bit of a hole-in-the-wall," I say, and Penny smacks my chest but laughs.

"It was your idea."

"You're still good with this?" I ask, cupping her face looking down at her. As bad as I want it, I'd understand if she said no.

But this is how our relationship works, zero to one-hundred with everything we do. Her hands drag down my chest and she looks back up at me.

"I don't know how I'm going to tell my parents that I got

married without them and it's to you. But I want this, I want you, Lincoln."

I kiss her as we enter the door, and the hostess runs us through the packages.

We go with one of the mid-tiers that includes a witness and photos. It's almost serendipitous that she's in a floor length dress and I'm wearing a suit as we get situated in front of the officiant.

He's fast and concise.

"Little lady, do you take this man to be your lawful husband?" he asks.

"I do," Penny says, holding her shitty looking bouquet with a massive smile on her face.

"And do you take this little lady to be your lawful wife?" he turns and asks me, he isn't dressed like Elvis, but it's clear he plays the role often enough.

"I do."

"Then, by the power that's vested in me by the state of Nevada, I pronounce you husband and wife."

The officiant moves out of the way as I grab Penny by the waist and the back of her head, crashing her lips to mine. It's a messy kiss filled with smiles and laughter as we pull apart and pose for a few photos.

We sign some more paperwork and it's official. We're married. In a matter of minutes and a few signatures we've tied ourselves together forever.

"What do we do next?" she asks, both of us looking at where we just signed.

"We celebrate," I tell her, grabbing her face and kissing her roughly. "I love you," I whisper against her lips.

"I love you too," she says softly, with no fear or regret, only pure happiness written on her face. She's the most beautiful woman I've ever seen and she's finally all mine.

Lincoln

No Regrets

KEEPING my hands off of her the ride back to the hotel is nearly impossible. Trying not to push her against the elevator wall and fuck her is even harder. But somehow I persevere as we speedily walk to our room.

As soon as the lock churns, we're pushing through and I have her back against the wall in a moment. My hand tangled in her hair, preventing the back of her head from resting against the hard surface while another grips her ass.

She's shrugging my jacket off of my shoulders and I have to move one arm at a time to get it off and immediately go back to having my hands all over her.

I pepper kisses along the side of her throat, licking and tasting and not being able to get enough.

She's mine. She's not going anywhere.

Her fingers are messily unbuttoning my shirt, her lips swollen from our kisses, and I can't get enough.

"You're my wife," I say and she pauses, undressing me for a moment to give me a smile.

"I am."

"I love you," I tell her. It's like now that I've said it, I can't stop saying it. I need her to know how important and deep saying those words out loud is to me. "I've never said that to anyone else before."

"I haven't felt it with anyone else before. I love you too," she tells me honestly, and I can't fault her for that.

I capture her lips in another kiss as I walk backward toward the bed. Penny tugs my shirt out of my pants and works on my belt buckle while I untie her dress and push the thin straps over her shoulders. The sparkling material pulls to the floor, and she steps out of it, only wearing a nude pair of panties and her heels.

I grab her by the back of her thighs, tossing her on the bed, making her laugh as her breasts bounce and her hair pools around her head like a halo.

My fingers wrap around her ankle as I press kisses against her calf before unfastening her shoe and then moving on to the other. I bend over her body, placing a tender kiss against her covered pussy, and her hands run through my hair.

I roll the offensive material down her smooth legs and toss them to the floor as I undress myself. The carpet is riddled with our clothes when I'm finally naked and Penny scoots down the bed and I follow her, covering her body with mine.

She licks her lips and spreads her legs wide for me, making room as I grind my cock against her wet cunt before pushing into her entrance.

Her back arches, pressing her tits against my chest, and I push myself closer to her, resting enough of my weight on my elbows and my fingers tangling in her hair.

Each thrust is slow and sensual as we look at each other while she takes me. It's like no matter how hard I try, not enough skin is touching, we aren't close enough.

I don't know that the reality of us being married has sunk in, but at this very moment, all that matters is us.

Her nails dig into my shoulder and she grips my ass while I fuck her, slow and deep.

"Are you going to come for me, pretty wife?" I ask, leaning down to whisper against her face, my pelvis dragging along her clit with every thrust.

Whoever said missionary isn't a good sex position clearly never had sex like this. I'm so deep inside of her with so much skin touching, it's like I can't get enough.

Her hand moves from my backside, cradling the back of my head as she holds me closer to her. My heart aches, knowing she feels the same way as me. She loves me too; she wants me too; she tied herself to me without a second of remorse.

I feel so much love for the woman underneath me, I'm not even sure how to express it.

"Right there," she moans and I pick up my pace slightly, rubbing my pelvis against her clit faster.

Her moans ring out around me as her cunt grips me tightly, and she falls apart. Penny holds me tightly against her with her hands and her thighs as I fuck her through her orgasm.

I pant as my body meets hers and I reach my release, spilling my cum inside of her. We lay like that for a long moment, her cunt keeping my cock warm as I pull back and look at her face.

Nothing has ever felt like this—ever.

I think for the first time in my thirty-six years of life I finally made love to someone, and she just so happens to be my new bride.

"No regrets?"

"Not a single one," she whispers, cradling my face in her hands.

It might as well be my heart, because she has the power to destroy me like no one else ever has.

I hold my weight on her, still not pulling out and twirling a piece of her hair in my finger.

"We can wait to tell our families, but I'd like it if you moved in with me."

"Moving a floor down seems like a downgrade," she jokes. "I want to tell them. I don't want you to feel like a secret, Lincoln. I'm tired of secrets."

I lean down and kiss her softly.

"Or we could buy a house, move somewhere else, whatever you want."

"Would you mow the lawn?" she asks with a smile.

"Don't get fucking crazy now."

Her thumbs graze my cheeks, and she searches my eyes. "You're my husband."

I grin down, finally pulling out and willing my dick to harden again so I can fuck my wife another time tonight. In the meantime, I kiss down her body, with her hand in my hair as I put my mouth on my wife, wanting another orgasm out of her on our wedding night.

IT'S the last day of the trip and we have a team building excursion that was booked. Even though I'd much rather have stayed at the hotel with Penny all day.

While the bulldozer company experience was a great add on by Penny and working heavy machinery is funner then I imagined, I'm ready to have her to myself again.

There was no regrets in the morning, just my pretty wife stealing the majority of the sheets and telling me to fuck off when I tried to wake her up.

Life is good.

Half the team seems to be a little hung-over while the other half are enjoying the event that Penny set up. It's fitting being in the field that we're in, though most of us sit behind desks all day.

With brunch already out of the way, we finish up our team building exercise and it's time to tell everyone to fuck off and I'll see them in the hotel lobby tomorrow morning to head home.

I look down at my watch, and Penny glances over at me skeptically. "What do you have up your sleeve?"

The rest of the employees take a van back to the hotel while we wait in the parking lot.

"You'll see."

The white Ford Mustang convertible and another vehicle pull up into the lot. The young man smiling as he opens the front door and greets me.

"Mr. Carlson?" I nod, and he hands me the keys as he jumps into the car that was following him.

We're already a ways out of the city for the event and I thought the middle of the desert would be the perfect place for Penny to practice.

I grab her hand and put the keys in them.

"I don't know, Linc. I haven't driven in over a year." Her cheeks heat, like she's embarrassed about it.

"If you don't like it, we'll switch. But there's hardly anyone on these back roads. They're straight and usually two lanes, way different from home."

She bites her lips and nods, looking at the flashy white convertible.

"Okay," she sighs, getting into the driver's seat and moving the mirrors and making adjustments to her seat so it's just right. "Are we going anywhere in particular?"

"Nope, just drive," I tell her.

With her sunglasses in place, she starts the engine. She's nervous and hunching over the wheel like a grandma as we leave the parking lot.

"Relax," I say, reaching over and placing a hand on her thigh.

"You relax," she snaps back and I bite my lip to hold in a laugh.

"Go right."

She puts her blinker on and waits a ridiculously long amount of time to make a safe right-hand turn. She's tense for a while, but the dry desert air flings her hair around as she drives. Nerves quickly dissipate as she relaxes in her seat and we enjoy the endless scenery around us.

Eventually, she gives me the okay to put on the radio and we listen to music while she drives us with no destination in mind.

When I look over at Penny, smiling as she drives for the first time in a year, my heart feels full. We pass a sign for a truck stop and I point at it and she nods, expertly taking the exit and pulling into a parking spot.

"How'd it feel?" I ask as she turns off the engine.

"It feels like I've been holding myself back for a long time and I'm tired of it," she says, and I know she means more than just driving.

"It's just you and me, baby," I say, leaning across the console to grab her chin.

"Yeah, it's just me and you," she replies dreamily, capturing her lips with mine.

I don't know what I expected to gain from this trip, but Penny making this large of a commitment wasn't even on my radar. I grab her hand and bring it to my mouth.

"When we get home, you can pick something out," I say, kissing her ring finger.

"Are you ready for when we get home?" she asks.

"We can stay in this bubble for as long as you want, but I'd really like to introduce you as my wife to people, and that doesn't seem fair to do without our families knowing."

She nods, looking down at where I hold her fingers.

"Maybe we can tell your brothers first, and then our parents?" she suggests.

"We can do whatever you want, but we have one more day till we have to face reality. So let me take my bride into this shitty truck stop and show her off."

She grins, kissing me again as we get out and step into the largest truck stop that doubles as a bar and restaurant.

We eat peanuts, order burgers without a care in the world.

No matter what tomorrow brings, we have each other and right now, that's all that matters.

COMING HOME, back to the humidity and looming reality of what we have to do, is daunting.

At least Lincoln isn't pushing for us to go over to my parents' house and tell them right now. It has to be the perfect moment to break news like this... I just have no clue what that moment looks like.

Maybe when we're over for dinner one day we just stand up and announce that we got impulsively married in Vegas and they need to learn to deal with it if they want us in their lives. It makes me feel guilty.

I suppose it's not newfound guilt. I feel like I owe my parents everything, not that they ever act like I do. They constantly give and give and I feel like all I do is take, and this will be just another moment where they have to deal with me being a disappointment of a daughter.

I'm quiet as Lincoln opens his apartment door and we head inside. He parks our luggage in the foyer and empties his keys as I go and sit at a stool under the island.

"Would you…"

"What?" he asks.

I go to open my mouth to speak, and my phone vibrates on the counter. I furrow my brow when I see my dad's name, but pick it up.

"Hey Dad."

"Oh thank God," he says on a sob.

"What's wrong?"

"Your mom is in the hospital."

I stand up off the stool and pace. "What happened? Is she okay?"

"They think she had a mild heart attack. They don't know if she'll need surgery or what the next step is. Could you grab some things from the house and bring them to the hospital?"

"Of course, is she okay? Is she awake?"

"Yes," my dad sniffles. "I'm sorry to scare you by calling you like that. She's alert, in some pain, but she's getting the care she needs."

"Okay, text me everything you need. Lincoln and I will be right there."

I hang up the phone, and Lincoln's arms are wrapped around me in an instant. My heart is racing and as much as I hate myself for thinking it, it somehow feels like this is my fault. How did I not keep better tabs on her cholesterol? I've been so lost in what's going on with me, I haven't even asked about her health.

"Hey," Lincoln says, forcing my eyes to meet his. "We're going to get into the car, drive to your parents' place and get what they need, and then we're both going to the hospital to see your mom."

I nod and try to even my breathing.

"She's going to be fine. I'll call my mom as soon as we get to the hospital and find out what's going on."

I HAND my mom her iPad as soon as we get to the hospital room and she automatically pulls up one of her online card games.

"Thank God. I was getting so bored I thought I was going to die."

"Jesus Christ, Holly," my dad grates out from his visitor's chair.

"Oh calm down. I swear he didn't even listen to the doctor. He said I need to work on maintaining a lower blood pressure and work on lowering my cholesterol. Avoiding stress, eating better, and adjusting to my new medication. It was minor, Tim," my mother tells my father like he's being dramatic.

My dad rubs the bridge of his nose and glances up at me.

"Mom, this is still really serious."

"Serious as a heart attack," she whispers under her breath as she plays solitaire. "You know, you all not talking about it would be really great for my blood pressure."

I glance over at Lincoln and he just shakes his head at my mother's antics.

"Should I call my mom?" he asks her and my mother huffs.

"Yeah, so I have another person in this room giving me grief? No thanks."

"Mom," I scold her.

"Fine, call Maggie. But I swear, if you make it out to be a bigger deal than it is, I'll throw a fit."

Lincoln gives her a salute and leaves the room to call his mother.

"Now, how was Vegas?" my mother says with a smile.

A part of me wants to blurt everything out and tell her how truly amazing the trip was because I came back a married woman. But now is far from the time to tell her that. I can picture it now, telling her I married Lincoln and her heart monitor flaring up as I give my mother a real fucking heart attack.

I rub my forehead, knowing it's going to take some time and planning on when to tell them and not fear I might send her into cardiac arrest.

"I loved it. I haven't had a chance to speak with Krystal yet, but I think I've got the job."

"As you should, she'd be an idiot not to hire you," she says and I shake my head. "What? You've been fantastic at planning events since you were a small child? You wouldn't even let me plan your birthday parties. You wanted to do it yourself so they would be perfect. I think you found your niche, Penny. I told you things were starting to look up."

My eyes well with tears and my mom tsks at me.

"None of that. Come, give me a hug."

I wrap my arms around her, avoiding all the cords attached to her.

"I'm so proud of you, sweetie," she whispers in my ear and I swear my heart sinks in my gut. I wonder if that's the last time she'll ever say that to me.

IT'S BEEN multiple weeks of keeping our marriage a secret and everything seems to be getting in the way of us being fully out to our family. Meanwhile, everything in our little bubble is going fantastic. I left Kemper's and I'm now working for Krystal full time. I'm driving again. Lincoln helped me pick out a cute Volkswagen that I love. And our marriage is going better than I could have ever expected.

We're in complete newlywed bliss. We eat dinner together,

sleep together, and wake up and do it all over again. I don't think there's a spot in this apartment where we haven't fucked, but I'm willing to make sure we haven't missed a spot.

My mother has been healing from her heart attack, milking every second of it. I can only imagine how much money she's spent online gambling, but she's truly doing better.

Tonight's the night.

We're going to walk into Lincoln's parents' house and tell them everything—well, minus the details of how this all started. There's no reason to traumatize our families to that extent.

I take a deep breath as Lincoln opens the door and when we do, there's groaning from our family and my heart stills, did they find out?

"It's not them," Maggie says. "Well, shut the front door before you ruin the surprise," she says and I look around at the balloons and the massive congratulation sign next to two wedding rings.

I furrow my brow and look at Lincoln.

"Get out of the way, they should be here any second now," Maggie says, moving us to the side as Aiden and Jessa walk through the door, and our family gives out rounds of congratulations.

I look over to Lincoln, who looks up at the ceiling for strength. I dust off this feeling of resentment as my best friend and cousin walk into the room beaming.

"Why didn't anyone tell us about the surprise?" Lincoln says in an irritated tone to his brother, Gavin.

"Probably because they didn't want Penny spilling the beans before it happened. Not everyone knows how good she is at keeping a secret." Gavin winks and walks away. Lincoln looks like he's considering throttling his younger brother as Aiden and Jessa approach us.

She holds out a hand, showcasing the ring, which I automatically recognize as Lincoln's grandmother's ring.

"Congratulations, Jessa," I say honestly, wrapping my arms around her in a serious hug.

"Thank you. I seriously had no clue," she gushes. Aiden's smile is wide as he looks down at his fiancé.

The smile that takes over my face is genuine. What's another week or two?

AS SOON AS the appropriate amount of time passes after Jessa and Aiden's engagement, we agree that we can't wait any longer.

We've gotten through Jessa's trial with her ex-boyfriend. My mom is doing well, and I honestly feel sick over the idea of hiding Lincoln for another moment.

Everything seems relatively normal as we head to my parents' backyard, where everyone else is waiting for us. My newly-sized ring is on my finger. It's gold with a large cushion cut diamond in the center. Lincoln went simple with a black band on his finger. It feels weird to actually wear it out, but I'm ready. We've got this.

I pull the sliding door back and my mother is on her feet, dragging a tall, brown-haired man in my direction.

"Oh, there you are. Penny, this is Oliver. He works in the legal department of—"

Lincoln is still next to me, and it seems like everyone is facing in our direction.

"Mom," I say her name softly, trying to resolve this quickly and quietly.

"I know you said you weren't dating, but that was months ago. You have your new job with Krystal. You seem happy."

"Oliver, I'm so sorry," I tell him and my mother looks affronted.

Lincoln says nothing next to me, but I can feel the tension rolling off of him.

"Oliver, I think you should go," I tell him gently. He looks around uncomfortably and then back down at my mom.

"Come on honey, just give him a chance. He's not a loser like—"

"Mom, Oliver needs to go because I'm not interested in dating anyone, because I'm... I'm married," I say, holding up my left hand and she gasps.

"Holy shit," Gavin whispers.

"Oh, fuck," Jessa adds in.

"What am I missing?" Maggie asks, looking at me.

Lincoln takes a step next to me and I take a deep breath. Lincoln has fought for us to be together since the very beginning. This is my time to prove that I'm all in. This is the moment where I prove that I was worth all the effort, that I love him as much as he loves me.

"I'm married. I'm sorry, Oliver, but if you could go," I tell him and he grumbles under his breath before leaving.

"You're married? I didn't even know you were dating. You had a wedding and didn't invite your family? Who is he, where is he?" my mother questions her tone nearly shrill and I wince, worrying about her blood pressure.

"Mom, if you could sit down," I ask.

She gapes at me, looking pissed as hell as she takes a step back and sits next to my dad.

None of them seem to be connecting the dots, minus the twins, Jessa, and, surprisingly, Aiden. I suppose I don't blame her for telling Aiden if she did. I know I tell Lincoln everything, it would only make sense that Jessa slipped up, I don't blame her. If anything it probably prepared him for this moment.

"We're married," Lincoln says, holding out his hand, clearly tired of the bullshit.

All four of our parents have similar expressions of shock. I try to not let it bother me, I knew there would be push back, that this wouldn't go over well, it's what I was so afraid of.

"Excuse me, you fucking what?" my mother asks and I swallow, my heart sinking with her disapproval.

"Lincoln and I are married. We got married while we were in Vegas," I blurt out.

"That was nearly two months ago," my aunt Maggie says in a soft voice, clearly trying to process it all. I don't fault any of them, I get it, I really do. But haven't they seen the change in both of us? They had to know something was going on in each of our lives.

"How long?" my dad asks, crossing his arms over his chest.

"How long what?" I ask as he leans forward, resting his elbows on his knees.

"How long has this been a thing?" He waves his hand between us, clearly in disapproval.

"Since the beginning of summer."

"It's nearly Christmas," Maggie gasps, clutching her chest.

"You took advantage of her," my mother says, pointing at Lincoln. "She was going through a hard time finding out about her biological mother and you manipulated her."

I stand in front of Lincoln, feeling pissed and possessive.

"You will not talk to him like that," I say sternly to my mother. "He was there for me when no one else knew. He's the reason I'm so happy. He's the whole reason I'm doing okay right now. You will never ever speak to him like that again," I say, hating the downtrodden look on her face, but I just couldn't let her speak to him like that.

I look over at my aunt Maggie, who seems pleased with me standing up for her son.

Lincoln grips my hip, and I watch as everyone collectively follows the motion. My heart sinks as I look at my mother's disappointment, but Lincoln's touch grounds me.

Lincoln

My Girl

I GRAB Penny's hip as she stands up to her mother for me.

The woman who was so scared about the damage our relationship would cause is choosing me, and I'm not sure how to handle it.

I've never been someone's first choice before.

"Penny, you've been through a lot lately. I'm sure this can get annulled. What will people think?" her mother asks.

I know my aunt Holly isn't meaning to be as hurtful as she is right now, but it just goes to show that she doesn't really know Penny. She loves Penny, would kill for her, but she doesn't know her, not like I do. I'm not sure anyone in the world knows who the real Penny is besides me. She gives people pieces of who she truly is, but I get the whole package.

My wife is strong and beautiful. Every time I think I couldn't love her more, she just proves me wrong.

"I don't want to get it annulled. You're not listening. We're married. It's the happiest I've ever been. I've felt more like me in these last few months than I have in the last ten years. I don't expect you all to get on board right away, honestly. I know it will be an adjustment. I love Lincoln. He's my husband, and I really hope you can learn to accept it."

Holly sits there for a moment, taking in Penny's words as my mother glances over at her other sons, who are all very obviously not shocked.

"You all knew?"

Ben shrugs, Aiden rubs his jaw, looking away, and Jessa mouths a sorry in Penny's direction.

"Since Labor Day," Gavin says with a shrug.

"Jesus Christ," Penny's dad mumbles under his breath.

"And you're just okay with this?" my mom asks.

"When is the last time you remember Lincoln being happy? When he wasn't moping around sitting by himself in the back-yard. He fucking smiles now. It's terrifying, but it's because of Penny," Gavin says, and I make a note to get him an additional Christmas gift.

My mom nods her head and takes a heavy sigh.

"Have you two thought about what people might think?" she asks, not judging, just asking. My aunt still looks like she's wrapping her head around everything that just happened and I know Penny is worried she might falter in her recovery.

I've been patient and the only reason I was content in waiting so long is because Penny and I have been so happy in our private little newlywed bliss. I'm not going to let them ruin it for us.

"It will probably be strange for family friends we've known for a while, but like I give a fuck what they think? We're not blood related, everything is legal. Her last name is Carlson already," I say, grabbing Penny a little tighter.

My mother glances between the two of us and rubs her forehead.

"I already love you, Penny. It's going to take a minute to get used to this, but I know Lincoln wouldn't be impulsive about something so serious." Penny stills next to me and I pray she doesn't think too hard about my mother's backhanded compliment, that Penny is the impulsive one, when that's the complete opposite.

"I think I'm just going to lie down for a while," Holly says getting up.

"Mom," Penny says, taking a step forward towards her mother.

"I just can't right now, Penelope. I need some space," Holly says, walking back into the house.

Her father stands up next and squeezes his daughter's shoulder.

"We'll figure it out, kiddo. We love you no matter what," he tells her, kissing her hair and following his wife.

Penny turns to me. She looks beautiful in her dark blue sundress and her hair is down in messy waves, but right now her big blue-eyes are welling up with tears.

"Hey," I tell her, cupping her face, and she blinks up at me. "They'll come around. They love you. It was a shock. It will be okay," I tell her, kissing her forehead. She leans into me and when I look up, I see my mom's shocked face.

She gives me a small smile and nod. "Not that you need it, but you have our blessing. Congratulations," she says softly. She grabs my dad's hand and starts heading toward the house.

My dad just slaps my back as he follows his wife.

"Thank fucking God. I didn't know how much longer I could hold it in," Aiden says, wrapping his arm around Jessa, whose cheeks are bright pink.

"I'm really sorry, Penny. He just dragged it out of me," Jessa apologizes.

Penny wipes under her eyes and nods at her friend. "It's okay, I get it more than ever now, trust me."

"Maybe now is the time to tell them I never actually graduated college," Ben says suddenly.

"Wait, you never graduated?" I say, tilting my head at him.

"Neither of us did," Gavin says with a shrug.

"Maybe take that one to your grave. I think our news was enough for today," Penny says, wrapping her arms around herself.

"Awe, it will all work out, Penny. Your mom has always been the high-strung one. She'll come around. Worst-case scenario, just get pregnant. How is she going to refuse a grandchild?" Gavin asks.

I'm retracting his additional Christmas gift.

"I think I want to go home," Penny says softly, not sitting next to my brothers or Jessa.

Jessa stands, wrapping her arms around Penny.

"You have our support no matter what," she says, squeezing her tightly.

Aiden stands up and gives her a hug, too. "Congratulations."

"You mean it?" she asks.

"I was shocked and had other feelings when Jessa first told me, but you two make sense. You're happy and that's all I'd want for the both of you," Aiden says, giving me a hug.

We hug my twin brothers and go through the side gate to avoid walking through the house and dealing with our parents.

Penny stares out the window the whole ride home. She's driven my car a few times, but right now she's too lost in her thoughts as I take us home.

"Well, I can officially move all my stuff downstairs now," she says as I hit the elevator for our floor.

"Or better yet, we can move all of our shit into a house."

"I thought you liked the building?" she says, leaning against the wall.

"I never wanted a house because I didn't like the idea of

living alone. When I'd visit Aiden before he was with Jessa, it felt depressing. Also, you have a lot of shit."

She gasps. "I do not."

"Remember that closet you stuffed me in? It was basically spilling out into your bedroom."

She approaches me, sadness still written on her face, but she isn't crying.

"You'd like to share a house with me?"

"Baby, I want to share everything with you."

IT'S Christmas Eve morning and things feel tense. Mostly because Holly is avoiding both Penny and me like the plague.

My side of the family has taken everything in stride, like I knew they would. I guess I didn't expect such a cold shoulder from Holly. My uncle is kind and accepting, but is sticking by his wife—I guess I get that now.

Even if Penny is wrong about something, I'd still take her side.

The meal is less lively than years past, but I try to make the best of it. It's a shame that there's still straining tension when there's so much breakfast food on the table. Holly watches as I touch her daughter's shoulder and comfort her.

We're free from our secret, but we aren't free from judgment, at least in Holly's eyes.

"Mom," Penny says across the table, and Holly glances up at her daughter. "I was really hoping you'd come and see the place we're under contract for. I'd really like help decorating it."

My wife takes the higher road, extending the olive branch, and I squeeze her shoulder in reassurance and support.

"You bought a house?" she asks. Her tone is hard to decipher.

"We did. It's in Jessa and Aiden's neighborhood."

"That is a nice area," Holly says with a nod. "Do you have a color scheme picked out?"

Penny nods, handing her mother her phone. Holly puts on her glasses and swipes through her inspiration pictures.

"I'd love to help," she says, only looking at Penny.

It might not be the warm welcoming I was hoping I'd get as her son-in-law, but I can tell how much this means to Penny.

"We close on the fifth. Maybe you could come over, see the place and we could all do lunch?" Penny asks, looking at both of her parents.

"We'd love that," my uncle Tim answers for both of them.

I don't know if it's the holidays or seeing how much her disapproval was hurting Penny, but I call it a win.

"Oh shit," Penny says, looking down at her phone. "I've got to go. Thank you for having us."

"Where are you going?" Holly asks, having been completely out of the loop from her daughter's life. I let it slide because they've made peace. Plus, any chance I get to brag about my girl, I'm going to take it.

"She helped plan the Ray's holiday party," I say proudly, and Penny beams.

"Thank you again for introducing me and Krystal to the owner," Penny directs at Aiden.

"It was a no brainer. Go do your thing," Aiden says, waving her off.

Holly looks at her daughter again and I think she finally realizes how truly happy she is. I know I'm a part of it, but more than anything, it's all Penny, she's finally figured out who she is. I take pride in knowing I was part of that journey, but in the end it was all her.

She leans down, no embarrassment or shame as she kisses me on the lips.

"I'll see you back at home?" She pulls out her keys and Holly tracks the motion, realizing her daughter is driving again.

"Yeah, baby, take lots of pictures." She grins, pulling away in her tight little red dress and higher than needed black heels as she clicks her way to the front door and heads to work.

Holly stares after her daughter for a minute and takes a deep breath.

"So... tell me more about the house," she says, looking right at me.

It feels like the weight of the world falls off my shoulders and it's no longer Penny and me against the world.

I HANG the last dress onto the hook on my side of the closet, the dress I married Lincoln in, knowing the closet will never be as organized as it is now.

It's wild thinking about how I got here. A freaking glory hole brought me to my future husband, who was right in front of my face the whole time. It hasn't been easy going, at least in the sense of getting to where we are now. But when I think about my relationship with Lincoln? It's the easiest thing I've ever done.

I slide my fingers against the sparkly material, thinking back to that day and how happy I was, how I still am. But there is a lingering sensation of wishing our families were there to watch us get married.

Lincoln's parents and brothers were onboard quickly. I think because they never expected him to get married, and it was easy for them to see the change in him. It's been slower for my parents—mainly my mother—but she's finally coming around. She's even coming over tomorrow to check the new house out and help me design.

I rub the material between my fingers sighing, not knowing how my life got here, but happy that it did.

As soon as I turn around, there's a huge clang, making me jump and clutch my chest as I gasp. I spin around and the entire fucking rack, with all the clothes I just hung, is on the floor.

I sigh, considering shutting the door and making this a problem for another day.

The door flies wide open, to where it was previously ajar.

"Are you okay?" Lincoln says louder and more aggressively than the situation requires. Clearly having run down the hall worried for my safety, I like it more than I should.

I wave a hand at the disaster before me, indicating the noise and that I'm perfectly fine.

"Yeah, the shelf just fell down."

"What the fuck? This is a new house."

"I guess new construction isn't as great as people say it is," I joke.

He arches a brow at me. He's wearing mesh athletic shorts that show the bulge of his dick and a tight black t-shirt. Casual Lincoln is my favorite, and he's all mine.

"You know, we haven't christened the house yet," he says. Eyeing the absolute mess behind me. Both of us are clearly on the same page—fuck this closet.

I smirk, thinking about what we watched together a few weeks ago and what I'd like to emulate. One of the best things about Lincoln is he's ready to try anything at least once, and so am I.

When I can keep the man on his toes, I take the opportunity.

"Meet me in the laundry room in five minutes," I tell him.

He arches a brow at me. "The laundry room?"

I rub my hands over his chest. He's a little sweaty from moving shit, and I like it. I know that when he takes off his shirt, his chest will be speckled with a glossy sheen that I'd happily lick off. But that's not in the plans for tonight.

Honestly, most nights we just have sex, in a numerous amount of positions. But now and then we like to play.

And I really feel like playing right now—with my husband—in our new house that we bought together. Both of our names ending in Carlson as I signed the dotted line.

"Don't you trust me?"

"I swear to God if you bring me in there to hang something up... my arms hurt."

I lightly tap his biceps.

"Poor strong man. If you're too tired..."

"I'll meet you in the laundry room," he replies sharply.

"Excellent."

He slaps my ass hard as I walk past him, making my way down the hall to the laundry room. They're both front loaders.

It's probably silly, in fact I know it is, but isn't that what marriage or being a long-term partner is about? Being silly and turned on with one another.

If anything, it kind of reminds me of the very unique way that we met. I take off my panties and shorts and decide I might as well get completely naked for the whole experience. I get on my knees, the tile cool and harsh against my skin, as I rest my front half of my body in the dryer.

The wait feels endless until the door to the laundry room clicks and Lincoln lets out a dark laugh.

"Oh no, did my wife just so happen to get stuck in the dryer with her bottom half completely exposed?"

"I'm really not sure how this happened. Do you think you can help a girl out?" I say, trying to stop myself from laughing.

His hand cups my ass cheek and he squeezes. No doubt his fingers leaving an imprint in their wake.

"Seems like a wasted opportunity."

"Help me out, I'm stuck."

His fingers slide down my ass, and he cups my pussy.

"Why are you so wet? Were you hoping I'd find you like this and want to sink my cock deep inside this greedy little pussy?"

"Of course not. I was just taking off the sticker from the inside of the dryer."

He pauses for a moment, clearly trying to hold it together.

"I think you wanted this. I'll give you what you want. All you had to do was ask," he says.

"I really just wanted—"

My words die out as his cock slides deep inside of me, forcing me to stretch around his length. My only saving grace is how attuned our bodies are. My body nearly drips with need anytime he says something dirty.

"What was that, Honey?" He thrusts and I have to hold my hands up so I don't hit my head on the dryer. "What is it you wanted?"

"Fuck," I hiss as I feel his spit slide down the crack of my ass. His thumb collects the moisture and pushes into my back entrance.

"You want it harder?" he asks, but it isn't a question as his thrusts increase.

My hand slips, and I go careening against the bottom of the dryer.

"Fuck," Lincoln groans, pulling his cock out and grabbing me by the waist to tug me out. I eagerly fall out of the dryer and as soon as I look at Lincoln, who is biting his lip, trying not to laugh, I lose it.

Tossing my head back and laughing as he follows suit, shaking his head.

"Come here, you fucking psycho," he says as I continue laughing. He picks me up by the waist, sitting me on top of the dryer as he cups my face and kisses me.

No sooner is he lining his hard, wet length against my pussy and pushing in. I keep one hand behind me for balance as I drag my other hand along his chest. Lincoln holds my face, kissing me, while he fucks me.

The dryer rocking and slightly banging against the wall with each thrust.

I'm so close, right on the cusp of my orgasm, and Lincoln knows it. He pulls away from my face, placing his hand between my breasts. I use both arms to hold my weight, my tits bouncing with each thrust as he grips me by the thigh with one hand and strums on my clit with the other.

He watches where we're joined with rapt attention, like it's the most fascinating thing he's ever seen, like he'll never get enough of me.

I watch him in the same way, wondering how I got so lucky and if there will ever be a time where being with him doesn't feel transcendent.

His fingers work quickly against my clit. He knows my body so well. I shutter, my muscles tensing as I let out a moan and fall apart.

"That's it. I'm going to fill you up with my cum and watch it leak out," he groans as he does just that. His grip on my thigh is bruising as his hips snap and he fills me with his release.

He leans forward, his messy hair slightly damp as he captures my mouth with his, a smile pressed against my lips.

"That was a nice surprise. But I don't think being trapped in the dryer is our thing," he says with a laugh, which I follow suit. Which makes Lincoln wince as my muscles tighten around his length.

"I thought it was kind-of glory hole adjacent."

He shakes his head. "Now that I have you, I never want anything to get between us again."

Lincoln Carlson truly is the most romantic man on the

planet and I'm the lucky woman who gets to call him my husband.

Two Years Later

MY BUMP IS huge in this flowy white dress, but I still feel beautiful. The sun is setting as I walk down the sand in bare feet. It's just our family and some close friends, like Krystal, her wife and daughter, and Lincoln's assistant, Marie and her husband, that are seated along the aisle.

Lincoln is wearing a white shirt and tan pants at the altar.

My mom is crying tears of joy. How did we get here? I'll never know, but she's truly accepted Lincoln as my husband beyond all else. It probably doesn't hurt that we've been happily married for two years with our first kid on the way. With the way this pregnancy has been going—definitely our last.

Lincoln is grinning as I approach and I take his hands in mine. There's no minister or anything. We just wanted something symbolic and with our families. My mom had a heavy hand in planning and at any moment I have to publicly show Lincoln I love him, I do.

"Can I start?" I ask, and he nods his head. He still looks at me like I'm everything to him. He still holds me at night and orders my favorite food. He's truly my other half and I don't know what I'd do without him.

I clear my throat, hoping I don't ruin my makeup with tears as I speak. "I can't pinpoint the exact moment I fell in love with you, because you've always owned a piece of my heart. But I can tell you the exact moment I knew I wanted to be your wife one day. It was here on vacation, when we were dancing at that dive bar while it poured rain. I knew then that I could spend the rest of my life searching and I'd never find a fraction of what we have."

Lincoln squeezes my hands, his own eyes filling with tears.

"You've helped me become the person I've always wanted to be. When I fell in love with you, you helped me fall in love with myself. You're the best husband I could have ever asked for and I know you'll be the best father to our daughter. I love you, Lincoln Carlson, and even if we lived a thousand lifetimes, I'd always choose you."

I pull one hand away to wipe my face and Lincoln does the same. I don't dare look at our family or else I'll cry harder.

"How am I supposed to follow that?" Lincoln jokes and there's a mix of laughter and sniffling.

Lincoln clears his throat, grabbing my hands and holding them again.

"I thought I knew who I was, what I wanted, and then you came along. I never really envisioned myself becoming a dad or growing old until you. I didn't think I'd be a good husband or a half decent partner, but with you it came easy. Not that getting to this point wasn't tumultuous at best. I know I was needy and adamant, but I've never wanted anything more than I wanted to be yours. You are the sun of my life and I love you for putting up with me," he says and everyone laughs. "For being my wife, and being the mother of our child. I love you Penelope Carlson, and I wouldn't trade a single moment to get to where we are today."

I grin as he leans forward and kisses me, our family clapping and the waves trickling in from the distance.

This wasn't the life I ever imagined. It's so much better.

ACKNOWLEDGMENTS

Hugest thanks to Leisha and Nikki for reading as I write and really pushing me to continue even when I got into my own head.

Jess and Kim thank you so much for alpha reading and continuing to motivate me to make this book the best it can be.

Laura and Tia thank you for sensitivity reading and using your life experience while reading through the book.

Stephanie and Lindsay, thank you for having eyes on the final draft before it goes out.

Sandra for my beautiful cover.

Anyone who has been in support of this book or sent me encouragement when I was worried about the pushback I was getting during early marketing.

High Roller Omegas (Shared World)

Queen of Hearts

Dead Palms MC

Nobody's Darlin'

Pucked Up Omegaverse

One Pucked Up Pack

Don't Puck With My Heart

Puck Around & Find Out - Date TBD

Heat Haven Omegaverse

Heat Haven

Omega's Obsession

Protector's Promise

Too Tempting

Heat Haven Holidays

Lavender Moon

Lavender Moon

Lavender Moon Meets Las Vegas

Want to take a walk on the paranormal side?

Charming Your Dad

Charming the Devil

<u>**Charming as Hell**</u>

Love in the Veil

Petty Cupid

Lucky Cupid

The Carlson Brothers - Contemporary Romance

Swallow Your Pride

Forget Your Morals

ABOUT THE AUTHOR

Sarah Blue writes contemporary sweet omegaverse, erotic, why choose romances. She loves romance in nearly any genre. When she isn't writing you can find her nose buried in a book or lit up from her kindle. She loves the sweeter side of romance and creating interesting characters while adding adventure and spice. Writing strong female characters and male characters willing to show weakness is something that makes her gooey on the inside.

Sarah lives in Maryland with her husband, two sons, and two annoying cats. If she isn't reading or writing she is probably working on a craft project or scrolling on Tik Tok.

www.authorsarahblue.com
@sarahblueauthor on Instagram and TikTok
Sarah Blue's Reader Group on Facebook